"The relationship between addiction and creativity, as I see it, is not causal. Rather there is a parallel process occuring in the psyche of the addict and the creative person. Both descend into chaos, into the unknown underworld of the unconscious. Both are fascinated by what they find there."

Linda Schierse Leonard, from *Witness to the Fire, Creativity and the Veil of Addiction*

1

CHAPTER 1

He walked through the bathroom door, his feet sticking to the floor and saw how the small black and white tiles were covered in a pool of blood, the source of which was the severed ulnar arteries of a sixteen year old boy sitting on the toilet alive, but unfocussed and staring into the fog that drifts somewhere between consciousness and whatever lies beyond. He knelt in the blood in front of the boy and held the boy's arms aloft and looked into his eyes, speaking his name in between shouting for someone to help and call for an ambulance. A sixteen year old life brought back from the brink in the bathroom of an adult ward secured by locks and airlocks deep inside a Victorian building somewhere on London's westernmost outskirts and where the boy should never have been.

He remembered the boy's name - Kendrick Wells - and he rolled those two words around in his head a few times and thought how often the boy would now come to mind, the curly-haired slight-framed boy who used to wear a blue denim jacket and jeans and who needed to be told to take a bath and to change his clothes and to wash his underwear. A life saved that time but only for the boy to break open a disposable razor one early morning just a few days later and use the blade to cut through his torso and into his bowel and die a slow deranged death in a surgical ward somewhere far away from his home.

Kendrick Wells was on his mind as he entered the toilet cubicle and smelled the vomit and saw its traces on the floor and a spray of fresh blood on the shiny blue laminated divide as he chopped a line on the top of the cistern and wondered why the police hadn't closed this place down. He checked his nostrils in the mirror before re-entry and saw a trickle of blood emerging from one of them that mixed with the powder to create a pink viscous flow tasting of salt and poison.

After that a blur of sounds and images intangible and lost somewhere not so far from the surface of his mind yet impossible to retrieve. He didn't know how or when he had reached home. He looked at his tan suede boots left by the door. They were stained wet. He remembered there had been a cloudburst and how he had walked on through it and how he had thought the amber glow of streetlights in the rain had now become one of the enduring images that gave identity to his restlessness. Observed through such a blur, pain lost clarity and became temporarily disempowered.

At some point he had gone in search of something ill-defined and perhaps as mundane as just wanting to feel again how it feels when the switch is switched on two or three drinks in and the conversation is uninhibited and everybody's getting high. Or maybe it was something deeper and always out of reach, some truth that was one minute in his grasp and the next gone but once its momentum built it was irrepressible and he would always be impelled to look for it again and again. He always headed to the same place those days to see the type of people he was drawn to at such times and that they were gathered there in such numbers was an affirmation of sorts. Dealers, working girls, pimps, outlaws, musos, road crew, addicts, misfits and lunatics. Members of the fringe all just about accommodated by whatever life was and all together in the dull glow of one of the worst bars in town. He had ordered a glass of porter and a whisky from the barmaid who never used a measure. Who knows what happened next? He now stood in the conservatory looking out towards the garden feeling as though some animal was scratching at his guts having taken up residence there and now wanted out. Saturday morning and a lifeless sky sat over the tile-red rooftops and every now and again a wren flitted on and off the woodpile by the shed twitching its tail and looking fearful. The support bandage on his right elbow felt as tight as a tourniquet. He had just checked his jacket pockets for his wallet, making sure his bank card was where it should be. He didn't find any receipts or tickets offering clues as to whether he had been anywhere else. He checked his phone and texts in case he had sent something he wished he hadn't and then checked his body for abrasions and bruises. All was intact and as it should have been. He knew the score and had done this many times. The night before he would have reached that higher plain of unrestraint where he believed he was incisive and able to see the world at large with a keen clarity, perceiving himself as confident enough to be shining. He would never know how it had unfolded as it had all vanished the way it always did.

He was standing barefoot on the polished tiles. He liked their look - Spanish and weathered – and liked how they felt to walk upon when without socks or shoes and the underfloor heating was on in the winter or the cool relief they brought on warmer days. Whenever he stood there he thought of the word *ambient*, the word the guy who installed the heating had used to describe its effect. *Ambient* as opposed to *dramatic* he had said as though the nuance needed explanation. Not convinced he could sense the ambience he was meant to he did feel a sense of satisfaction regarding something he and she had got right. The purpose found in life had to be meaningful and in this case the meaning came with tiles looking good and feeling good to the bare foot. He pondered this while reading a flier for a local Turkish restaurant settled on top of the kindling in the wicker basket by the conservatory door. A free litre of coke if you order a *Supersize Mixed Kebab*. One of the menu items read *Large Mate And Fries* and he was intrigued by the possibilities.

This was home whatever that meant and it was where he and Amelia, common-law partner of eight years, found a sanctuary of their own making and where they kept the outside world at bay in order to process what needed to be processed in order to prevent any influences with malign intent from encroaching too much on their lives together. They could choose what to let inside and if over time the choices they made proved to be compatible then all was well and if not they either ignored them or worked them through. That way the world inside stayed calm. Whether any choice they made was the result of negotiation or unilateral action, all choices were made with the intention of creating or maintaining the peace. Many aspects of the outside world could still invade this interior to greater or lesser extents but they aspired and mostly succeeded in keeping a tight control on who or what had access. Neighbours would knock and the mail would come through the letterbox and occasionally they invited people over to drink and eat, resulting in a convergence of the interior and exterior worlds which mostly created a resonance, sometimes of orchestral dimensions. If there ever was any dissonance they worked at dismantling its cause in order to smooth the path towards restructure and balance. In the early days of their living together they would willingly expend the necessary effort for this to happen but over time they had both become less willing and over-wary of conflict and its oft-visited residuum of introversion and resentment.

He heard his phone vibrate on the coffee-table in the sitting-room and walked through to get it. She was sitting on the settee doing a crossword with her arm outstretched towards him holding the phone.
Elliot, your phone, she said in an irritated voice too loud for his proximity to her.

He indicated his awareness of its ringing by widening his eyes in irritation and directing his gaze towards her which had no effect as she wasn't looking at him. This was a fairly typical interaction on such a day when they were sharing mostly the same space but engaging their minds and bodies in separate activities. Hours could pass when only a cough or a sneeze from another room or a flushing toilet or footsteps on the stairs betrayed their existences to one another. It wasn't an unpleasant way to live but he didn't find it particularly meaningful either and he wondered if she found it any more meaningful than it being the manifestation of two people mostly comfortable together as they cohabitated. That might be meaningful enough, he thought. She once described their relationship as a journey on twin tracks going in the same direction without any need to converge unless absolutely necessary or there was an intensely felt desire to do so on the part of either one of them.

During their time together there had been career changes - she was on an upward curve and he was trying to change his following early retirement on grounds of ill-health - and family issues - his two daughters, Iris and Isabel - and no more than the usual ups and downs of a life lived neither particularly well nor badly. They didn't feel the need to impose too much of their selves upon the other. Life together was comfortable enough in a midstream kind of way as they began to contemplate reaching the other side some time in the indeterminate future. For now the waters were still enough and they knew how deep they ran without feeling the need to dive down into them too much anymore. Her intellectuality, as keen as it was functional and unobtrusive, insulated her like an extra layer of clothes so her usual demeanour was one of understated confidence and self-sufficiency. He was less certain. As he reached for the phone he felt the pain in his elbow. It was Michael from across the road.

Hello, Micky, he said using the shortened version of Michael's name and knowing Michael hated it.

Fuck off don't call me that.

What do you want?

I'm going to the brewery. Fancy a pint?

How can I resist?

He believed Michael to be a psychopath albeit one with redeeming qualities that would satisfy other people he was nothing of the sort. Elliot had worked with personality disordered men in his time and knew the difficulties associated with the diagnosis of anyone on the cusp between psychopathy and so-called normality. Familiar with the many inconsistencies in that branch of psychiatry he conceded Michael could in certain situations demonstrate the capacity to feel and express appropriate emotion, particularly if talking about his children or his dog. He always without question supported the underdog and this suggested a capacity for empathy but Elliot remained unconvinced. Michael was quick to anger at anything he believed was the result of an abuse of power and his fervour when challenging such perceived injustices would often override any contrasting truths within the given situation and his responses were therefore usually disproportionate. It's something you had to watch when in his company and his drinking could precipitate the bypassing of any filter system there to remind him to think things through before taking action. His subsequent impulses included violence and threatened violence, all of which made Amelia wary of him, whereas Elliot saw him mostly as engaging and funny and good company and considered him a friend who also served as a conduit to sluice him away from the boredom of everyday life. Michael worked as an accountant for a small logistics company and was apparently good at his job for which he was paid considerably more than his neighbours. He lived in apparent harmony with Linda and their two young girls and a black Labrador. Unmarried, they appeared to be people who would have followed an alternative lifestyle had they not decided that money and a sizeable house with modern conveniences were more important than following what may or may not have been a life more congruent with their youthful values. She worked as a legal clerk and said she didn't get on with her colleagues whom Michael believed bullied her. A recovering heroin addict and a depressive with low self-esteem she nevertheless stood up to Michael and he accepted boundary-setting from her that he wouldn't have accepted from anyone else.

Their first meeting with Elliot and Amelia had taken place at an event their next door neighbours had billed as *A Festive Evening of Mulled Wine* the first Christmas after they had moved there. Over their mutual preference for beer instead of hot sweet cheap red, Michael and Elliot started to bond. The evening allowed Elliot and Amelia an opportunity to be introduced to neighbours in the immediate vicinity whom they were yet to meet. Jack and Gill – in their seventies and devout Roman Catholics and the hosts for the evening, Evelyn and Rory - sixties and devout Anglicans, Tom and Jerry - forties, gay and prone to bickering in public, Bert and Betty - sixties or possibly seventies, naturists and swingers, Biddy and Tom – fifties, part-Romany and also naturists but they didn't commune with Bert and Betty and then Cheryl and Bill from next door who said nothing unless asked and looked uncomfortable throughout. There were other neighbours there but these were the ones they got to know enough to feel comfortable waving hello to or accepting a parcel for or putting back their bins for them after the Tuesday collection. It helped place them during the phase after their move into a new house when they were feeling displaced and uncertain.

I just need to shower and change.
Twenty minutes.

I'll come over.

He shaved and brushed his teeth and washed his armpits, adding deodorant and after-shave to be sure. Most mornings he and Amelia would discuss the arrangements for that day's evening meal – who would cook or if anything needed to be defrosted or if it was one of her fasting days or if there was a need for any shopping. It was as though knowing what was in store for them later on determined something of the day ahead but that day they hadn't had any such conversation and he said goodbye to her sensing he was leaving something unresolved and trusting that a carry-out or home delivery was on the cards for later. He wondered if that night was the night for the *Large Mate and Fries*.

On closing the front door he saw Cheryl whom he felt was indirectly responsible for the pain in his elbow. She was about fifty and worked in IT mostly from home. Ex-army with a heart condition and diabetes and some kind of social phobia meant she and her partner were neighbours who didn't like to socialise. When they did she would drink more than she could handle, becoming self-disclosing to an inappropriate degree, mainly about her health but occasionally detailing aspects of their sex life. Her husband Bill was epileptic and also diabetic and several years younger than her. He kept two pet white mice with pink eyes in a cage in their kitchen and made jewellery he tried to sell on market stalls. Their dog Marley was their second border collie, bought after their first one Jock, an agoraphobic, had died a couple of years before. Bred to *show* not to *work* as Cheryl described him, Marley was marginally less neurotic than his predecessor though suffered separation anxiety whenever they went away or left him alone. This is where Elliot usually stepped in if the kitchen calendar allowed him to do so. To his knowledge they had never *shown* Marley and his idea of how to keep a dog, even one bred to *show,* was very different to theirs. Marley was the boss in their house and got his own way but knew his place when walking with Elliot and the two of them had reached an understanding early on in their relationship.

Being bred to *show* Marley wasn't one for long walks and preferred to just sniff around and mark areas of the common at the end of the road.

The only interaction anyone could have with this single-minded animal came when they threw a frisbee for him which he would fetch enthusiastically only to carry it further away and then drop it on the ground before he crouched *working*-dog style and pointed to it with his snout, refusing to bring it to the thrower's hand. The repetitive action of throwing the frisbee had led to Elliot straining some minor muscle or tendon in his elbow when Cheryl and Bill had gone to her mother's for most of the day before. When they returned they gave him a box of chocolates as a token of their gratitude for looking after the dog.

Thanks for looking after Marley, she said, her hair wet and sticking to her face.

No worries, he replied, and no need for the chocolates but thanks all the same.

He crossed the road and noticed an unfamiliar car - a shiny, ultramarine five door, indistinct but for the three letters HTL at the end of the registration number. In that particular order they formed the initials of his late father and as such had been in his consciousness for as long as he could remember. Henry Thomas Longman, born 1919 and died 2009, father of two and husband of one who served with distinction in World War Two in the Forgotten Army then worked his way up in the oil industry at first on the rigs in Venezuela and later in Trinidad where he was based for most of Elliot's childhood and teenage years. He had been an all round good man in Elliot's eyes, one who didn't deserve the end he had endured as a sufferer of Parkinson's Disease. HTL – it wasn't just the names the letters stood for but their very shape as though each one of them had its own characteristics representing different aspects of his father's personality. They had been etched into Elliot's memory and whatever it was that then generated a process so influencing the way he saw the world. The strong upright letters symbolised his mythical vision of the man who had been his father and about whom he sill felt he would like to know more.

He thought of the grave on a hill overlooking the Thames near Cookham and recalled the funeral on a bitter January morning and how his mother stood on the slope leaning on her stick defiant against the wind and sleet with her jaw set in resolution and resignation like some warrior queen who had seen everything the fates could ever throw her way. He remembered the way his father would raise a conspirational eyebrow at him when he visited during the last few years of his life as if they were about to do something naughty and secretive together. Those last years were dominated by carers and hoists and incontinence pads and falls and bruises and cuts and confusion - all the paraphenalia and failure of faculty that amplified the indignity of old age. Elliot remembered seeing and hearing his father sob like a child a few weeks before he died as he lay in bed unable to speak and surely knowing his time was just about up and equally as surely wishing it wasn't. The hideous long-drawn-out drama of his father's death came to the fore of Elliot's mind at the slightest prompt even then six years on. He regretted with a depth of feeling almost too painful to bear being unable to alleviate his father's demise and now missed him more than he ever imagined possible

Michael answered the door, already in his coat – an enormous, shiny green parka with enough faux-fur attached to the hood that an Eskimo might have found it excessive, a baggy cream coloured jumper, drainpipe jeans and beige boots. A big man with the build of a modern-era rugby player he swept his flat blonde hair away from his eyes and smiled his best winning smile full of cheek and mischief.
All right cunty bollocks?' he asked.

Even though going out for a drink was something they often did together, Elliot wondered if at his age it should be, not least because each time he would have to contort his spine, sciatic nerve screaming in protest, into the bucket seat of Michael's sports car. However, there remained something attractive about sitting in a small uncomfortable fast car as though the prospect of speed and glamour combined might still turn him on. Michael accelerated unnecessarily to the junction at the end of their road, immediately setting off a chain reaction in Elliot of anxiety and involuntary phantom-braking and shooting pains which took barely a second to discharge through his left buttock and down the back of his thigh all the way to his big toe. He gasped, provoking a snort of amusement from Michael who took the first S bend, slick with the rainfall from the night before, at an inappropriate speed, barely keeping to his side of the road. Then his foot went down as they hit the straight. Elliot tried to ignore the warning voice inside him shouting *what the hell are you doing here?*

He thought about and acknowledged the genuineness of their friendship and how they shared confidences and humour and the ridiculousness of drunkenness. It's just there was an edge to Michael that was hard to describe. It was as though Michael lived on another plain of consciousness, one dominated by forces unique to him and remaining unexpressed by him. He could step out from whatever universe he was in whenever he wanted to be, or had no choice but to be, in the company of others. People could feel ill at ease when with him and if he sensed their disquiet he became uneasy in theirs. He knew he was burdened with something unresolved from his past and he also knew Elliot acknowledged and understood this tacitly so they never had to discuss it. This made Michael as relaxed as he was ever going to be in the company of an acquaintance and thus allowed them to talk meaningfully if the circumstances demanded or just be as stupid and shallow as they pleased. But was there something else to it? Elliot was definitely attracted to Michael in terms of his star quality, his charisma he supposed, as though by being in his presence Elliot's life experience became enhanced even if sometimes that enhancement came about from doing slightly more dangerous than normal things with him. Michael often drove when over the limit and Elliot with little pause would get into the car with him. He would use cocaine and Elliot would sometimes join in. He would ignore *trespassers will be prosecuted* signs when they were out walking and Elliot would, albeit with a do-you-think-this-is-wise kind of protest, walk with him. Elliot wondered what it was about charismatics that made them so attractive to those of more ordinary character. Is it because they want a sprinkling of stardust to come their way? But he was not starstruck by Michael. He was actually uncertain about him and only too aware of the turbulent undercurrent beneath his outer layer that threatened to overflow every now and again. Friendship with Michael was like walking around the rim of an apparently dormant volcano that every now and again would emit sulphurous gases, the origins of which were way down in the nether regions of the Earth and a reminder it could erupt anytime, taking Elliot and his non-judgemental positive regard with it as he became overwhelmed by whatever malevolent force it was. If that happened, he concluded, he would have no choice but to become familiar with the place from which it originated.

CHAPTER 2

The Beech Brewery was run by Jonny and Carol, a couple in their forties who gave up careers in something like marketing in order to take the leap into the unknown that was establishing their new venture while at the same time speed-learning the pitfalls of the trade and the challenges of maintaining a positive interface with their suppliers and clientele. They had made a good enough go of it to never have to return to the corporate world they were happy to have left behind. They had swapped the lifestyle of well-paid commuting middle-managers - and all its paid holidays, tiredness, ill-health and caffeine - for a seven-day week of hard graft in order to establish something they could rightly call their own. It was a different kind of tiredness. Their bar opened on Fridays and Saturdays and locals, mainly men, would enjoy drinking and socialising in what was a basic but pleasant enough setting.

As they stepped through the door Michael spoke under his breath.
Bollocks. Miserable Bastard's here.
They had never ascertained Miserable Bastard's real name nor had they wanted to. They had named him thus because he was prone to grumble and grouse to anyone who would listen to him about the way things were in the world – prices, immigrants, the European Union, the young, the cost of renewal for his golf club membership – he was the type who would land in paradise and then complain the sky wasn't the right kind of blue and would then want to find someone to blame for that and give them a piece of his puffed-up self-absorbed little mind. When floods had affected large parts of the West Country the previous winter he opined the misery experienced by his fellow human beings was not the result of unprecedented weather conditions or cuts to flood-defence budgets but was instead caused by the inherent laziness of the people who lived there and who could have done more to help themselves.
Like they do in Yorkshire, he added.
That where you're from then? Michael had asked.
Yes what of it?

He had then cast a disapproving look towards Michael as though he was of an inferior class and had no right to breathe the same air. Michael had the last word.

      That figures.

There followed a murmur of laughter among those standing at the bar.

They walked past him without any acknowledgement and Jonny welcomed them with handshakes before pouring the pints and telling them about a new porter that would be available the following week. Carol came down from the office and double-cheek kissed them both and joined in the conversation for a while before Michael and Elliot sat down at one of the tables fashioned from old kegs. Along with Miserable Bastard they were at that time the only customers. Elliot adjusted his position on the stool several times before feeling comfortable and they sat in silence for a few minutes staring into their glasses. Such neutrality of time and experience was comforting and Elliot wished to himself time would now stand still. In such momentshe experienced calmness, acceptance and affirmation. Michael spoke first.

      How's the pain?

      Which one?

Michael jerked his chin in the direction of Elliot's groin.

      Sorry mate.

And Elliot knew he was and that he meant well. It touched him in the same way as when people had shaken his hand and said *sorry for your loss* at his father's funeral. Any words offered to demonstrate condolence were appreciated but only in the knowledge that they made no difference in the end and that platitudes could never bring relief to those who grieved. Everyone had to deal with their own stuff and even those who had suffered similar pain could only ever just acknowledge it however empathic they were. Elliot believed life meant suffering alone.

A couple of years before he had attended a pain-management group one day a week for six weeks having been referred by a consultant neurologist who had told him there was nothing he could do medically that wouldn't run the risk of making his condition worse. All Elliot could do was learn to live with it but the group might help him to do that. The consultant had reached this conclusion after a prolonged assessment during which he was accompanied by a female houseman who was learning the ropes. She was impossibly tall and attractive and winced when Elliot thought she meant to smile. The assessment involved a series of questions and in answering them he tried not to sound too hopeful or desperate as he retold his ages-old clinical history. Then the consultant examined his prostate gland. As the tall attractive wincing woman looked on Elliot dropped his trousers and underpants and climbed up onto the trolley-bed and lay down turning towards the wall as he tried to find something to focus on. He drew his knees up to his chest and heard the snap on skin when the consultant donned latex gloves as though he was putting on a pair of marigolds and resenting with all his heart that it was his turn to wash the dishes. There followed the squelching of lubricant onto his fingers and then the unnatural sensation of his fingers being inserted into Elliot's anus, inducing a phantom sensation of an imminent and uncontrolled bowel movement - a *normal* feeling according to the consultant. Elliot thought it would have been anything but normal to lose control of his bowel all over the consultant and in front of her – that really would have really made her wince - as the consultant began to massage and prod that tiny male thing, the possible core of his troubles, the seat of his disharmonious relationship with the world. The tall attractive wincing houseman looked on silently and Elliot felt as though a pair of fireside tongs were searching through the passageways of his lower intestine.

You're very tense, said the consultant.

The idea of the group was for its members to bond over their genito-urinary pain and help each other find some way of living with it. One of the first things they had to overcome was that the facilitators were all women – two psychologists, a nurse, a physiotherapist and a consultant anaesthetist, all for the most part younger than they were, meaning it was difficult to talk openly in their company about subjects pertinent to their genitals and their functioning or dysfunctioning. Of the mix of men, most were forty-plus but there were two in their twenties who struggled more than the rest when listening to the exchange of war stories between the veterans that took in a whole range of relevant subjects, including the procedures peculiar to genito-urinary medicine as well as STD clinics, misdiagnoses, prostate examinations, cystoscopies (you're going to put *that* in *there*?), endless antibiotics, alternative therapies, Chinese medicine, acupuncture, the curtailing of sporting life, sex life, working life, the challenges to relationships, depression, alcohol, drugs, impecuniosity, homelessness, even prison sentences, to name but a few. They soon overcame their embarrassment because needs must but also because it felt as if they were in the last chance saloon where there were no magic cures (always the hope) and no magic side-effect-free analgesia and no choice but to get used to the fact this condition was going to be with them in one form or another for the rest of their lives. They all at times shed tears of grief and also laughed with a freedom and disinhibition they could only have felt as a result of being in one another's company. They had reached there via different paths – some through botched surgery (one a vasectomy that went disastrously wrong but not as disastrously wrong as the subsequent corrective surgery – I would have killed the surgeon if he'd done that to me, Michael had said), others like Elliot through accidental injury but all through some simple, vicious, twist of fate that changed their lives forever. *You are not your pain* was one of the oft-repeated mantras devised by the well-meaning young women but it often felt to these men they were exactly that and they always would be. Acknowledging this as a truth, Elliot concluded he had become a nihilist who had lost faith in the world and its systems which he perceived to be full of false hope and false promise. He began to silently sneer at anyone trying to offer hope because he knew no one but himself could find ways to transcend the pain. It was existential and so could only ever be his own experience. His and only his and no one else would or could ever feel it. The group helped to challenge this paradigm and helped him to see, even with a lack of enthusiasm for it, that life could go on but he would have to give up investing hope in medicine to cure the cause or the physical and psychological effects of his condition. From that point on he resolved to rely only on his own self to see him through and if he failed then so be it.

One of the younger men stepped in front of a tube train and died instantly about a year after the group finished for good. Elliot was one of only three members of the group who stayed in touch and met from time to time to drink themselves into the ground over a few immortal hours of mirth and sadness before hugging their goodbyes and returning back to their unknowing worlds. The other two were both called John, one of whom was a hostage negotiator with the Metropolitan Police, the other a trumpet player who said he never *got* Miles Davis and who had worked six nights a week in a long-running West End musical. Most nights he hadn't been able to sit for the duration of the show because of his pain so he left and was now running a small sawmill in the Hertfordshire countryside. Work was difficult for them both and they envied Elliot's semi-retired status courtesy of his ill-health pension. They were far from being *best* friends but when together they felt as close to one another as you can get.

Then there was his other pain although the two had been around one another for so long they often merged within his mind into an overwhelming all-consuming force. He avoided the word *depression* as a descriptor, thinking it didn't do justice to the true and varied nature of the condition and anyway it provoked unhelpful reactions in others, ranging from awkward attempts at understanding, usually expressed in platitudes, inappropriate advice, or both, all the way to disbelief and scepticism, none of which ever constituted genuine sympathy or empathy which was exactly what most depressives needed and wanted. Michael wasn't averse to talking about it, being someone who asked genuine and insightful questions about anything he didn't understand. He was was not afraid to go where others feared to. Elliot had lived for most of his life with the disharmony depression can cause, as both a witness to and survivor of its fickle manifestations. At times in the past he had swallowed everything that came his way, believing he was dealing with it and then later, when trying to stay dry and clean and deal with physical pain, he was prescribed benzodiazepines and opiates so he just combined those with booze and that is what did for him, accelerating him down his path as an addict. A few months ago he decided to be more open about it all, feeling like he was coming out the way a gay person might, finally telling his family and friends an undeniable truth – a confession finally made in anticipation of and in spite of all the subsequent misunderstandings and wide berths. He hadn't used benzodiazepines or opiates for years now but remained easily tempted by other substances. He still drank. In the end, coming out as a depressive and an addict and acknowledging that for him these were not separate phenomena, unsurprisingly meant more to him than it did to anyone else and of course didn't change anything at all, just helped him accept more the person he had been and now was. He did N.A. and A.A. but they weren't for him as he refused to succumb to a higher power and told himself even if he believed in one he still wouldn't kowtow to it. All that introspection and self-flagellation and subsequent structure and restriction bored the hell out of him.

He was currently emerging from a depressive bout which had lasted six months or so, though the recovery felt tentative as his eyes blinked into the light and he remained wary and self-conscious and inclined towards solitude. He saw depression as a physical condition, one affecting mood and emotion like many physical conditions do when their symptoms are aroused and on the attack. The first signs were the poor quality of sleep, then the early morning wakefulness which led to a state of lethargy and apathy making him irritable and self-loathing. The vicious circle was closed by an accompanying anxiety-state severe enough to make him believe he was finally losing his mind.

Amelia dealt with it all and, as she did so, avoided making demands on him but also did not allow him to wallow in it which was his natural inclination. This time a regime of exposure to light, Vitamin D, brazil nuts, dark chocolate and walking had kept the bastard at bay but he was not convinced that this was a permanent solution. It didn't feel deep enough. When tears came to his eyes as they often did those days, they were often provoked by random stimuli such as soap operas, crap films, news items of pets going missing or being found and reunited with their owners or anything to do with children hugging their parents. This made him suspect the damage done was deeper than he was admitting or was beyond his capacity to deal with so God help anyone else, including Amelia, daughters, friends, ex-wife, former colleagues, doctors, homeopaths, counsellors, psychiatrists, cognitive-behavioural-therapists, kinesiologists, reflexologists, reiki therapists and, as he put it, Uncle Tom fucking Cobbly and all. He decided he was too old to keep on trying to find a cure and if he needed the pills he would take them, if he had to withdraw from all human contact he would do so and if one day he had to end it all then he would do that too. If the dog slipped its chain then so be it. He knew the signs and often imagined a drill whirring and spiralling down inside him with viscera and shredded organs spraying outward, splattering over anyone who got too close. He used to think one day it would reach an end point and it might be worth the pain to get there but now he knew it just carried on until it bored a hole right through him, eventually leaving him incapacitated or dead. Meanwhile he was enjoying the beer and the company and Carol's hazel and green-eyed smile as she served the next round.

Roxy the barmaid came to collect the empties, smiling at them and saying over her shoulder to Miserable Bastard,
    Couldn't get out the bloody driveway.
Miserable Bastard widened his eyes in exaggerated horror, shook his head and twisted his mouth, looking down to the floor as though he'd just heard of an uncle dying or a favourite pet being run over. He appropriated a tone of moral outrage.
    That's terrible. But bloody typical intit.
    I think there was a funeral judging by the cars and people. Didn't look like a wedding...no one looked very happy.
    They have big families but it's no excuse. They just ignore the rules...and then laugh in our face.
Michael rolled his eyes and mouthed *wanker*, provoking Elliot into a smile of suppressed laughter. Roxy started to wash glasses behind the bar and Miserable Bastard stared at her chest.
    So did you get them to move?
    Yeah, yeah. They were fine about it once I found someone who knew the owner.
    Still not right. It's like the double-parking in front of the school gates at the end of our road. No consideration for others and the way

we do things in this country. I bet you didn't know this...they don't even teach their children how to cross the road. Allah's will if they get run over apparently...Allah's will.

Then, after a few moments he said,

IPA's a bit cloudy Rox.

Michael picked up their glasses and went to the bar. He grinned at Roxy.

Nothing wrong with mine. Two IPAs please Rox.

You all right Mike?

Elliot noticed he didn't mind her using an abbreviated form of his name.

Good ta...you?

Yeah yeah just late for work once I'd been to the childminder's but mustn't grumble.

She smiled a toothy smile at him.

No you mustn't Rox.

He gave a big smile back at her before taking the pints to their table. Elliot had watched the interaction with Roxy and noted how Michael had an easy way with young attractive women like her who easily turned that how-hard-life-is-mustn't-grumble neutrality into something flirtatious to which Michael could respond with the knowing look of an older experienced and kind-hearted man. They had got to know Roxy a little bit and something of her life after the three of them had sat on the barstools getting drunk not so long ago – the father of her children had left two years previously and he defaulted on the maintenance most months. She had three jobs – office cleaning, caring for a disabled woman and working part-time at the brewery. She drove a beat-up old Civic she couldn't afford to replace and she often wished she had met someone better but still asserted she could manage perfectly well without a man in her life.

Michael looked away from Roxy and back to Elliot.

What are you up to tonight?

Elliot was unsure whether he wanted to be up for anything at all and decided to leave all options open including the declining of whatever suggestion was about to be made.

Nothing particular.

Get Linda and Amelia on board? Carry-out? Our place?'
Yeah could do.

Michael started to text. A few moments passed before Elliot said,

I don't want to keep drinking all day though. I could do with a break.

Yeah yeah.

He was still texting as he spoke.

Come over about half six? See the kids and order for about half seven eight?

Elliot sent the suggestion by text to Amelia and she immediately replied *OK*. He didn't know what to make of that and wondered if that was an OK with a smile born of enthusiasm and happiness with life, including an eternal love for him, or was it a resigned and eyes-rolling bored OK meaning she wanted her home-time to stay as peaceful as it had been since he had gone out? An unsatisfactory exchange ensued.

sure?

yes

I love you

don't get too drunk, me too

He considered her last message as giving him the green light to press ahead with the plans and he asked Michael what he was doing the rest of the weekend.

Nothing much. Quiet day with the wife and kids.

You're not married.

Good as.

He was looking at Roxy. They laughed and touched glasses and Michael's face lit up in a way that Elliot thought could make the whole world feel good were it watching. There was no need to think about anything else because life was feeling grand again and the two friends were happy to be sharing *that* feeling in *that* moment. The good feeling was enhanced when Michael pointed to the door and Elliot looked round to see Biscuit coming in, swinging his growler and grinning like a mischievous child when he saw them. He walked over and awkwardly hugged them in turn with genuine warmth. He looked triumphant.

Geezers! he said.

Biscuit and Elliot were of a similar age and had trodden a similar path in terms of work, children and relationships but differed in that Biscuit came from Leith, supported Hibs and still sported a younger man's haircut of number one back and sides with a untidy mop of curls on top. They had met at the local reggae club. It had been a surprise to find a reggae club at all in their town but the Natty Congo Lounge had live acts and a resident DJ every Wednesday fortnight. Elliot and Michael would go along whenever they could and had become friendly with some of the regulars who were mostly older West Indian men, some of whom were Rastas and a smattering of whites, most of whom were women. Biscuit and Elliot had started chatting at the bar and soon recognised a kindred spirit when they reminisced about music in the seventies and early eighties - Rock Against Racism, the Clash, the Pistols, the Jam and how punk and reggae had often been mutually respectful bedfellows during the days when the likes of Biscuit and Elliot had searched for alternative ways to express themselves. Never party political but political all the same, they had been feeling their way in the world as they spliffed, sped and drank their way through the years with a fuck-em-all attitude. Then they burned out and got mortgaged and cynical but had still carried on looking for the hit. For a while back in the eighties, so Biscuit told them, he had favoured shaving his head completely, leading to his pals calling him Baldy then Garibaldi then Biscuit, the name that stuck and the one he always used to introduce himself. His real name was Eddie. Only ma fuckin ma calls me that, he had said.

He told them he was buying them a pint and went the bar giving Miserable Bastard a friendly nod to which he got no response. He made an indistinct jerk of his head in the direction of the older man which only Roxy could see.

Three IPAs please Rox.
She smiled as she pulled the pints. Biscuit brought them over to the table and sat down.

Just went wi the missis ta the fuckin Dolphin man, he said, ta eat ya know. Fuckin useless fuckin dump. Ya been in? See the fuckin menu? Ya wouldn't fuckin believe whats on it.

Unbefuckinlieveafuckable. Treasure of the gatherer. Yever hear a that? Fuckin treasure… of the fuckin… gatherer. What the fuck do ye think that is?'

The two of them shook their heads.

Aye on the fuckin menu. Treasure of the gatherer. That's what they fuckin called it.

What?

Mushroom soup! Fuckin mushroom soup. Fuckin mushroom soup is now *treasure* of the *fuckin* gatherer. Fuck that and up their fuckin arses man. And there was more ta come.

Michael and Elliot were now both laughing. Biscuit continued in an exaggeratedly camp voice,

Jewels of the sea on a bed of peppery rocket. Imagine that! Fuckin prawn and chewy squid wi a few green leaves and them baby tomatoes…that's what fuckin jewels of the sea are. Fuck's sake. She loved it mind so she did but I couldnae wait ta get oot. Spent forty fuckin quid n all!

He sees Jonny leaving the office.

Jonny! Hey Jonny yever hear a this?

He retold the treasure of the gatherer story to more laughter and then declined the offer of another drink from Elliot.

No ta. Just come in to fill my fuckin growler. Have to get hame. She's pickin up the kids from some fuckin party and we're all gonna watch fuckin Toy Story Ten or some such shite. Promised I wouldn't be late.

Miserable Bastard looked round from his perch and said loudly enough for it to be meant for an audience,

Small mercies.

Fuck off ya miserable cunt. Away and suck yer ain dick. Lads it's been a pleasure.

He blew a kiss at Roxy and then one at Jonny.

Adioski good people.

The bar area began to fill with white men over the age of forty and the atmosphere was one of neutrality with busy conversations, mickey-taking and laughter. It served as a place of refuge where no one ever caused harm or trouble, more like a private club and more familiar than a pub. A regular they recognised but didn't know arrived accompanied by a young Asian-looking guy who ordered a couple of pints. The Asian-looking guy was tall and well-built with his hair shaved at the back and sides with shiny spikes on top. Miserable Bastard spoke out loud without looking up from his glass.

Thought you lot weren't allowed to drink.

The young man looked at him and said in a West London accent,

I'm sorry? Are you talking to me?

You heard. Don't want to offend your bloody prophet now do you?

He looked to his audience for recognition and approval but didn't get it.

I'm not Muslim and even if I was you prick…what's it to you?

This was the first time they had sensed trouble in there and the crowd was transfixed with that familiar mix of adrenaline, fascination and wariness which always accompanied the preface to violence. Miserable Bastard spoke again.

Kin pakis. Fuck off back to whatever shithole you crawled out of.

This unleashed an agitation of outrage and shouting from some of those standing nearby. It was loud and full of swear words and insults and all directed at Miserable Bastard.

Dave enough. Enough! said Jonny.

So that's his name, thought Elliot. Through it all and in what Elliot remembered as a muffled silence he saw Michael rise from his chair and push his way through the crowd towards Miserable Bastard who looked at him for no more than a second in at first defiance and then in fear as Michael pushed him on the top of his chest with both hands so forcefully that Miserable Bastard was launched backwards, taking his stool and pint with him. His head hit the wall. His glass broke and Elliot watched the beer staining Miserable Bastard's jacket and shirt. The older man looked both surprised and stupid lying on his back like a stranded beetle with no one moving to help him up. Everyone was quiet and Elliot started to feel sorry for him.

Jonny put his arms around Michael from behind and told him he should leave it and leave. Elliot picked up Michael's coat and pulled him away. They stood on the steps outside for a minute or two. Michael was breathing heavily and looking at his feet. He sat down.

Okay?

Yeah yeah.

He didn't look up. Carol came out and touched him briefly on the shoulder and then rested her hand on Elliot's arm in the way a nurse might do when reassuring a patient about some forthcoming procedure. It felt gentle and friendly, surprisingly intimate and arousing.

Are you okay Michael? she asked with her hand still on Elliot's arm,

I'm sorry Carol.

He's an arse.

She gestured dismissively so her hand left Elliot's arm. He moved closer to her in the hope she would touch him again.

And we are going to ban him. Surprised it hasn't happened before. He's saying he wants you arrested…Jonny's talking him down just now.

Elliot put his hand on her arm before speaking.

Don't worry Carol. Best we go now though eh?

Yes. Thanks. We'll see what other members and the staff say but as far as I'm concerned you're both always welcome here.

They both thanked her and she looked at Elliot catching his eyes. He raised his eyebrows and gave her an exaggerated grin, then thinking he maybe looked foolish he changed his expression to something more serious and gave her a sageful nod instead, hoping at the same time to convey how attractive he found her. '

Let's go.

Michael stood up and took his keys out of his pocket and pressed the remote to unlock the car. Elliot watched the rear view of Carol in her jeans and fleece walk towards the brewery door.

Before he started the engine Michael spoke.

Not straight home eh? I need another drink. Sorry.

Elliot wasn't sure what Michael was sorry for – the assault on Miserable Bastard or the delay in taking him home. He couldn't remember ever hearing Michael apologise before.

Dolphin?

Yeah why not?

Michael smiled a half-smile then puffed out his cheeks and exhaled as though he was extinguishing a candle.

The Dolphin was crowded and noisy and full of a much younger crowd drinking lager and watching the results on a big screen. The two friends sat mostly in silence but agreed not to mention the incident to Linda. Elliot assured him he wouldn't tell Amelia although he was already thinking it was something he didn't want to keep from her. He wanted to ask Michael about his anger and why he had acted that way and how he now felt but something in Michael's demeanour made him think this wasn't the time. Michael drove slowly on the way home as though reluctant to reach there.

See you about half six.

They then did something they rarely did and shook hands. It was at Michael's instigation. They were making a pact.

CHAPTER 3

Amelia was still sitting on the settee, the crossword replaced by a book entitled *The Mind and Work of Paul Klee*. She glanced at Elliot over her glasses before speaking.

Hello dear. Good time?

He couldn't hold it in a second longer despite the promise to Michael and told her there had been a bit of an an incident and he described the scene and chain of events, how the peaceful atmosphere had been spoiled by Miserable Bastard and his loud casual racism and the obnoxious nature of the insults he had directed to the Asian-looking guy. He fabricated a version of events where Michael had demonstrated heroic restraint under provocation, describing the assault as only a push and that Miserable Bastard had lost his balance. Amelia was quiet for a moment before asking if Michael was okay. Elliot said yes but didn't believe what he was saying and Amelia sensed that, so she asked if he was sure. He reassured her with more confidence this time. He was feeling shaky and tried not to show it whilst continuing to wonder how Michael was really feeling. He had seemed so calm after the event, albeit detached and withdrawn but who could possibly have known what was going on in his head? Amelia was also calm and appearing disinterested, which he thought was typical of her. It was also difficult for him to know what was going on in her head. He would have liked more of a reaction and felt piqued by her apparent indifference.

Elliot ran a bath, something he often did when wanting to remove himself from a situation in which he felt uncomfortable. He wanted to be asked if he was feeling okay and was annoyed she hadn't done so then he was annoyed with himself for being annoyed but still couldn't avoid the fact he had wanted her to show some concern for him. He hated it when she appeared so self-contained she became detached and dispassionate. Now he wanted to cut himself off and relax so he could reflect on what had happened at the brewery but instead of thinking about Michael, his thoughts kept returning to Amelia and her lack of reaction. Was his wanting a reaction and her not giving one a symptom of their relationship being in the throes of a terminal decline or was it normal behaviour for people who had been together for a few years? Did they *know* each other any more? Did they ever? Who *was* she? Who was this person who spent so much time in close proximity to him but with whom he now seemed to share so little? How could the things that happened to *him* be so separate from the things that happened to *her*? He put his head under water and thought he would like to stay like that for eternity.

He stayed there until the water started to cool. Maybe they had been spending more time apart for a reason. If so, what was it? What had provoked him to spend more and more time with Michael? He knew Amelia believed Michael to be someone who might be better kept at arm's length but Elliot rationalised his likeness for him, describing him as intelligent and unpredictable, someone who was different and so much more stimulating than others in their social circle. All through his life he had come across charismatic and potentially dangerous people like Michael and all had been different from his regular friends – the ones who were close on the surface and with whom he had shared some of life's milestones but whom also, when he examined them with his critical eye, were mostly concerned with what *they* did and with what *they* felt. Self-centred rather than selfish but so preoccupied with the minutiae of their own lives they found it difficult to truly listen or see even though they would no doubt have denied this if challenged about it. The sort of people whom if they saw him with his leg hanging off or one of his eyes gouged out would say that had happened to them once, before going on to describe their experience while completely bypassing his, all the time believing they were acting as good friends and doing what good friends do. He concluded friendships could easily disappoint and that he shouldn't have had unrealistic expectations of any of them even though he had always been someone who had wanted to be smothered by the constancy they offered and the affirmation he gained from them. He was less like that now.

Maybe ten years of living together hadn't been enough and maybe they had to go through this stage of doubt and uncertainty in order to reach the true meaning of what their relationship was, although ten years seemed to him a significant amount of days and hours to have shared the same space with the same person for it not to have been truly meaningful. He thought back to when they first met in the members' restaurant at Tate Modern. She had sat down on one of the few spare seats which happened to be at the table where he was sitting. He was immediately interested – her skin darker than his and he wondered if she was South American. He noticed her green eyes and the silver bracelets she wore on both arms. They talked about Bridget Riley whose exhibition they had both just seen and during this neutral discourse he started to find her likeable and attractive. Her hair was tied up loosely and secured by what looked to him like chopsticks and she wasn't wearing any make-up as far as he could tell. A brooch of an intricate Celtic design was pinned to her lapel and he avoided looking at it too closely in case she thought he was looking at her breasts. She appeared relaxed and confident and not at all wary of him. Her opinions were well-informed and articulately expressed. She had that slightly distracted air characteristic of some artists or academics and when she learned he was a painter she showed what he took to be genuine interest and asked him some unusual questions including why he only worked in two dimensions. When he said he just couldn't be arsed about the third, her face lit up and she laughed out loud with a harsh honking animal-like laugh which he found appealing and which provoked his further interest in her. He hesitated to ask about her work in case it sounded too clichéd or where she was from in case it sounded too superficial but then thought it would actually demonstrate genuineness on his part and would also show he was the type of man who didn't just want to talk about himself even though he did. He asked her where she was from.

London.
And your roots?
London.
She honked at his discomfort before adding,
My mother was from Sierra Leone where I was born and my father was half-Spanish and half-Scottish. But I've lived here for most of my life.

They went for a drink in the Market Porter and she insisted on buying the first round. As he stood behind her the barman asked looking beyond her if Elliot was being served. Elliot told him, nodding towards Amelia, that they were together. The barman smiled at them,

Congratulations mate…how long for?

Elliot put his arm around her and said,

About two minutes.

This made the three of them laugh. He feared he had acted with too much familiarity too soon and he apologised but she told him not to worry and seemed comfortable. It had been good to feel so carefree in her company and that quality pervaded the next few times they met. Sleeping together was easy and without neurosis. Their first breakfast as calm and natural as he had ever known.

She lectured in aesthetics at the University of London. It was a subject whose worth she said she was unsure about, her doubt provoked by the philosophy lecturers she worked with whom she mostly distrusted and disliked. She described them as not having an original thought among them despite their presuming an air of erudition and pomposity which was designed to discourage anyone questioning their intellectual prowess and opinions, let alone the worth of their highly-paid positions. Aesthetics was a discipline she said she understood instinctively and so it felt natural to her to encourage her students' critical thinking in relation to the subject and all it encompassed. Her intellectual capacity seemed well-suited to the rigour required of philosophical discourse and analysis and she was in the process of writing a book about how the essence of aesthetics had been lost somewhere up the arses of those who had abstracted it too much in their perpetual self-justifying discourse. Aesthetics is simple, she assured him, and who was he to argue? She once said to him she could never be an artist because she couldn't feel at ease allowing her unconscious mind all that ascendancy but she could understand the need for artists. You do enrich the world, she said, even if you're all barking.

The tension between their two disciplines had seemed unimportant in their shared space. If anything, in the early days it provided a stimulus to their discussions and an impetus to the things they decided to do together. Now it went mostly unacknowledged. He hadn't really talked to her for a long time about his own art and he had never sought her approval for it. Their consideration of and respect for one another's work had been thus far one of tacit appreciation. To him she resided somewhere in the middle of existence as he went out to seek its extremities. She had once told him if the world was flat then he would have to travel to the edge and peer over its side whereas for her it would have been enough to just keep a safe distance and know the abyss was there. They went at her instigation to Finisterre for a holiday – her birthday present to him - a choice of destination at once humorous, worldly and imaginative in a way only she could be. He had loved her the more for it.

This was now a different kind of love, he realised. One that older people find before they grow old. Where you're not afraid to show the scars but don't feel the need to explain them or develop a persona around them. Where a bit of loose flab or an unsightly vein doesn't matter. Where it's understood that what's gone before belongs in the previous chapters and the story has now moved on. For now together. No rush, let's see how this thing goes. Ten years later it was still going but he was troubled by the thought that something somewhere along the way had been lost or sidelined and put up on a shelf because they were not quite sure what to do with it anymore. It had become convenient to leave it there because it didn't challenge the inevitable slide towards mundanity that they had become comfortable with. Until now, he thought.

The brewery incident and its precursors – all the little scenes, the *dramatis personae* involved and Amelia's reaction to it all had fomented this sudden questioning in him and had made him feel a sense of guilt as if he was taking part in the preliminaries to an act of sedition against the institution their relationship had become. Everything he had chosen to do that day and so many days before he had done without her. All the perceptions of life around him with the ensuing thoughts, emotions and reactions had been experienced without her. Maybe there was nothing strange in such a development but that autonomous way of experiencing the world now happened more often than the less singular episodes they at least still shared in part but used to share much more. The only events they now shared involved being with other people – his daughters visiting in their various combinations, going out for meals with old friends or sharing a carry-out with the neighbours. The rest of the time they were on their parallel tracks, barely glancing over at the other to see how they were, let alone where they might have been going. In the short space of time he had been with Michael that day he had felt and thought many things and now he couldn't find the motivation to articulate any of them to her. What he had shared with her was the dramatic bit and he embroidered even that. He had basically been asking her to look at *him*. *He* had been involved in an incident. *He* was interesting so could she please give him some attention.

Rain pattered onto the frosted glass of the bathroom window. He heard cars go by and tried to think of credible excuses not to go out later but found none. An indolence permeated his being. The light-heartedness he had felt earlier was gone and been replaced by something much more burdensome - the weight of a conclusion yet to be reached and which was nevertheless obvious. It was biding its time and was all the more intrusive for its lack of insistence because he knew it was there, telling him he would have to stop ignoring it soon enough. He felt the need to park this uncomfortable thought somewhere before getting out of the bath to dry himself, deodorise and dress.

Years before he and Amelia crossed paths he had met a working girl in a pub somewhere in Edinburgh New Town. He was leaning on the bar looking into his whisky and listening to the clack of pool-balls and the players' banter when she approached with a view to getting his business. He declined but maybe because of her London accent or because of how she looked - mixed-race African or West Indian and boyishly thin, albeit with the over-applied make-up of her profession but beneath it all he reckoned her to be vulnerable and beautiful and because of how he was feeling alone in a city not his home he offered to buy her a drink. She accepted and they fell into conversation about where they were from in London, what they were doing in Edinburgh and some of the challenges she had faced doing her job, many of which were alarming but described in such a matter-of-fact way they could have been discussing shoe-sizes or the lateness of trains. She told him she used to think she would like to meet a decent guy one day and give up her work but the more time went on she knew this was less likely to happen. He told her not to give up and suggested her view of men had been skewed by her working experiences. She laughed. She hadn't met a man yet who had a clue about women, how they worked or what they wanted or how they could be satisfied.

Most men are useless, she said, and the rest are brutes.

She described how she used an imaginary box to help her get through the days. All her uncomfortable or unrealistic thoughts could just be put inside it and then she would close its lid and carry on. I asked if this included her aspirations for a different life.

Yep, she said, especially the aspirations. Why want something more from life? It just stops you from doing what you have to do now and from getting on with it.

Doesn't the box fill up? Overflow?

Then I open another one.

Where do you keep them? Under the bed? On the mantelpiece? Don't they just look at you and remind you of what's inside them?

Then I chuck them out and they're gone forever.

She told him she had to get back to work and then leaned forward to put her face close to his and their eyes looked into one another's, their breath on each other's lips.

I reckon you and me could have been all right. I feel like I know you. Shame, she said.

A kiss on the cheek and she was gone. When he walked back to the hotel he had hoped to see her. He wanted to find her and sit down with her, open up those boxes to help her find ways to realise some of the things she had given up on. He had hated how patronising he was being. His life no better than hers and probably less honest. Now he thought about using such a box for his own thoughts. That conclusion waiting in the wings. There was a knock at the door. He heard Amelia answer it as he stepped out of the bath.

Oh hi, she said with a fake enthusiasm designed to show the knocking person how *pleased* she was to see them in that way people often do in order to demonstrate friendliness and how much value they place on the other person when in reality they weren't at all certain of how they felt about the knock on their door which was unsolicited and not part of their plans. It was obviously someone they knew so he guessed it was a neighbour and he stood without drying himself so as not to make any noise that would prevent him hearing their conversation. He recognised Cheryl's voice.

Hi Amelia. Er…that hole under the fence.

Yes?

It's not Marley.

No. I didn't think it was.

He doesn't dig.

No. I wonder…

Bill thinks it's a badger.

Really? I…

There's one living under Biddy's shed.

Really? Yes I remember that Jack and…

But I can't talk to her about it. Not since…you know…when…

The previous Christmas Biddy had torn up Bill and Cheryl's card and posted back the shreds through their letterbox following a row about a hedge and they hadn't spoken since.

No. I'm sure.

So, we need to fill it. The hole.

Yes.

Bill can do it. We'll do it.

Okay but we can help.

I'll help, he shouted from the bathroom but didn't know if they had heard.

Tell Bill we'll help if he wants.

The badger might do it again though.

Yes but…

That's life isn't it? It's nice in a way.

Yes it's lovely.

Living here. All this wildlife.

Yes we love it.

Okay then. See you soon.

Bye Cheryl. Let us know won't you?

Yes I will.

And that was that - a pleasant neighbourly exchange. Life was back to normal.

CHAPTER 4

He moved into the bedroom to finish drying and then picked out some clothes, choosing a beige shirt with a worn collar. It was his favourite shirt but he knew Amelia didn't like it. She preferred him to wear colour and didn't like him wearing clothes showing signs of wear and tear. He recalled when during the previous summer they had gone to a members' evening at the brewery where there was a barbecue and free beer with some folk singers performing (one of them, a bustless middle-aged woman with untidy grey hair and round glasses, sang a song about watching a squirrel playing in her garden) and a large number of men (Elliot included) were wearing beige shorts and polo shirts mostly in shades of blue. He had looked out at this sea of beige and blue as he and Amelia sat at a wobbly barrel, drinking and not communicating much with one another nor with anyone else, save for the occasional smile to someone they didn't know but whose eye they had caught. Something in those smiles, he thought, that was like the way people said hi to neighbours calling round unexpectedly – not really sincere, almost apologetic and really saying don't come any nearer, don't speak to me, I don't want to talk to you, go away, but does just enough to appear polite and demonstrate civility. They were all there together having such *fun* in their bland and beige and blue way so they had better not spoil it by being real. Elliot had wanted to lean over to the next table where a particularly beigey couple were sitting and ask them if they were swingers. He had whispered the same thought to Amelia who struggled to keep the beer in her mouth as she laughed. The next day he went to Marks & Spencer and bought new shorts, described on their labels as salmon pink, maroon mood, mellow yellow and mystery black. No more beige for him, he thought. Except for his favourite shirt. Amelia groaned when she saw him.

I knew you'd wear that.

The familiarity in this instance was comforting and he smiled at her in a familiar way. She smiled back. This is going well, he thought as they walked down the stairs and into the sitting-room.

Shall we have a drink before we go over?' he asked.

Bit early.

She looked at him with incredulity. He persisted.

We could go to the pub.

Which one? I don't want to drive anywhere.

The Oak then.

Really? I don't like it there.

Something to do.

We haven't got a lot of time. By the time we walk there…

It'd be nice. Have a stroll. Get out the house. We could collect the curry afterwards so we don't have to phone for it.

We don't know what they want.

We can text them. Order it from the pub and pick it up on the way.

Then we'd have to eat it straight away.

Could leave it in the oven…on low.

Or we could just order it from theirs when we get there.

Where?

Michael and Linda's.

They were silent for a moment before he spoke again.

That would be simpler.

Or we could just have a drink here.

Be nice to get out but up to you, dear.

I'll go if you really want to - *dear*.

I don't *really* want to do any of it.

Well why did you arrange it?

Oh I don't know.

He stood at the conservatory door. She sat down and picked up her book. He remembered the knock on the door from Cheryl.

I wonder if it is a badger.

Could be.

We could put peanuts out and watch for it.

Like we did in Scotland. With fish and chips.

Yes. They eat anything.

He continued to look out towards the garden and his mind turned to Scotland. Amelia's family owned a small house on the coast near Kirkudbright where they had stayed many times but not for over a year now. The house was part of a small collection of cottages called

Knockbreck and was about a hundred weather-beaten yards from the exotic sounding Barlocco Beach. They both had good memories of their times there and they looked back on them through only slightly rose-tinted lenses. He loved the expanse of the mudflats when the tide was out and the view over the Solway Firth towards Cumbria. He pictured the two of them walking there at low tide with a cold wind in their faces and Amelia's arm linked into his, the light changing constantly with the rapid movement of the clouds. He thought he could paint there. Some watercolour sketches. He could take photos of the sands and the sky then bring them all back to the studio and stretch a large canvass. Canvasses even. A series of sea and landscapes like he had always wanted to do. He turned to her.

Why don't we go?

Where?

The cottage.

When?

Now. Next week. You know. What are you working?

I told you.

Forgot.

I'm free after Monday's tutorials.

Shall we? If it's not booked.

Not likely to be this time of year.

Shall we then?

I'd love to, she said smiling. Her smile told him that she too had been thinking about their relationship, that it was still worth their efforts and they could still find purpose and they still loved each other despite their both doubting whether that was the case. He returned the smile and acknowledged that was the most intimate they had been for weeks. He then understood these sorts of conversations constituted the glue that held together the disparate parts of a relationship and were in many ways more important than when they spoke of more sophisticated subjects such as art in its various forms or politics or philosophy and even though he recognised the worth of doing that he concluded those apparently more shallow unthought-through exchanges were the ones that gradually stimulated the manifestation of their inner selves and the way they chose to be together. At first they had been cautious lest they betrayed their doubts or insecurities, then as they had become more trusting they moved into the shared middle ground where they homogenised, feeling reassured enough to drop their defences. He started to pour two gin and tonics when Amelia re-entered, putting on her coat. She looked at the gins and he looked at the coat. They laughed.

Lets go, she said with mock impatience and her eyes bright.

She slipped her arm through his as they walked and he pressed against her. A fine rain blew into their faces. '

I'll phone Elvis tomorrow, she said.

Great bloke. It will be good to see him again.

He envisaged their friend Elvis Elwood who was, as well as being the Knockbreck postman, a coastguard, a poet, a Bob Dylan obsessive and the keeper of the house keys. A hairy bear of a man with a gentle lilting accent and a preference for quilted checked shirts and who generally kept himself to himself but who once quite happily sat up with them until the early birds had started to chirrup as they drank a bottle of malt whisky and listened to Blonde On Blonde. He was more worldly and informed than he appeared but kept his opinions to himself even when asked for them and he had quietly written a couple of slim volumes of poetry which had been published to favourable reviews. They both reckoned it was great to have someone called Elvis in your contacts list.

They entered The Old Oak Tree via the saloon bar. It was busy and noisy and they recognised a few of the regulars, noticing a man known to be having two affairs who was sitting at the bar alongside one of of his lovers. He was a weasily little man in his fifties with an excess of product on his swept-back, dyed-black hair. It made his head shine and reflect the light. They didn't even bother saying hello to him but did to the lover who grimaced a smile and turned away without saying anything. She owned a little dog with two-inch legs and she would walk it down their street. Always dressed smartly, always with her nose in the air as though there was a foul smell somewhere nearby as her stilettos sounded against the pavement and the dog with two-inch legs whimpered as he was dragged behind her.

Welsh Jenkins and his rugby-playing Samoan partner, Lucy, waved to them and they waved back. Elliot made a sign of necking a pint and pointed towards the public bar door. Welsh Jenkins gave him a thumbs up as Lucy and Amelia carried on waving and smiling enthusiastically to one another. Then there was Gary who pronounced all his r's as w's, supported Spurs and sported a tatoo of a geisha girl on the left side of his neck. He was sitting with two men Elliot hadn't seen before, both of whom were wearing England football shirts. Gary shouted across at them.

Aw wight, my lovelies?

His two companions turned at the same time and only had eyes for Amelia, scanning her body from head to foot in seconds. Tempted to say gwumble, Elliot replied,

Mustn't grumble.

They moved through the dividing door. Everyone in the saloon bar had been white and most of those in the public bar were black and Elliot was reminded of a segregated bar near New Cross he used to frequent in his art student days where the barman told him coloured in that one, mate, whites in here. Elliot and Amelia also knew a few of them in the public bar too and the atmosphere immediately felt more friendly. Elliot had opined many times that white people often presumed where mixed-race couples were concerned (especially if the man was white) that it is the non-white person who would have to assimilate white culture and its encumbant attitudes. He soon realised that in terms of feeling comfortable it was the opposite - in as much that, as a mixed-race couple, they collectively were *non*-white and whilst he didn't consciously try to assimilate blackness he felt more at ease in environments which were predominately black or of a happily mixed-race base. Brendan, one of their favourite people in the neighbourhood and with whom Elliot shared a studio space, came over to them. He kissed Amelia on both cheeks then shook Elliot's hand brother-style and then gripped him above the wrists with both hands.

Good to see you guys, he says smiling.

Then he looked Elliot in the eye and said,

Haven't seen *you* for a while.

Nah I know. Keep missing you.

Elliot could tell Amelia had picked up on this so he avoided her eyes and pushed his way to the bar. If the truth were known he hadn't been going to the studio when he said he had. He had not been doing anything else particularly but had just been feeling stuck as regards his work for some months now. It felt as though he had nothing left to say, that there was nothing left inside of him worth bringing out. That there was nothing there or if there was it was hidden and he couldn't find it. He didn't want to admit this to Amelia, wanting to keep this part of his life separate to their life together but he realised he needed to work out why he wanted that. He didn't want to be made to analyse why he felt blocked. It was as though it was something to be ashamed of and by telling her he would be admitting guilt or failure and didn't want her to think of him like that. He had aborted several attempts at new paintings, all of which he had started and got going with to varying degrees until for one reason or another he had abandoned them. Now he couldn't bear to go into the studio and look at them. He didn't know how long it had been since he last felt he was working on something worthwhile. It had been months since he had been lost in that space. He remembered the last time, probably more than a year previously when he had been drawing a self-portrait using chalk and charcoal. It was February and the studio windows were wide open because of the fumes of the fixative he periodically sprayed onto the drawing to stop it smudging. He had been immersed in his work, not noticing that the CD he was playing (Thelonius Monk's *Monk's Dream*) had repeated several times over. When he finished the portrait by giving it a blood red background and he then sat back to look at it. Suddenly he became aware of how cold it was and that he was shivering as he was barefoot and wearing only a t-shirt and track bottoms. His hands and forearms were covered in chalk and charcoal, he had smudges on his face, his lips were dry and the light in the room dim with the early winter darkness as icy air blew through the windows. He didn't know where he had been in over six hours of drawing and hadn't noticed the near-freezing temperature. When he worked like that he felt he was transcended, maybe in the way Zen masters were when meditating or that he was in a similar state to the ecstasy some could achieve through prayer. It was as though another force took hold of him at such times, primarily anxious and adrenalised and then flowing like an engorged river, unstoppable and all-powerful as it swept away any obstacles in its path. It was an addiction itself, the yearning for that high and the blissful timelessness within which it sits, the perfect state of mind born out of chaos and ordered by whatever it was he had within him. Was it a spirit? Was it a positive force or did it have a malign intent? He no longer felt able to handle the low that followed and so he would fill that desolate space with anything he could – alcohol, drugs, socialising, travel, exhibitions, reading, exercise, sex – but none of those came even close. He had asked himself over and over again why did the creative force exist and why did he feel so burdened by it? Now he was blocked he wished he had never had it, wished he'd never been cursed with it.

He spent the time he should have been at the studio wandering - taking a coffee here or there, walking in the woods, popping up to the brewery, going to see an exhibition before he even stopped doing that, finding the experience too dispiriting as the originality and vibrancy of other artists only confirmed what he perceived as his own impotence. He did anything but confront the reality of mediocre unfinished work stacked up in the studio waiting to be either brought to life or put out of its misery. The thought came to mind more and more often that maybe it was over and he was no longer able to paint. Whatever and wherever the source was it may have dried up and he would now be forced to contemplate the desert that life would feel like without it.

Brendan told them there was going to be a little blues in the back room at the Wanderer later if they fancied going along. Amelia told him they had plans but looked at Elliot as though to say she wished they hadn't. Brendan left them to rejoin his crew who were all jazz musicians (Brendan played trumpet) and they noticed George the bass player who waved both his hands at them and smiled. They drank at the bar and talked about the week ahead, both looking forward to Knockbreck. He told her about the blues he used to frequent somewhere near Ladbroke Grove in the seventies. This one would be a different affair, he told her, tamer than in those days when he had walked down a stairwell to a basement flat in the early hours of the morning and a wooden hatch slid open to reveal a pair of eyes that silently scanned him and his friend Redman before whoever it was opened the door and let them enter. Inside the basement had been knocked through to form a single large room. The bass was loud, the air thick with smoke and the smell of weed and as the only white man there (there were several white women) he was the focus of some attention, though mostly benign some of it was hostile and Redman had insisted he didn't go alone to buy the beers that were served from a hatch at the back of the room for fifty pence a can. The first time he had gone there the toaster, a tall Rasta with waist-length locks and a beard reaching his chest, made an announcement over the sound system while looking at him with a smile and to the amusement of those standing near him.

I see we have reggae international tonight, he chanted.

Elliot's phone vibrated and he saw a message from Linda.

girls have friends 4 sleepover tonite mind if we cancel? come 4 late lunch tom instead? xxx

He showed it to Amelia who with a smile ordered another round. He replied to Linda.

No worries. Yes re tomorrow x

Amelia looked him in the eyes.

How come you haven't seen Brendan for a while?

Just keep missing each other. Different time zones these days.

Are you working on anything?

Yes. Well no actually. Kind of. It's not working though. How's the book?

Slow. I'm not disciplined enough.

Don't give up. It will be good.

For now he had diverted her but he knew she had registered a doubt. After another couple of rounds they headed for the blues about a ten minute walk away and took in a shared shish kebab on the way. The Wanderer had once been a thriving pub but was now on its last legs and it was hard to imagine how it could stay viable for much longer. It was a large space dominated by a dark wooden U-shaped bar, behind which a solitary barmaid with dyed black hair and lip-piercings stood waiting for one of the three or four customers to come for their next drink. The lights were dim and sparsely situated across the flock wall-papered walls. A fruit machine flashed in the corner, emitting electronic beeps and whistles. A television on one of the walls was showing the news with the sound turned down and anyway nobody was looking at it. *Crocodile Rock* played intrusively through the speakers above the door that led to the toilets.

They walked to the function room where Augusto Pablo's *Baby I Love You So* boomed from a pair of giant speakers. A Rasta with grey locks sat behind a small table from where he gave them a morose welcome as they paid him a tenner each. There weren't many people there yet as it was still relatively early for a blues which would normally go on until three or four in the morning, police permitting. The lighting was mellow, the music good and a whiff of weed was in the air and Amelia started to move in rhythm, not quite dancing, not quite standing still. The lagers were cold, the rums golden and they each had one of each. He sensed they were about to get hammered and a couple of tokes from a friendly spliff offered to him (Amelia declined) added to this. They were relaxed together and communicated mostly without words – little squeezes, touches to the lower back and arms as they went effortlessly with the flow. The room gradually filled and they found themselves dancing cheek to cheek. Then she leaned back and clasped her hands behind his neck pulling him towards her and kissed him on the lips. He told her she was beautiful.

They went back to the bar, Amelia sashaying in front of him as Brendan, George and crew arrived. More brother-shakes, fist-bumps and man-hugs for him and polite respectful cheek-kisses for her. Both of them were stifling yawns. George puts one of his hands on Elliot's shoulder. It felt heavy and strong.

You want a little something to keep you going? It's quality, he says.
Elliot looked at Amelia who frowned as if to say oh no not now please I'm tired and so he declined the offer. After more hugs, brother-shakes, bumps and kisses they were heading out of the side exit and into the

cold. It was nearly one o'clock and the walk home was slow and wayward.

As soon as we get in I'm going straight up, she said.

Okay, I won't be long.

He sat on the sofa and switched on the television and wondered why he was watching the news at that time? He woke up about two hours later, cold and dry-mouthed. Once upstairs he could hear Amelia snoring softly and he got into bed without waking her and he remembered how he used to find those little noises so alluring. We are too familiar now, he thought before trying to remember if he had brushed his teeth and locked the front door. Fuck it, he said out loud before getting up.

CHAPTER 5

Sunday morning and he watched the sunlight edge around the curtains. He hadn't there for a few minutes and contemplated the day ahead as a flutter of tiny heartbeats palpitated through his arms all the way to the tips of his fingers. He had experienced more disabling hangovers than the one now lurking inside of him and he believed he would be able to handle it, having evolved into the kind of person who knew how to deal with this level of toxicity so as to appear to the rest of the world he was fully functional. He would manage this and the process would begin with a walk, the rationale being that fresh air, light exercise and a brief engagement with the world could counteract or compensate for what would inevitably be more excess when they were with Michael and Linda later on.

Drinking had become difficult to avoid and then impossible to resist. It had got to the point when early in the day he would start to look forward to the first one and how quickly it would blunt reality's keen edge and gradually return him to a state of loquaciousness and sociability that made everything seem okay again. He resolved to go a few days without it, starting the next day but immediately reminding himself he would *have* to drink on Tuesday (maybe with Elvis) after they arrived at Knockbreck. He rationalised that drinking up there was different and somehow permissible because it was part of the experience of being there *and* it was a holiday so it didn't count. It was unimaginable to be in Knockbreck and not sit by the wood burner drinking whisky, it was also unimaginable to be in Knockbrek and not enjoy a pint or two with the locals in The Galloway Arms. He also believed Amelia would be more relaxed about his drinking when they were there. If only he could stop after two or three, if only he could lead a life in which he was able to drink but not every day, to be able to enjoy alcohol's modest effects and stop, instead of allowing it to consume him as he answered its siren call.

He decided to walk to the parade of shops at Easy End, about a mile and a half away, to buy newspapers and have a coffee and bagel in The

Aficionado, a café where good food and coffee was served by young people who smiled at whoever caught their eye. He dressed without washing, brushed teeth and put on boots. He gulped down a glass of water hoping to keep the developing thirst at bay and walked out of the door into a world covered by grey cloud and buffeted by a cold wind. It was good to be sentient again, even if the stimuli had to work hard to penetrate the residual fog surrounding him as a result of last night's booze and weed. This made him realise his ability to fully engage in life was being compromised by drink, so he promised himself he would cut down, start exercising again and be mindful of what and how he ate. This could be a turning point, he decided.

The walk was more difficult than he imagined it would be, the honeymoon period between his conflicting impulses lasting about ten minutes. It had been an effort since then as the hangover had kicked in with a viciousness so malign and cruel it surprised him, bringing with it a self-consciousness that bordered on the paranoid as people he passed said good morning and made him realise he was incapable of behaving the way a human being in was expected to on a Sunday morning. He wished he had stayed in bed.

He reached Easy End, a basic parade of shops and services that just about met local needs. It was 10.40 and he headed to the café. He looked through the window, saw it was empty apart from one of the young women who served there cleaning the steam attachment to the coffee machine with a vigorous up and down motion. He pushed the door and met resistance – it was locked. He looked at her and she smiled and mouthed *closed* while shaking her head then pointing to the sign on the window which he hadn't noticed: *Sundays – 11am to 3pm.* He mouthed *ahhh* at her and she smiled again before going back to her attachment-rubbing. He wondered if he was looking deranged. What to do now? His temples began to throb. He decided to go to the Co-op for newspapers and so walked the fifty yards or so to the end of the parade, glancing in the windows of the mostly closed shops along the way. The wait will be worth it, he mused. The bagel would be the perfect antidote to the hangover which was now threatening to reduce him to a write-off. An Asian Big-Issue seller was setting up by the trolley stack.

Hello, boss, he said, how are you?

Elliot struggled to find words but managed to reply.

I need to get some change. See you when I come out.

Okay boss, no worrying at all.

Papers and Big Issue bought, conversation with seller avoided apart from the necessaries, he still had fifteen minutes to kill so he pondered the worthiness of waiting. The bagel was taking on such exaggerated proportions it was becoming the only meaningful purpose in his life so he decided to walk around the block behind the parade to kill some time. He was on a residential street of new houses, all with the same sand-coloured bricks, maroon roof tiles and slate-coloured paving on the driveways. The parked cars suggested home-owners who earned above the average and who had all borrowed hundreds of thousands to buy their houses, vehicles and appliances. The pavements were separated from the road by a grass verge punctuated at uniform distances by spindly rowan trees. It was quiet and peaceful but he felt as though there were eyes behind every net curtain and they were looking at him with suspicion, so out of context did he feel. He wondered if they would question his being there, believing himself to look like an alien who had just landed with the intent of disturbing the peace of their bland but trouble-free neighbourhood. An old woman walking a small dog on the other side of the road stopped while it defecated on the grass.

Good girl, Misty, she said, before taking out a roll of blue bags, tearing one off and bending with some difficulty to pick up Misty's shit which Misty appeared to have deposited in copious amounts, making Elliot wonder what the woman fed her. The woman didn't register his presence. He walked on and tried to imagine what life would be like if he and Amelia lived on this road and his sense of being an extra-terrestrial developed further. Another woman, middle-aged, face covered by the hood of her expensive-looking waterproof was also picking up dog shit, this time from the pavement in front of him and which was the produce of an older-looking dog who was fat and could hardly walk. They caught each other's eyes. A fine rain began to fall.

Morning, he said in an overly-friendly tone of voice hoping this would reassure her despite his unwashed, dishevelled state and the fact he'd been drinking far too much and taking drugs. He wanted his voice to convey that he was a nice middle-class professional man who was just killing some time. She ignored him, confirming the rationale for his self-consciousness.

There was still a few minutes to kill as he arrived back at the parade so he looked in some shop windows: an estate agent displaying photos and prices of houses that made him realise he couldn't afford to live here even if he had wanted to; a charity shop with the usual discarded and superfluous jetsam of the western world, including rack upon rack of second-hand clothes, shelves of books, CDs and DVDs in such countless numbers that they could never be and never would be sold. He stopped in front of the pharmacy where a sign in the window read:

Free! NHS Service Medicines Check Up – lets make the most of your medicine!
Free! Repeat Prescription Service –lets text you when your medicines are ready to collect!
Free! NHS New Medicine Service – lets help you manage your medications!
Travel Health – lets prepare for the take-off!
Cancer – lets go through it together!
Healthy Heart Support – lets show your heart some *love*!

Apart from the assumption that anyone would want to go through their cancer *together* with *them* (whoever *they* were) or he would allow *them* to show his heart some *love*, he was disturbed by the random capital letters, exclamation marks and absent apostrophes.
A few minutes to go and the hunger was beginning to claw at his insides. He leaned on the wall outside the café and opened one of the papers, hoping to appear nonchalant and at ease, thinking she would come and open the door soon. A man and a young woman stepped out of a four-wheel drive. He was tall, broad and wearing a corduroy jacket with leather elbow patches. He looked confident as though he owned the place, as though he owned the country, and he pushed at the entrance. For an instant Elliot thought, Hah! Idiot! It's not open yet.

Then he saw the man breeze through what was now an unlocked door. Feeling nearly disabled by his self-consciousness, Elliot followed him and the young woman into the café. Worse, the corduroy-and-patches man was on first-name terms with the young woman working there and he spoke to her in a loud posh accent, engaging her in a conversation about mutual acquaintances before ordering a pot of tea and eggs benedict. His companion ordered coffee and toast with marmalade.

It was Elliot's turn. He asked for coffee and the avocado and smoked salmon bagel for which he now had such an overwhelming need that he didn't know how he would cope with having to wait for it to be served.

Sorry, no bagels, she said with that smile.

Words failed him for a few seconds, his mouth wide open, head jerked forward as though someone had just hit him by surprise on the back of the head.

Oh, okay, just the coffee then, he said.

She smiled again even more broadly and walked away, possibly aware he was looking at how tight her jeans were.

The coffee was tepid and weaker than usual so he drank it quickly, all the time trying to focus on the newspaper but only managing to listen to corduroy-and-patches man telling the waitress about the *amaaaazing* deal he had got on his wife's new car. Elliot had to leave. The waitress told him to have a nice day and he told her to have one too. He headed for the bus-stop as he couldn't face the walk home. He just wanted to get there, eat something and go back to bed. He had imagined returning heroically with the papers and making a pot of coffee before sitting down with Amelia for some peaceful, wholesome and warm-hearted time together. That was now out the window.

The timetable told him he had nearly ten minutes to wait. A dumpy grey-haired woman of indeterminate middle-age, wearing glasses and a grey waterproof approached from his left.

Good morning, she said enthusiastically.

Morning, he replied, trying not to look horrified that she was speaking to him. She looked at him as though he really had just landed from a distant galaxy but persevered in trying to engage with him.

Not too bad is it?

He didn't know what to say but answered after an unnatural pause.

I thought it might be brighter.

Well they did say it was going to rain, she said, as though admonishing the alien for not listening to Earth's weather forecasts.

Oh, did they?

He had tried to sound more worldly but was beginning to panic. What if he had to sit next to her on the bus? A man approached from the same direction she had come from. He was stick-thin and wearing a blue baseball cap with a yellow embossed *NYC* on its front as well as an oversized brown tracksuit top, brown trousers and blue suede shoes. He was bow-legged and walking with a slight limp.

Morning, Barry, said the woman.

Morning.

Have you got arthritis?

I've got everything.

Right.

Then there was silence between the three of them. They were standing in a line facing outwards towards the road. Occasionally one of them glanced in the direction the bus would come from and Elliot made himself stare in the opposite direction in order to avoid eye contact. Another woman arrived, not quite so dumpy and with blonde hair variegated by a stripe of grey roots running down the middle of her head. Her face was so cracked and fissured and it resembled the aerial view of a mountain range. Elliot surmised she was a smoker who enjoyed several packs a day, confirmed when he heard her rasping voice as she spoke to the first woman.

Morning. Yokay?

Morning. Yeees. You?

Yeees. My granddaughter's coming back today.

Right.

Wasn't expecting her till next week.

Right.

Then some silence. The two men listened to the women, the first of whom had turned her back on Barry who subsequently looked uncertain of the world. He glanced at Elliot who turned his head away. The first woman spoke again.

> Not *too* bad, is it?
> No, said the second.
> They said it would rain.
> Yes they did didn't they?
> Nice to see the blossom.
> Oh it's lovely isn't it?

They all looked towards the cherry tree on the opposite side of the road. The bus arrived and they waited for Elliot to board first as he had the status of being first-in-queue. He gestured for them to all to go ahead in order to minimise the danger of one of them sitting next to him. He smiled at them as though chivalry and generosity were his only motivations and then found a seat on his own. Safe at last, he fixed his gaze outwards.

He walked through the front door, threw the newspapers onto the settee and headed for the kitchen. Amelia passed him in the doorway like a ghost in silence.

> Papers, he said.
> So I see.

She sat holding her mug with two hands as though she was feeling cold. She was wearing a long white t-shirt, her hair tousled and her eyes still swollen from sleep. He poured a glass of water and went upstairs, undressed and got under the duvet. Then he got up again to close the curtains, returning to lie on his back. He thought how beautiful she looked sitting there with the sunlight catching the side of her face and her breasts easily accessible under her t-shirt. He imagined the softness of her skin and the gentle way she used to say *shhh* as she climbed on top of him. He resolved not to sleep for long so they could spend some time together before going over the road. He had to divert his thinking and so he started to plan the compositions of a series of paintings, the genesis of which would be his sketches and photographs of the Solway's sky and sand. All those purples and greys in streaks across the canvass. The view from the headland – that vast empty space, save for seabirds and the Cumbrian hills on the horizon. He imagined riding a horse along the coastal path that led upwards from the beach at Knockbrek and which afforded for him an unsurpassed view of the world. He was dressed in chain mail and a surcoat and on his way to a distant castle he had to reach before nightfall. Wild primroses were turning the fields to gold and a gaggle of geese waited to take flight en masse from the side of a hill like an army ready to march, its sentinels wary of his approach. He drifted in and out of a peaceful sleep.

After an indeterminate time he became aware of Amelia getting into bed beside him. She pressed against his back. He was surprised and so waited a few moments before turning to slip his arm underneath her and draw her towards him. Her t-shirt had ridden half way up her back and he placed his other hand on her buttocks, his fingers pressing between them. She gasped and he started to move his hand but she held it there, pushing it into her. Her arousal aroused him more than anything or anyone else ever could, the intimacy as natural as it was extraordinary. She spoke in whispers.

I couldn't wait any longer. I've wanted to since last night.

You should have said.

She pushed him onto his back and knelt over him, bending her head to kiss his face. He leaned forward and through her t-shirt sucked gently on one her breasts and then reached between her legs where she was wet. No feeling could arouse him more as he touched her there, pressing his fingers gradually inside of her. The thought crossed his mind that she had masturbated before coming upstairs. She rocked to and fro.

I've been downstairs thinking about this. Now I've got you, she whispered, moving up to straddle his face.

It was in that place where she became unpossessed and feral, grinding against his mouth until she decided to move. She slid slowly down his body, her breasts brushing briefly against his face before guiding him inside her. He took off her t-shirt. Her small breasts, childlike and womanly at the same time, quivered as she moved above him. He looked into her eyes as she looked down on him and they held the gaze. She smiled briefly before returning to wherever she had gone. She sat up and he let her control the speed and rhythm of her movements. She pounded herself against him. Then her orgasm – loud, her back arched like a diver plunging to the depths of a mountain lake, then louder still until she let out a cry and fell back on top of him. Within seconds she started to move again, deliberately allowing him to nearly slip out of her several times before taking him back in. He couldn't hold on any longer and cried out in pain as he climaxed from what felt like the depths of his very being as his life-force surged into her with an irresistible and pulsating violence. He was in awe of this intimacy and overwhelmed by his love for her. Tears seeped from the corners of his eyes. She laid on her back and he traced light lines and circles around her nipples and stroked her pubic hair.

So soft, he said sadly.

They laid like that for just a few minutes before she looked towards the window and said,

Let's go for a walk.

He looked at her, searching her for something.

What are you looking at me like that for?'

Nothing, I'm just trying to take you all in.

We don't have to go over there for a while still. How about the woods? We've not been there for ages.

He would have been happy to stay exactly where they were for a while longer and wanted to tell her this but he also liked the idea of their going out and doing something together. The way they used to not so long ago.

I love you, Am, he said, his hand reaching for the back of her head as she sat up, wanting to draw her towards him again but she was on the move. She stood at the window with her back to him. He looked at her naked form, that which he always wanted to draw just so he could have a prolonged time to look upon its beauty.

I know. No doubt I love you too, she said.

It felt to him there was a *but* to follow. It didn't materialise.

Let's just go now, she said, shower later. Look at that sun.

CHAPTER 6

They walked across the scrub towards a stile over which they crossed into a field bordered on one side by black a iron fence from where droplets of dew hung like tears waiting to fall. Behind the fence through large rhododendron bushes they could see Hatch House, a centuries-old mansion that had recently been bought with a large amount of new money. They heard a game of tennis being played. Ball on racket, ball bouncing on tarmac, someone shouting *forty-fifteen*. After climbing over another stile they stepped onto on an unmade road leading to a livery stable where a ruddy-faced buxom woman in filthy jeans was brushing a pony. Cheery good-mornings followed before they climbed yet another stile into a field that sloped down towards the woods. They had to bypass a group of muddy horses before reaching a kissing-gate through which they passed in silence. He used to insist they kissed whenever they passed through one of these gates and Amelia would sometimes accede immediately and other times play hard to get, flirtatiously denying him before drawing his head to hers and kissing him with a lustiness and passion that would take him by surprise. Once some other walkers chanced upon them, coughed as they approached and said *excuse me*, making them both laugh.

The path widened into a clearing where the overhanging branches of beech, ash and oak showed the first signs of Spring creating a pale green awning between them and the sky. There was birdsong all around and a rustling of leaves somewhere away from the path suggested the presence of a larger animal, perhaps a deer or wild boar. She linked her arm through his and he could feel her breast brushing his arm in rhythm with their footsteps. He wanted to make love there and then, on the ground, against a tree. She broke the silence.

So are you not going to the studio?

He didn't know what to say and hesitated, trying to choose his words.

No. Not much anyway.

Where do you go then?

Nowhere really. Coffee shops, the bookies, you know, the brewery.

The brewery?

Sometimes.

Why?

What?

Why do you not go to the studio? Why do you go to the brewery? Why do you tell me you've gone to the studio?

She had released her arm.

I don't, he said, I just don't tell you I haven't.

Why?

Sometimes I do go. Just don't stay there.

Two women walking their dogs were coming towards them. Elliot and Amelia returned the women's good mornings with good mornings of their own. The mood between them had changed.

Why? she asked again.

Because I hate it.

What? The studio?

No. My work. Or lack of it. I hate it. I'm not able to work there.

Well, move then.

It's not the studio.

What is it then? Brendan?

No he's great. It's me I guess.

What for God's sake?

Her sudden irritation stung.

I can't fucking paint, he shouted.

She looked at him, frowning, twisting and puckering her mouth.

What does *that* mean?

I can't paint. Can't draw. Can't see. Can't think. I'm finished.

How?

I just feel blocked. There's a million-foot thick lead door between me and it.

What?

Where I should be. Or something like that. I can't explain.

They had emerged from the wood and were now walking over to the brow of a hill. There was a bench at the top where they sat and looked down towards the town. They could see the supermarket car park, the railway station and endless rows of houses, all brick-and-tile red, winding up the hills surrounding the middle of town where its eyesore shopping centre called *Destiny Mall* dominated the skyline. A four-carriage train passed, slowing towards the station. He broke the silence.

Humanity. So much of it. Maybe Knockbreck will help. I think it might, you know. He reached for her hand and she pushed him away.

You should have told me. What if I needed to find you? Also, did it ever occur to you if you would ever let me in that I may have been able to help.

May have been?

Why have you got to be just so fucking secretive?

Her anger was so apparent he didn't dare to reach for her hand again.

It's not secrecy. It's shame.

' *Shame*?' she spat, About what, for God's sake?

Impotency. Uselessness. Not the man you think I am. I don't know. All those things.

There was silence for a few minutes, the breeze fresh in their faces as a red kite glided above them, its forked tail steering it one way then another as it swooped down and then back up and all without a single flap of its wings, its feathers shining like burnished copper. She broke the silence this time.

How fucking male. Scared how I would react if you had the droop. Scared of not being the great big phallo-centric prick to my accommodating legs-akimbo quiet little wife. So you fucking withdraw. Become deceitful. Lie to me. Disappear.

It's not like that.

Well that's how it looks. How it's felt for ages in fact. I see it now. Your distance. All because creatively you can't get it up. It's not my fault is it?

He thought of saying *well actually it might be* but thought better of it.

Why are you so angry? he asked

Because you're so distant. Or drunk.

So are you. Distant. For fuck's sake.

He was now angry and another uneasy silence hung over them like a threatening cloud. Then she spoke, calmer but still tight-lipped and staring out in front of her.   Chicken or the egg.

What do you mean?

Which distance came first? Yours or mine? And why?

Does it matter?

Maybe not. But your dishonesty does.

I'm not having a fucking affair for fuck's sake.

He thought of Carol smiling at him from behind the bar.

Maybe you should. Might *un-block* you, she mocked.

Don't say that.

He took her hand and this time she let him, returning the grip with enough pressure to let him know there was a possibility of at least some reconciliation. They sat there in silence still holding hands and both hesitant to be the one to break it. She then released her grip, patted his arm and stood up. She had decided it was time to go.

Fucking artists, she said and he laughed.

Yep. We're selfish useless bastards. I know.

What are you going to do about it?

He told her about his plans for taking photographs and sketching at Knockbreck and how he could then use them as the basis for him to start working the images onto large canvasses. Trying to sound positive, he said he was thinking of using a limited palette and mixing just a few shades of purple and grey, maybe yellow, using broad brush-strokes and applying the paint in layers. He made it sound as though he had been giving it some real consideration when in reality it was just their conversation that had sparked this particular train of thought.

You've never done that before. Landscape. Seascape. Whatever it is.

No. Not since I was a student.

It's a good idea.

Really?

Yes. Do something different. Take a step. Anything but the fucking no-man's land you've drifted into.

He told her about wanting to draw her looking out the window.

Naked?' she asked.

Yes. Of course.

You want me to pose for you?

Yes.

We could try at Knockbreck. On a rainy day.

He wanted them to get home quickly so there would be time to make love again before going out. He held her and looked into her eyes.

Let's go get the wine, she said.

On the walk back he asked about her book and she told him she too had reached an impasse with her work, unable to home in on the points she was trying to elucidate through her writing. He felt guilty that he should have known about thisand asked her about it before. She explained to him she wanted to reclaim aesthetics from where it had, she believed, become stuck up the backsides of the academic philosopher elite – the *prizewinners* was how she scornfully referrred to them and whom she described as being limited, self-serving and vain. She warmed to this particular theme.

Philosophy is such an archaic bastion of...of... male one-upmanship and...ghastly Institutionalised sexism. You can probably add racism to that as well.

Really? I always imagined la *académe* to be full of liberal lefty pinkos, admittedly a long way up their own arses but generally politically correct, even if a litle superior in their attitudes.

Well, not in philosophy. Certainly superior but so *un*worldly as to be worrying. If they were working on splitting the atom or something as esoteric as that then maybe their self-obsession and blinkeredness might be understandable. They live and think in a small world and it's one that's narrowing all the time in my opinion.

But aren't they meant to be explaining life...for the rest of us...surely?

Exactly.

She paused for a few moments and then said how she wanted her book to describe what she believed to be the essence of aesthetics in a way and using language everyone could understand. She believed she could only do this by going back to where that particular branch of philosophy began and translate what she found there into her present day thinking and writing but she was beginning to worry this was too laborious a process.

Like preliminary sketches, he suggested tentatively, not least because he knew she was able to just swat away suggestions which didn't reach her level, usually without realising she wass risking offence to whoever was making them. She looked at at him quizzically but he persisted.

It makes sense. Going back to the basics. For me it would be like life-drawing again. You know I'd do some exploratory sketches and then bring them back to the studio where I would try to turn them into something new and real. Something original, a new way of seeing something. For someone with your knowledge and experience, going back with older wiser eyes may be refreshing.

Exactly! Look. Imagine you are looking at an object.

A piece of art?

Any object. Could be a work of art. Could be something mass produced. Could be something from the natural world – a stick, a tree, a bird, I don't know, just *something* that you're looking at.

Okay.

He felt hesitant as though he was about to go somewhere he wouldn't understand but wanted to show interest so he nodded at her, encouraging her to continue.

How are you going to interact with it? she continued, How do you relate to it?

He looked earnestly at her, knowing he was not meant to answer. She continued.

Not all of those interactions will be important or relevant but what *does* matter is if there is an aesthetic re*lation*ship between you the onlooker…the viewer…and the object. If there *is* a unique interaction that is aesthetic in nature and which produces something new – i.e. your new knowledge, your subsequent growth as a human being, even what you pass on to others in your own actions or dialogue – then this is how aesthetics changes our existential perception of the world and thereafter the world itself.

He felt dwarfed by her intellectuality but nevertheless encouraged her to continue.

What about things which aren't objects?

Yes! But like what?

He was watching her become more animated, passionate about her subject.

Like music. Sport.

Exactly!' she shouted, eyes wide, smiling at him, If you look at a musical score it means nothing to you because you can't read music. Hieroglyphics, Martian, whatever. But if you hear that music being played and you *react* to it, what is that reaction? It's not a universal experience is it? – I might react in a different way. What does it *do* to *you*? What has happened? The world has changed.

Draw a line on a blank page and you have changed the world.

Yes.

She was nodding and smiling in recognition of what he had just said and continued.

I love that. Or build a pond, build a wall and you change the world. And then every other interaction with that line, that pond, that wall, that bit of music - if it is of an aesthetic nature then it *is* unique. It's existential. The stuff of life. Even with the performance of that musical score – depending on who, what, why, how and where - the result will be…different. The experience of it will be affected by who the audience are, their level or receptivity, the environment, the acoustics, the conductor. Just one musical score could produce millions of different reactions.

So it's about perception then and how different individuals perceive any given thing. That process of garnering the information, moving it through the mind, how it's affected by memory…or emotion. Like a photo of the San Remy Asylum compared to Van Gogh's painting of the same scene. One is reportage and the other the result of his unique experience. How his expression of what he perceived through his own senses is so much more powerful…how it conveys the reality much more effectively.

Yes, she agreed.

She was thoughtful and silent for a few moments.

But then we have to consider the physics.

How? Why?'

Because we cannot prove how perception works.

I don't understand.

Take colour. No two people are likely to see the same colours when looking at the same thing. Multiply the complexity of that by the number of the people on the planet. The number of eyes there are, notwithstanding all the other senses. Look, every *thing* or object has a unique system of energy surrounding and emanating from it.

Okay, he said, not understanding at all.

That system determines what the object, the *thing*, absorbs and then sends back out as either reflected or refracted electromagnetics. Radiation. That's what the eye sees. And it's variable depending on the intensity of the radiation and whichever way it's being transmitted. Colour doesn't even exist at this stage.

What? No colour?

No, not yet. There are millions of retinal cells in every eye. When light enters the eye it travels through the cornea then the lens before it is coloured, if you like, by a kind of system of dyes. There is still no colour as we know it at this stage. This is where the brain starts to process the information received from the retina in order to transmit it to the individual. We still don't know how this happens but we do know that the brain then recognises what we call blue, red, yellow, the different shades, all the millions of colours.

So you could see...my blue sky coloured in what is my red for all I know. And even if we are looking at the same thing, what we are both looking at is different to whatever eachother's individual interpretation of it is.

Yep...light is made of particles...photons...and what we see is made up of atoms that emit and absorb photons thus allowing us to see things...every one of those atoms contains a nucleus and loads of electrons...and every nucleus contains protons and neutrons...and every proton and neutron is made up of quarks...these are the components of everything around us...and that's where I'm stuck. Because what I am looking at...trying to explain...is but one small part of our universe's activity. What about the rest of it? How do all those different interactions and occurences relate to one another? And how do we make sense of it? That's consciousness I guess. But what is that? Some say that's where God comes into it.

Why? I don't mean why God but why are you stuck?

Because I don't know if this is the realm of philosophy or neurology...or religion...or is it just physics? And what I want to write about is perception. If we are looking at the same thing but seeing it differently then how are we recognising its beauty or its ugliness or how do we know if music is discordant or harmonious? I want to simplify the complexity of it all.

You just have...forget about the quarks.

Maybe. It's just if aesthetics can be reduced down to a point where it's just physics then what's the point? Especially as physics is still at an embyonic...no micro-cellular...stage in terms of our understanding of the universe. If it all comes down to quantum mechanics or relativity then I question the worth of aesthetics to be honest. We are just a dot in this solar system which itself is but one dot amongst millions of others. Our sun...our source of light...the source of everything on our planet...in our lives...without which we wouldn't exist...is just a star...one of billions.

Hang on a minute...why do we do it then?

Do what?

Anything...from the cave painters of forty thousand years ago to Picasso and all of the little old ladies doing watercolours and all the rest of us hovering between mediocrity and greatness...what do we do it for? What is the point of it?

Civilisation...from the Neanderthals onwards...we had a need to be civilised....whether it meant our belief in deities to order our lives or the development of all our institutions...like politics...the arts and sciences...we had to create these structures to become civilised...to order our lives...to record our lives. Art has existed for longer than physics and probably has more to say about us than physics will ever do.

There you go then...there's your answer...so when I put paint on a canvass I'm contributing to civilisation...that's great...I've never thought of it like that.

It's what art does...especially great art...it simplifies all the mystery of the cosmos into something recognisable...something that stirs your thoughts or your feelings but without seeking an explanation for it or a description of it. It takes you away from the finite and demonstrates the infinite...it's like when you're watching sport...Roger Federer's backhand or a football bulging a net...the balletic lines of a striker hitting through the ball...how it can thrill us...affirm something in us that is innate...instinctive.

We recognise beauty in that as much as a Matisse cut-out or a Canova sculpture...maybe we should go and watch some sport?

She looked at him with a slight frown, causing a near-vertical crease between her eyebrows.

You know, she said grinning, that just might be a good idea.

They wandered down into a small valley then up the steep hill towards The Avenue, a residential street just a short walk from their house. As they approached a wooded area half-way up the hill a man and his dog emerged from the trees. He was obese, his breasts and stomach emphasised by his wearing a tight-fitting Arsenal shirt. His grey track bottoms were stained down one leg. The dog was some kind of lap-dog on a lead and baring its little teeth at them, growling as they approached. Elliot and Amelia said a good morning each and the man replied.

It's afternoon now innit.

He chuckled, showing them his yellow teeth. Elliot grimaced a smile back as Amelia took his hand and they headed up the steepest part of the track, through the kising gate at the top and onto the road. The Avenue was a road of large detached houses he couldn't help but covet, resenting that he was unable to afford one. Most of them had double-gated driveways so a car could enter through one way and exit through the other. He imagined life inside these houses to be comfortable and settled and the people who lived there functional and calm.

CHAPTER 7

He passed by the open bathroom door and saw Amelia standing naked at the sink applying her make-up. She was looking into his shaving mirror, her eyebrows arched and her shoulder blades taut and pronounced. His eyes followed the lines leading from her neck and shoulders all the way to her waist and then on to her buttocks and the backs of her thighs. He stood behind her and lightly kissed her neck while looking at her eyes in the mirror and they widened in surprise. She pushed her buttocks against him and he traced a gentle line between them.

We haven't got time, she said.

He kissed the back of her head and went to the sitting-room where he poured himself a whisky.

He carried four bottles of wine, knowing that if he took any less he would have to come back to get more as Michael and Linda never had enough of their own. Amelia carried a spray of daffodils and a bag of sweets for the girls. Linda answered the door and spread her arms out wide, saying *hiiii* in such an exaggerated fashion Elliot suspected she was trying to convince them that all was well when in all likelihood it wasn't. She looked like a female version of a 1970s Keith Richards, her straight black shoulder-length hair spiked at the crown and wearing a velveteen sleeveless top, black flared jeans and cowgirl boots, black kohl eyeliner, red lipstick and an abundance of silver jewellery on her ears, nose, lips, eyebrows, forearms and fingers and her bracelets jangled . as she greeted them with double-cheek kisses and hugs. Elliot noticed her eyes looked watery in front of her near-black pupils as if the surface tension of her eyelids was holding back a pool of tears would soon overflow and wash down her cheeks. He wondered if she was on anything so quickly scanned her arms, seeing nothing, but something in her look and manner made him suspect she was under the influence of something more than just an overstated sense of *bonhomie*.

Linda had hepatitis C, a legacy from when in her teens and early twenties she had been a regular user of heroin. It was period of her life she had always been open about with Elliot and Amelia – all the needle-sharing, gouching, rip-off dealers, estrangement of her non-using friends, sex when unconscious and in the end a diagnosis of liver disease. The whole lot bar fatal overdose. The fact she hadn't passed hep C on to either of her children or to Michael was a source of motivation for her to stay clean. She believed the healing power of nuclear family life was the driving force behind her continued abstinence and recovery. However shit her life had been, she asserted, she had learned there was always hope and that she possessed within her an indomitable life force. She had wanted to be an illustrator for children's books and over the years had produced hundreds of pen and ink drawings, mostly of mythical characters and landscapes, all small in scale and painstakingly detailed. Her increased use of class A drugs during her college years meant she never graduated. Once the girls were older, she said, she would like to go back to drawing but for the time being she felt content to continue with her office job and only occasionally make use of her collection of pens.

Elliot watched her tall lithe form lead them into the sitting-room. He couldn't' get the thought out of his head that she was on something. But who gives a fuck? he thought, it wasn't his business. They had spoken together many times about their addictions, having recognised each other's addict behaviours almost as soon as they had met. It wasn't just their addictions to drugs, alcohol and sex that they spoke about, they had also discussed the labyrinthine dimensions of what it meant to be an addict, the reasons behind it irrelevant, the only acknowledgement necessary the one that accepts addiction in all its complexity, whether an individual's junky status was in the denial phase, in so-called recovery or active. When two addicts met they usually recognised the addict in each other. It was in the eyes, the body language, the determined efforts to appear normal, to be all things to all people, to be the life and soul of a gathering - anything please, but to be outed as a dirty, low-down, manipulative, untrustworthy junky. Once denial between junkies became pointless the next steps were all about whether they could trust each other and this involved much testing of the ground they were standing upon, how comfortable they were with sharing and to what extent they could be honest. Junkies were often happy to share needles but not emotions. As Linda had once said, you can't wash an emotion through with bleach. Trust could only be established between junkies if they both had the same junky status at the same time as it wasn't easy to be abstinent when in the company of someone who was still using. Once trust was established, however, the bond felt eternal.

Linda and Elliot were both in recovery and they had often talked about what that meant exactly. They both thought it was another meaningless descriptor used to compartmentalise individuals for the sake of expediency, to paint over a bleak and monochrome picture with bright and positive colours in order to reassure significant others, the police, the courts, doctors, nurses, counsellors and the rest that things were going in a socially acceptable direction. It denied the addict their existential reality, which was for most a daily, second by second, struggle to stay clean and sober. It meant having to retreat from what had become normality, it meant learning to carry the darkness as much as, if not more than, the light and it often meant swapping the most destructive addiction for one more socially acceptable or more easily hidden and denied. The term *in recovery* was disparaging as it implied the person afforded that status had characteristics unfavourable to an ordered society: weakness, self-indulgence, lack of moral fibre, untrustworthiness, lack of capacity to judge, discern, love, work, bear children, parent and so on. Every precept that a Western capitalist, consumerist society required of its citizens was deemed to be beyond anyone who had an addiction even though it peddled and profited from the very chemicals people became addicted to. The addict could never live up to those specious expectations and so had to hide or die. An addict's sense of their own failure was affirmed whenever they looked into the smoke and mirrors of society's eyes and felt its judgements rain down upon them. Eventually, in times unadulterated by whatever their particular poisons might have been, both Elliot and Linda had got to understand the game. Linda felt fortunate to have found in Michael a partner from whom she received unconditional affirmation and acceptance, which was how she defined love. Elliot felt fortunate to have found in Amelia someone whose intellectual capacity was broad enough for her to be non-judgemental about his past but she was clear she wouldn't accept his bringing that kind of chaos into their lives together. This made him wonder if her boundary setting was protecting him or preventing him express his true self, even if that meant destruction.

Their partners were not addicts and so could never understand them as fully as they needed to be understood. Elliot and Linda both invested much energy in trying to reassure Amelia and Michael, in being faithful to them, in denying their selves for their sakes, believing they would be loved in return, kept on whatever the straight and narrow might be and have done more good to them than they could probably have ever hoped for. Elliot knew though that when he had established trust with a fellow addict then he was bound to them forever in an impossible love that was hard to let go of because in sharing their insights they were admitting to each other and so to the whole universe that life was a lie. The whole premise upon which their hopes, aspirations and efforts were made was illusory. Addicts preferred to blunt their pain, so any hard-earned insights and health-consciousness would never be enough to stop them wanting, over and above everything else, to collapse into the arms of their anaesthesia again and again. When this happened it was called *relapse* and a relapsing junky caused havoc in the lives of their loved ones but knowing they would do so was not reason enough to stop it happening. Oblivion's call was irresistible. A few managed to stay determined, impermeable and, despite what society and its army of judges might say, strong enough to resist the call. Linda was as strong as anyone Elliot knew and stronger than most. He wasn't sure if Amelia and Michael could see that.

Michael was sitting at the dining table and he stood to greet them. Elliot was relieved to see him in an apparently good mood and full of smiles as he hugged him and then Amelia, their hands lingering on each other's upper arms. She was smiling warmly at him. Elliot looked away and placed the bottles on the table.

Ooooh thanks, said Linda as though he had given her an erotic novel to read.

Kids not here?

I'm getting them after we eat.

She linked her thumb and forefinger around the neck of one of the bottles.

So not too much of these fellas for me. Unless you save me some.

He laughed conspirationally and reassured her there was plenty more if needed.

Ooooh thanks.

Michael was showing Amelia a small circular ashtray made of brass. It had been a surprise to Elliot when Michael had told him that he like to collect artefacts, usually small and from the East or Middle-East, from junk and charity shops. He said their unkown histories and subsequent mystery were fascinating to him and so he liked to show them anything he had recently acquired, especially to Amelia, no doubt believing her erudition qualified her to appreciate them more. He never sold them on and just seemed to like owning them and their as-of-yet untold stories. The shelves in the sitting-room were full of them: ashtrays, boxes, bracelets, bottles, jars and coffee pots.

Persian, I think, said Amelia.

There's something else, he said, taking another brass-looking piece from the mantelpiece and handing it to her. It was an incence burner with a removable top, shaped like a miniature tagine.

Nice, she said, holding it at eye-level.

Elliot thought, is she *really* interested? It's a fucking incence burner for God's sake. Linda poured the first round of drinks and told them the food would ready in about an hour.

What's on the menu? asked Elliot.

Chicken.

Ooooh nice.

He groaned inwardly, knowing Amelia would be doing the same if she had heard. The last time Linda cooked chicken for them a pallid, unseasoned, soft-skinned thing was placed before them at the end of the table, barely a different colour to what it must have been immediately after it had been plucked. He was instructed to carve and where Amelia and he normally fought over the wings, thighs and fleshy underneath bits, he mischievously put most of these on her plate, a stage-whisper only the two of them could hear. She didn't thank him. The other notable aspects of that most under-whelming of meals were the vegetables – over-simmered mixed frozen vegetables and barely-coloured, crunchless roasted potatoes. A jar of cranberry jelly provided the only moisture apart from the bird's flaccid skin and the wine they drank in gulps to wash it all down. There followed overemphasised pats of their stomachs to show they were *so* full when asked if they wanted more.

The chicken now presented to them was of a marginally darker skin-tone and Elliot noticed a scattering of dried herbs on its back, indicating at least some accommodation to the concept of seasoning. Four bottles of wine were drunk by the time the pre-frozen treacle tart and ice-cream was served. Knowing she was about to leave to collect the kids, Elliot had the thought that Linda had to be over the drink-drive limit. He went back home to get two more bottles and wondered why hadn't just brought six in the first place. When he returned Michael was talking about a Spanish brandy he had bought in Waitrose. Some passable Stilton was polished off with the second pair of bottles, most of it drunk by Elliot and Michael. Then they moved onto brandy, served in glasses Linda had warmed in the micro-wave.

Everyone appeared to be in good form and the conversation flowed, sometimes breaking off into various permutations of pairings, but mostly with all four of them engaging together at the same time. Sport, books they had just read or were currently reading, films they would like to see and TV programmes they liked to watch formed the neutral subjects of their exchanges. Politics and work were the ones that provoked some raised voices but all in all they were an amiable, slightly bland group doing what many others were no doubt doing - filling up the empty hours of a Sunday afternoon with food, drink and light conversation.

Until they mentioned family or, subsequent to that, parents and parenting. Conscious that they were at a different stage in life to

Michael and Linda, Amelia and Elliot veered away from being too conclusive and know-it-all about the subject. Elliot kept to generalisations and clichés such as wanting to always be there for his kids or that it was more important to be a parent than to be their friend and Linda opined that it was all about love at the end of the day and there was no such thing as a perfect parent. Amelia agreed with a sage-like nodding of her head before offering her own view.

It's about being constant, a reference point when it all goes crazy.

Michael hadn't said much and Elliot watched him toying with the incence burner, twirling it in the fingers of one hand, repeatedly removing and replacing its top, all the time staring towards the table-cloth, his focus somewhere on a point in the middle-distance of his consciousness.

Linda's opinion that it was all about love was one Elliot thought was nonsense but he was loath to self-disclose in order to prove his point. He had talked enough about childhood over the years. Ad nauseam. To girlfriends, wives, children, friends and various therapists – all to the same avail, which was to say that the process of his sharing personal information and any subsequent well-meaning or therapeutic intervention hadn't changed one thing about his past nor his own perspective on it. His childhood had been fucked up. More so than many and also less so than many. He had dealt with it in both functional (creativity, relationships that lasted) and dysfunctional ways (addiction, relationships that broke up) and all the issues were still there: an absent father for much of the time, an absent sibling who was sent to boarding school and an all-too-often absent mother who had been an alcoholic depressive, a condition that led to her having numerous hospital admissions and being hopelessly ill-served by the patriarchal and moralistic mental health care system of the time. What would be the point of sharing these experiences? They were *his* memories, *his* insights and the way he now lived life was his unique way of being. He didn't think he could contribute anything helpful to the conversation as it developed so he held his tongue. Michael looked up, still toying with the burner and spoke slowly.

The worst thing you can do is frighten them.

Elliot cocked his head and made eye-contact with him as a way of encouraging him to speak in a way he hadn't heard before. Michael continued.

My father frightened me when I was young. Shouts. Threats.

They were all silent for a few moments before he spoke again.

A slap across the head if I didn't like my food or didn't understand my homework or couldn't sleep. Towering over me and shouting. Taking his belt off and whipping me. Big fucking man. And I became angry too. Enraged actually. Not so much with him funnily enough, but with her, my mother. For being complicit, passively part of it, allowing it to happen and then expecting me to get over it. As if a hug would make it all better afterwards. She never did anything to stop it.

Double-bind, said Elliot.

Oh yeah. I was double-bound all right. I know that. He made me frightened of the world and she allowed it to happen, all the while telling me she loved me and I was a lucky boy to have such a hard-working father who also loved me.

Do you ever see your parents?

It's Linda who answers.

He hasn't seen them for months.

Michael cast his eyes in her direction. No one could tell if he was irritated or grateful for her intervention. Elliot was irritated though. It was unprecedented for Michael to speak about himself in any depth, even when he had been drinking. In fact he would usually detach himself when within a social gathering, shutting his self away to just go through the motions of social discourse. Elliot realised Michael wanted to explain why he was the person they all thought they knew. He wasn't making excuses, he just wanted them to understand something of the burden he carried. Had yesterday's incident provoked Michael into this self-disclosure? He was slightly opening an inner door, one that usually remained shut and Elliot wanted him to continue speaking without anyone inducing his usual reticence by interrupting him. Linda broke the silence.

It's like they want to show each other affection but just can't.

Everyone's eyes were on Michael.

Fuck it, he said, enough of this. Too deep.

He laughed then addressed Elliot.

Cold beer? How about you, Am?

They both wanted one so Linda took three beers from the fridge, all jacketed in condensation. She stood behind Michael, put her hands on his shoulders and bent over to kiss him on the top of the head. He leaned his head back and pursed his lips in readiness for the kiss that she then obliged him with. She rubbed his back as though he was in pain.

I'll go and get the girls then, she said. You'll still be here, won't you?

Most likely, said Elliot, raising his eyebrows and nodding his head in order to reassure her.

Where are they? asked Amelia.

Not far, just up past Oakwood station. I'll only be twenty minutes, half hour tops.

Then we'll be here, said Amelia, drawing lines in the condensation on her beer bottle.

Elliot was still worried Linda was over the limit and possibly under the influence of something else so he felt he should offer to go with her. He analysed his motivation to do so. He felt protective and fraternal but also secretive and even incestuous. The addict in him wanted to share a secret space with another addict. He brushed the thought away – she was responsible for her own actions and she had to make her own decisions and judgements. He would only make things worse, more complicated and awkward. So she left alone.

More than forty minutes had passed, during which time the three of them had drunk more beer and listened to music while talking about nothing in particular. Elliot sensed Michael's unease as he waited for Linda's return, checking his watch, sending a text. Then the sound of a car on the gravelled driveway broke the tension. The kids ran in and give them all hugs. Linda leaned against the door frame, unaffected and elegant, watching the scene with a smile. Michael glanced up at her.

Come on, she said to the girls, time for bed.

What about baths? asked Michael.

I suppose they should. They can just shower.

She slurred the last two words and ushered the girls out towards the stairs. Michael's expression was tense, emphasising the lines of his cheekbones.

Fuck's sake, he said, still twiddling the burner in his hand.

It's okay, said Amelia.

Elliot sensed that Michael was about to erupt but didn't know if Amelia had realsied this. Michael looked angrily at her.

It's not okay.

Amelia tried to calm him, speaking softly.

It's been a long day. Everyone's tired.

Linda came back in and Michael looked at her.

Why were you so long?

She frowned, shrugged her shoulders, rolled her eyes and then gestured with her hands outstretched as though she was being asked a stupid question.

They took ages to get ready.

And you had a drink.

I didn't.

Well you fucking sound like you did.

I didn't!

I can't believe you would do that.

Michael, calm down, I didn't.

How could you get in the car like that with the girls? I don't fucking believe you sometimes.

Like what?

How many more fucking times?

Not now please, Michael.

Amelia and Elliot remained silent, both considering interjections but were unable to think of what to say.

I just don't fucking believe it, continued Michael.

Linda shook her head and rolled her eyes again.

Fuck off will you? Just lay off.

She left the room, closing the door forcefully behind her. Michael looked stung. He pulled back his right arm and it was apparent he was going to throw the burner. He was looking at the closed door. As he started to project his arm forward Amelia and Elliot heard the turning of the door handle and both felt an urge to shout a warning. Linda opened the door as Michael released the burner and it flew at force towards her. She had no time to see it, let alone react to it and it struck her in the face below her left eye. Her hands were raised in defence and then she fell to the floor, her head hitting the door as she screamed. The sound was visceral as though it had been howled by a wounded animal and they all leapt from their chairs.

Amelia was the first to her. Blood stained her hands as she tried to turn Linda over. A pool of it began to form on the carpet. Linda was crying. There were tears, snot and blood all over her face as Amelia and Elliot helped her to sit up. Michael was standing over them. He spoke with desperation in his voice.

Lin, I didn't mean that, sorry darling sorry, I'm so sorry
She sat up against the door.

You cunt, was all she she said between sobs.
Amelia took command and told Michael to get some water and a clean cloth and he hurried to the kitchen. The girls came into the room, hair wet from their showers. They were screaming and crying. Elliot tried to reassure them, betraying anything but calm as he hesitated and stumbled over his words. They knew something was wrong, they saw it in his eyes, heard it in his voice, in their mother's sobs, in Amelia's steady focus on no one but Linda and in Michael's hurried return with a bowl of water and a tea towel. The wound below her eye looked serious - jagged, about two inches long and despite Amelia's efforts at first aid the blood kept flowing down Linda's cheeks. There was another cut on her head, less serious, the result of her falling into the door but both would need sutures. Michael was crying as he took the girls out of the room trying to calm them. Elliot suddenly felt sober again and able to focus.

She needs A and E, said Amelia.
Ambulance then.
Elliot reached for his phone as Michael re-entered.
No ambulance, he said, I'll take her.

You can't, you're miles over the limit.

I'm fucking taking her.

Linda was sobbing, her eye ugly and beginning to close. She shouted at him.

I'm not getting in a car with you. I'm not going to be on my own with you, you cunt.

I'm fucking driving and that's it.

He had shouted in a way that made it clear no one could tell him otherwise. Elliot looked at Amelia and she looked back at him, opening her bloodied hands as though to say what do we do now? Elliot made an instant decision.

I'll come with you. Amelia can stay with the girls. Just fucking calm down, Michael, if you're going to drive.

Amelia and Elliot lifted Linda to her feet. He told Michael to wrap some ice in a tea-towel and then instructed Linda to hold it against her face. His feet stuck to the pool of blood congealing on the laminated floor. Kendrick Wells came to his mind and he felt the adrenaline of danger surge through him. Michael had started the car and Amelia was hugging the girls as she knelt beside them. One of them was wearing a yellow nightdress that had streaks of blood on it. Elliot put his arms around Linda's shoulders and led her to the car. It was somewhere after ten o'clock and the air was sharp and cold. Elliot calmed again, thinking the air felt good, clean and real. The world hadn't stopped turning. Linda was also calmer but for little sobs beyond her control. She sat in the back of the car with the dripping blood-stained tea-towel held against her cheek. Elliot could see Michael was still agitated and hoped he was controlled enough to be able to drive. By the time they reached the mini-roundabout at the end of the road it was apparent he was far from it.

Slow down Michael.

It's fine.

He slowed down to take the next bend in order to show he was in control. There were no cars coming from either direction at the junction and he accelerated down the hill, ignoring the speed bumps and making the car jolt. Pain shot through Elliot's lower back, feeling as if someone had stabbed him there. The pain spread like a river's delta through the lower part of his body and coursed its way through his buttocks and testicles before flowing irrestistably all the way to his left foot which was now pressed to the floor.

Please just slow down.

Michael ignored him and accelerated again, jerking the car in a spasmodic forward momentum that made Elliot me feel nauseous. Linda threw up and opened her window, trying to lean out.

Shut the fucking window! Michael shouted, taking his eyes off the road to look round at her.

She carried on vomiting inside the car. The smell filled the air. Michael accelerated again towards the junction at the bottom of the hill where he braked too sharply. They all lurched forwards. Elliot looked out towards the right and became aware of three men standing on the pavement outside the Dolphin. They were shouting and laughing, one of them holding a bottle. Michael turned left and shifted gears. The left hand side side of the road was lined with parked cars and Elliot saw someone walk in between them about fifty yards ahead. They were nearly upon him. He wanted to shout a warning as the figure stepped out in front of them. Michael braked sharply again. They all lurched forward, more violently this time. Elliot felt the weight of Linda hitting his seat from behind. A man was sprawled over the bonnet, body arched, eyes wide and arms stretched towards them. The car stopped and the man slithered down the bonnet in slow-motion and disappeared from view as he fell onto to the road. Michael opened his door, stepped out and walked to the front of the car.

Fuck, said Linda

Michael pulled the body and asked him if he was all right. The man was floppy with his arms over Michael's shoulders and a stupid expression on his face, his mouth wide and gasping for air. He pushed himself away from Michael who again asked if he was all right. The man nodded. Michael's voice was raised.

What the fuck were you doing?

The guy looked young, in his early twenties, wearing a parka, jeans and white trainers.

What was *I* doing? Crossing the fucking road is what I was doing.

You weren't fucking looking.

Nor were you obviously you fucking drunk cunt. Could have killed me.

Elliot couldn't believe what he was seeing. Michael turned away slightly then suddenly turned back again and swung a punch, connecting with the man's mouth. Blood and teeth sprayed outwards. He didn't go down. Michael punched him in the stomach and as the man bent over he followed up with another punch to his face. The man fell to the ground. Elliot was struck by the ugliness of it all and how violence, even though he had witnessed it countless times, was always shocking, always unnatural, an invasive force that so easily penetrated defences and that came from somewhere inside us all without control or rationale. He stepped out of the car and saw Michael kick the man in the stomach twice and then once in the face. He twisted his bloodied face towards Elliot in a silent plea for help. There was blood on the road and the man's face dropped to the ground. His prone body made no sound. His eyes were closed. As Elliot went to grab Michael from behind, shouting at him to leave it, he became aware of some other men nearby. It was the group of lads from outside the Dolphin. He recognised one of them. His name was Lennie, he worked for the firm who had built their conservatory.

One of Lennie's mates moved towards Michael and shouted.

Oi get off him you cunt.

Michael, despite Elliot's efforts at holding him back, landed a punch full in the mouth and the lad dropped to his knees holding his face. Elliot pulled harder at Michael. They were in the middle of the road. A passing car slowed down alongside them and the people inside were staring, stupefied, before they drove on. Michael shook him off. One of the lads shouted.

Call a fucking ambulance, man. Get the fucking feds!

Michael grabbed Elliot's and spoke calmly.

Get in the car.

Elliot hesitated and looked at the apparently lifeless body on the road.

Get in the fucking car, Michael said, urgency in his voice.

The three lads were shouting. Elliot saw the blade as Lennie shouted.

Stick him. Stick the fucker.

Michael pushed Elliot away and grabbed the wrist of the one holding the knife and twisted it. The knife fell from his grasp and onto the ground. Michael had the lad's arm twisted around his back and then he slammed his head onto one of the parked cars after which the lad slumped onto the road. He then turned to Lennie, who was backing away. Michael looked at him impassively and spoke.

Now fuck off. Go home to your mummy.

He appeared calm. For a moment Elliot felt everything was now going to be all right. It was over. They were safe now and they could carry on with what they were doing before. It felt as if they could just go back home and everything would be normal again. They got back in the car. Linda was silent as Michael drove slowly to the hospital. No one spoke. Elliot tried to imagine a way in which this would all end up fine and without serious consequences but he failed to do so. How could he extricate himself from this? How could he walk away from this moment in time and avoid those consequences? He realised he wouldn't be able to. The world had changed.

CHAPTER 8

So much had happened in the four weeks since Michael's arrest. They had come for him about six on the Monday morning. Eight coppers and a dog to whom he offered no resistance, going peacebly as though he had expected it to happpen. A little while later they knocked on Elliot's door. Two policewomen, polite in their assertiveness, told him that both he and Amelia had to go down to the station to make statements. They told him that for now he wasn't going to be charged because the CCTV footage showed him trying to pull Michael away from the victim but they nevertheless required some more of the background story to the evening. They warned him charges could still be forthcoming depending on how their investigations developed and that he wasn't to travel anywhere without informing them. One of them noticed the support bandage on his elbow and asked why he was wearing it. He said he had strained a ligament so she then asked him how. When he told her the injury had been sustained throwing a frisbee for a dog, she smiled and he couldn't determine whether this meant she believed him or whether she thought it an improbable excuse. Michael appeared in court that same morning, the charge Grievous Bodily Harm with Intent under Section 18 of the Offences Against the Person Act 1861. He pleaded guilty and the magistrate refused bail, remanding him in custody to HMP Woodhill some sixty miles away.

It was about three weeks (he couldn't remember exactly) since Amelia had left alone for Scotland after advising him as she struggled out of the door to the waiting taxi carrying two large holdalls (she had refused his offer of help) that she didn't want him to follow. She wanted time to herself. Even if he had wanted to go there the police had directed him to stay put as it was likely he would have to appear in court. The days in between Michael's arrest and her leaving were, for him, the worst of their lives together: full of fear, sleeplessness and blame. His eyes constantly stung with tiredness and he was consumed by a persistant sense of helplessness – he did not know how to make things better. For the first time in his life he felt impotent. All the mental strength he thought he had gained over the years had gone. All his ability to handle different types of situations, different people and their behaviours was also gone. His problem-solving skills had been rendered inept in these circumstances, the likes of which he had never known before. He had once believed the world had nothing left to show him, that he had seen it all, and then in an instance his complacency had been shown to be what it really was - a delusion born of arrogance and denial.

He wanted to phone Amelia but the signal up there was weak at best and he also suspected she didn't want to hear from him. If she wanted to talk it was easier for her to call him. He understood that if she was in the cottage or walking on the beach then she would be out of reach but if she was somewhere with a signal she could call. It made him feel anxious and he sensed that familiar scratching at his insides. It was a feeling that had been a constant companion since that Sunday night, albeit one superseded by unadulterated fear after the first of the threatening phone-calls. He couldn't remember what time of day (probably morning) or even which day it was (he guessed the Tuesday or the Wednesday) when he answered the landline. Amelia had just returned from the supermarket.

Is that Elliot?' asked a voice belonging to a woman who sounded as though she smoked sixty a day and hadn't had a glass of water for weeks.

Yes.

You can tell that black cunt of a wife of yours we just watched her come back from the shops.

We? Panic took hold of his insides and he tried to stay calm.

Who is this?

You like your cunts black don't you nigger lover?

Look who are you? What's this about?'

He knew full well what it was about but had no frame of reference to draw upon to help him respond.

You don't know me nigger lover but we know you.

Well fuck off... and tell Lennie the police are on to him.

You threatening?

No but you are. I'm just stating fact.

She laughed, sounding as if she was about to spit out a throatful of phlegm before she continued.

I wasn't threatening. Just pointing out we are watching you and your black cunt...just stating fact.

She laughed again.

You're just making things worse for yourselves, he offered, feeling weak.

You'll be hearing from us you sad fuck. You started something you ain't going to be able to finish.

With that she hung up. Amelia was staring at him and his hands were shaking. He felt his bowel loosen but resisted the urge to go to the toilet, wanting to convey to Amelia that he was all right and in control of things.

What did they say? she asked, the urgency in her voice making her words shake.

Just threats, silly stuff.

What did they say?

She was louder now, her eyes wide, so he walked over to her and put his hands on her shoulders.

They are obviously watching us, they saw you come home.

She screamed at him.

Who? Who did? Who for God's sake?

A woman. I don't know who.

He didn't want to show his fear but he knew he was in danger of losing control of his body so he walked quickly to the bathroom. As he sat there he tried to calm himself but tears began to well up and he couldn't stop the ensuing sobs. Deep, gutteral and grievous, his cries poured out of him. He was sitting on the toilet having nearly soiled himself, crying in an anguish he had never experienced before. It was as if he had been abandoned in a place so hostile, dark and remote that no loved one would ever find him again.

The phone-call had been the latest in a series of events seemingly triggered by Michael's actions. Lennie, the guy who had worked on building the conservatory, for whom they had made tea, fed with chocolate digestive biscuits, even shared a beer with in celebration of the work's completion, that cheeky young guy with a mischievous grin whom they had grown to like and with whom they often laughed, was apparently behind all this. Really? he wondered, is this what he had grown into? He surmised Lennie must have known Michael's victim and between them they had plotted a course of revenge and retribution best actioned through a campaign of threats and fear. But to what purpose? There was surely nothing to be achieved other than an eye for an eye – a crude and illogical motive if ever there was one but one he knew was hard to stop once it had gained momentum. He feared that unless it stopped quickly it could just go on and on. The only conclusion would be to move out and that would take an age, so until then there would be no escape. Unless they could somehow be stopped, but by whom?

When they returned from the police station on the day of Michael's arrest, a car was parked outside the house. There were four of them inside it, all with their hoods up, windows down, smoking and playing music loudly. Elliot and Amelia watched them for a while from the kitchen window, wondering whether to confront them. Elliot decided discretion was the better part of cowardice and tried to ignore them. Amelia adopted a stoical attitude, saying that their tormentors would soon get bored if neither of them reacted. The car drove away after a half hour or so after which they argued. There was no logic or sequence to it, just an outpouring of anger and recrimination on Amelia's part to which his only defence was to suggest she was being neither fair nor reasonable. She told him he should have stopped Michael, that he was so awestruck by him he had become blinded to his flaws and that their excessive drinking had contributed to the whole situation. Elliot felt indignant as to the injustice of this. He pictured Amelia touching Michael's arm, smiling at him while he went on about the latest piece of ethnic junk he had bought. He told her that she liked to flirt with Michael and enjoyed his attention. This increased her anger to the point she was screaming at him, telling him that he was the one who had brought a psychopath and a junky into their lives and that he was a weak, useless failure, from which point it seemed there was no going back. They had crossed a threshold. After they calmed down he hoped she would apologise. She didn't. He went to check on Linda.

Linda had spent a few hours in A&E on Sunday night, waiting for her wound to be glued and steri-stripped. She had been asked how she had sustained the cuts and she answered truthfully, albeit with an omission of the contextual facts, that it had been an accident. She was then asked if she was being physically abused by her partner to which she offered a denial. Linda and Elliot had been left alone together at the hospital as Michael had (at Elliot's insistence) gone home earlier. He had refused at first, but when Elliot told him it was likely the victim would be brought to the same A&E and that his mates or family and almost certainly the police could well be on their way as well, Michael saw the sense in going. Had he stayed Elliot feared he would have taken them all on.

As he waited for Linda he sat on one of a row of red plastic seats and watched the comings and goings of the drunk and the stoned, the elderly, the wounded, the crying kids, the fretful parents and the various healthcare professionals merge into an amorphous mass of constant movement and noise. He looked at the rolling digitalised green words above the reception desk moving so slowly that he had to read them in staccato.

THIS...NHS...TRUST...OPERATES...A...ZERO...TOLERANCE...POL ICY...AS...REGARDS...VIOLENCE...AND...AGGRESSION...TOWAR DS...OUR...STAFF...THE...POLICE...WILL...ALWAYS...BE...CALL ED...AND...THE...HOSPITAL...WILL..SUPPORT...STAFF...WHO... WISH...TO...BRING...PRIVATE...PROSECUTIONS...AGAINST...AN Y..PERPETRATOR...OF...ABUSE...OR...HARASSMENT...YOU...WIL L...BE...SEEN...AS...SOON...AS...

POSSIBLE...CASES...ARE...PRIORITISED...ACCORDING...TO...NE ED...PLEASE...BE...A...PATIENT...PATIENT.'

He went to stand outside and wanted to smoke a cigarette for the first time in years. One of the automatic double-doors was opening and shutting repeatedly. Just inside them a large man was struggling on the floor with two men and a woman, none of them in uniform, who were trying to hold him still. He was screaming and grunting like an animal in a trap. An ambulance pulled up and a person of indeterminate gender wearing an oxygen mask was carried on a stretcher through the same double-doors, the crew having to negotiate a route around the sprawling bodies, their demeanour calm as if this was a normal occurrence. He wondered if the person on the stretcher was Michael's victim. He went back inside and saw police officers in the waiting area. He sat down again on another red plastic seat. One of the police officers was talking to the receptionist, his radio crackling and spitting. Shortly afterwards Linda came out, her wounds dressed. She looked like a civilian casualty in a war zone. They took a cab home. Michael was calm, the kids were in bed and Amelia looked grim, unable to hold eye contact with Elliot. Michael's eyes were swollen from crying. Amelia signalled they should leave. As Michael hugged Linda her arms stayed limp and unengaged by her sides.

Elliot brought all this to mind, once more trying to make sense out of something that didn't make sense. How could life have changed so much? What if they had not gone over to them that night? None of this would have happened. How can something so mundane and normal as a meal with neighbours have resulted in this? Recalling the events and wondering *what if* and *if only* occupied his thoughts in a never-ending repetitive cycle. He was sitting at the table in the conservatory, laptop open, trying to sort out some overdue payments online but the signal kept weakening for some reason. It happened there occasionally. He had made three attempts at logging into his bank account, each time losing the connection mid-transaction, leading in turn to the bank's default security mechanism to kick in. He was now having to prove who he was. His identity was confirmed by his mother's maiden name, the name of his first pet and the name of his first school. Then he was the third, fifth and eighth digit of his password. He noticed blue tits busy feeding and flying to and from the nest box on the shed and he watched swifts diving in sweeps and arcs across the blue sky. They usually sparked a sense of optimism in him, a reminder of the warmth of summer to come: evenings on the patio drinking cold beer or having friends over and putting chicken wings on the barbecue with glasses of chilled white wine slipping down as they talked and laughed. Or just the two of them listening to jazz as the sun set behind them. He sent her a text.

When are you coming back?

It was the most urgent of questions, one loaded with both hope and anxiety, all sent out into the void via the touch screen on his phone. Five words, a collection of letters spelling a question, the answer to which he believed would determine his destiny. No timbre of voice, no body language, no facial expression could be attached to it. The last time he texted her the same question it took three days before she replied *no idea*. Nothing nuanced, just the two words looking up at him from the screen. He had invested so much in his words to her. Where had that force of emotion been for those three days? Had she just sat on the message for all that time or had she only just received it? Did she agonise over it or had she been irritated by his wanting to know? Did she understand the neediness behind his words? And if she did, did she care? Not knowing agitated him and made him despair.

The harrassment and threats had tailed off but he remained cautious, checking the street outside from a darkened room, taking cabs if he needed to go anywhere and even harbouring thoughts of revenge. The last incident had been three nights previously when a bottle was thrown at the kitchen window, cracking it. The day before that he had seen a young couple standing on the other side of the road opposite the house, the young male pointing over towards it as though he was explaining something to his companion. She was laughing. He had his hood up, but she didn't, so Elliot took a mental note of how she looked. Later that day dog shit was posted throught the letterbox. The morning before that he had found a cat in the recylcling bin. Its wailing, like that of a deranged baby, had awakened him. Some nights the landline rang so often he now left it unplugged. If he answered the caller only ever said the word *dead* often with laughter in the background. The numbers were always witheld. At some point he told the police he was being threatened and harrassed and they told him to keep a record and get back to them if he was worried. He did both. One evening WPC Liz

Brooks came round, telling him he could call her Liz if he liked. They sat in the conservatory drinking tea as if they were friends and she had popped round for a chat. She told him that usually these things died down but as they didn't know who was behind it all they couldn't take any action. He told her it had to be Lennie, the only one who knew him and who could possibly know his phone number and address.

I can pop round and see him if you like, she said, sometimes the police turning up on someone's doorstep can have an effect.

It can also make things worse. Escalate the situation.

Unlikely. He has no record, no known associates. He's just a little wanker trying it on.

What about the guy Michael beat up?

I can't tell you anything about him.

Is he still in hospital?

Sorry sir, I can't tell you anything about him.

But he could be behind all this.

Again unlikely sir. No record and no known associates.

He must know Lennie then. Otherwise what's the point of all this?

Like I say it will probably die down. Meantime let your neighbours know what's going on so they can keep a lookout as well.

She smiled and he thought she had nice eyes. She said she had to leave. He wanted her to stay so he offered her more tea which she declined. She stood, picked up her hat and walked to the door, high-viz jacket rustling as she adjusted her duty belt. She pressed a button on her radio and it crackled into life. He felt abandoned.

He phoned Biscuit. The only friends he had told about all this were Biscuit and Brendan. Both were of the same mind – he couldn't let this carry on and the only way to sort it was to take action himself and not involve the police. Up until now he had been too frightened to allow either of them to do anything even though both were willing. He felt ashamed that he couldn't fight his own battles, that he was allowing someone to fuck up his life to this extent while he just cowered at home, stuck, scared and emasculated. Biscuit answered.

Fella.

I don't know what to do. Police have just been round.

And?

Nothing. They don't think I should worry.

Well?

I'm still worried. I want him done. Warned off.

Sure?

No.

It could come back to you. You know that.

He doesn't have to be hurt.

Aye he does.

Really?

Aye. He needs to be frightened. You just have to prepare yourself for the questions that will follow from the police if he reports it. Just deny it. Over and over and over.

I'll come with you.

Nope.

Won't it make things worse? Escalate it?

Doubt it.

I don't know.

Look if we go down this road, two things. One, he needs to know we're serious. Two, the cops'll come to you if he gets done.

Done?

You said you wanted him done.

If you're gonna do anything it can't go tits up.

It won't. Just no point in him seeing you.

It's wrong to ask you to do this.

Yer no asking. I'm volunteering.

Let's leave it and see.

Up to you fella.

Nothing had happened since and Elliot wondered if Biscuit had gone ahead and acted without telling him. Part of him hoped that he had. He finally completed the payments and shut down the laptop. His phone rang. It was Biscuit.

I'm outside, he said and hung up.

Elliot opened the front door and saw a transit van backed up into the driveway. Biscuit stepped out from the driver's seat and walked round to the rear of the van.

Something for you, he said and opened up the van doors.

Lennie was inside. He was sitting on the floor which was covered in a polythene sheet and he was staring out at Elliot, visibly shaking. He was barefoot and topless. Elliot was struck at how thin and vulnerable he looked: his arms, taut and muscular, folded across his chest in a defensive posture, his hair spiky and shiny in the gloomy light. He addressed Elliot.

It's over, he said and then added after a non-verbal cue from Biscuit, I'm sorry.

Elliot stared at him. Part of him wanted to get in the van and beat the shit out of him, throttle him, bang his head against the sides and kick him into a bloody unconsciousness. He realised that this was what the polythene sheet was for – to stop any blood spilling onto the inside of the van. Lennie must have expected violence. Elliot felt he was about to be sick but swallowed it away.

Why Lennie?' he asked, Why the fuck did you do all this?

Lennie was still shaking. He looked down and several seconds passed before he answered.

He's family. My cousin.'

Who?

The guy your mate beat up.

But I didn't beat him up did I? I tried to stop it happening.

He beat my mates up too.

One was carrying a fucking knife.

Anyway. There'll be no more.

Really?

Lennie looked towards Biscuit who nodded at him, raising his eyebrows, encouraging him to answer, which he did after a pause.

Yeah…really…it's over.

And your cousin?

He's okay. No lasting damage.

Elliot realised Lennie thought he was enquiring as to his cousin's wellbeing.

I mean does he think it's over?

Yeah. He was never part of this.

Your mates?

Don't worry about them. It's blessed mate…over…no more…promise.

Biscuit walked round to the front of the van and brought out a phone, a pair of trainers and a polo shirt. He chucked them all at Lennie.

Put them on and fuck off.

Lennie quickly pulled on the shirt but took longer with his trainers as his shaky hands fumbled with the laces. Elliot felt sorry for him. He had been made to feel frightened that Biscuit was going to subject him to violence and now he understood his worst fears weren't going to be realised he wanted to get away in case they changed their minds. He shuffled to the edge of the van and Elliot started to make way for him but Biscuit prevented Lennie from standing up with a hand on his shoulder. Biscuit looked at Elliot.

I've told him we don't use the police. We sort things our way.

He slapped Lennie's cheek with the palm of his hand, making him cower.

And Lennie understands this now. Don't you son?

He sounded like a benevolent uncle even though his words were loaded with menace.

Yeah we get it, said Lennie.

He brushed past them and started walking down the street, not glancing back and trying to look calm but hurrying all the same.

You coming in? asked Elliot.

Biscuit looked at his watch and looked up smiling.

Nah...on a bit of a schedule.

Thanks mate.

Brewery Saturday? I'll pick you up.

Sure...thanks...and thanks for...

He jerked his head in the direction of Lennie's flight. Biscuit opened the driver's door.

Nae bother fella.

Biscuit.

Aye.

How did you…I mean did you…?

Biscuit held his hand up like a policeman telling a car to stop.

You don't need to know geezer. All you need to know is it's sorted.

Thanks.

Brewery. Saturday.

He climbed in and drove off with a wave and a toot of the horn.

CHAPTER 9

He hadn't seen seen much of Linda since the fear had started. He had visited her a few times in the days after Michael's arrest to check on her and she always assured him she was *fine* but once she understood he and Amelia were being threatened fear had got the better of her. He kept in touch via text messages and the occasional phone call and her replies were always noncommital and monosyllabic. She barely reacted when he told her Amelia had gone away, saying only *oh dear* followed by a silence during which he hoped she might offer him some words of hope or encouragement. None were forthcoming. Now and again he would see her from the kitchen window walking the girls to and from school but didn't call out to her lest someone was watching. It would have been disastrous if Lennie and crew had found out she was Michael's partner. Still, he felt resentful that he was the only one of them having to face the backlash of threat and menace. Michael was in prison, Amelia had gone and Linda had become uncommunicative. Why was he the only one left to deal with it?

Also, he didn't feel he had carried the burden well. He thought his suffering had been unheroic in the way he had complained about it to anyone who would still listen and he felt remorse about how often he had drunk himself stupid in search of some force that could release his fear and banish his impotence. He contemplated ending it all and only his love for his daughters stopped him from doing so but one early morning, sitting in the conservatory, he had come very close. He was listening to Bruckner's 8th and drinking brandy. He had placed three packets of paracetamol and a few valium on the table in front of him. He stepped back from the edge but subsequently suffered a storm of self-loathing that lasted days. Whenever Iris or Isabel suggested a get together he deferred skillfully, so practised had he become at the art of deception. He thought he should have reached by now a stage of post-event wisdom having heeded a lesson about existence – how he took things for granted and didn't notice the signs saying he was losing control of his life and destiny, but he still felt too raw for that. Something still seeped from the wounds, yet he could at least sense the next stage coming into focus. It felt calmer as if there had been a shift towards resolution.

He played Mingus at top-notch volume – the opening track *Better Git It In Your Soul* with it's start-up of bass, piano and trumpet all confident and teasing before the band bursts into the riff that now once more filled his spirit with something approaching joy. He relished the chaos of the brass section, the background shouts and handclaps as the only accompaniments to the sax solo. He felt alive again. He texted Linda *it's over!*, the daughters *family summit asap! love u x* and Amelia *call me, the nightmare is over, love u x*, then played along with the drum solo beating out the rhythm on the table top and screaming along to the *oh yeahs* at the end. Yes, he thought, I better git it in my soul.

Linda did't reply so he walked over to see her. A beat-up lime-green Fiesta was parked across the driveway. She answered the doorbell after turning keys in two locks and opened the door about an inch, not even enough to tauten the chain. He had to persuade her it was safe to let him in and that he had good news. After what seemed like an age and her muttering something to someone inside (presumably to lime-green Fiesta person, he thought) she opened up and he stepped inside. He realised he was still wary of strangers because he felt anxious at the prospect of meeting whoever it was in Linda's home. For her part Linda didn't exactly look at ease as she introduced him to Toni, who waved at Elliot instead of accepting his offered hand. He looked like he was of far-eastern origin with long spiky black hair and was dressed in a baby-blue jacket, white t-shirt, impossibly tight maroon chinos and white deck shoes. Elliot immediately thought *wanker* who was fake-smiling at him as though he was a child and had just said something sweet to him.

It's with an I not a Y, said Toni.

I'm sorry?

Elliot looked to Linda, holding his hands out as though to say *what's going on?* She said Toni was just leaving and as she saw him to the door, it clicked. He was her dealer.

Who the fuck is Toni?

It's not what it looks like. I'm not using.

You are, Lin. I can see you are.

He actually wasn't sure he could but thought the bluff might make her admit it to him.

Lin, we have always been honest with each other in the past and I hope we are going to be now.

I've just needed a little. I've stopped again though. Never really started.

I'm sorry, I know things have been awful, but...

They stood there in slience. The living room and kitchen were untidy, kids' toys and clothes strewn across the floor, dishes in the sink. He told her the threats had stopped, thinking this would possibly make her feel better but she barely reacted. Then he refocussed and remembered that through all of this the main issue for her, of course, was that Michael was in prison awaiting trial and most likely a likely custodial sentence. Their whole life together had almost overnight been made insecure and unsafe. Their future, once feasibly rosy, was now coldly uncertain. He took her in his arms and she sobbed on his shoulder.

I'm so sorry, Lin, so sorry.

It was all he could say.

She eased herself out of his hold and opened a drawer in the kitchen. She handed him a wrap.

Take it please, she said, and get rid of it for me...and these.

She opened another drawer and took out a carrier bag.

Works, she said.

He looked in the bag and saw a pack of needles, a syringe and a discoloured dessert spoon. He put the wrap in his breast pocket, trying to ignore the fact that he'd been given some skag to do with whatever he wanted and that some part of him was rubbing his hands in glee at the unexpected opportunity.

I only did it twice, she said, and I was so fucking sick the second time I realised I can't do it anymore.

She laughed.

Maybe I've grown up. Anyway that's what Toni was here for...I was telling him no more and to just get me some weed...that's all I want for now and even that's messing with my brain. I told him no skunk to get me old school weed. I'm not having any of that shit.

He asked after Michael and she said he was struggling but holding on even though he was pessimistic about the trial. Elliot wondered out loud if there was a chance Michael would get a non-custodial sentence. Linda looked at him for a few moments without answering.

Are you going to see him? she asked.

I don't know.

His indefinite reply made him reflect as to his ambivalence. Elliot had felt a fair degree of anger towards Michael for doing this to all of them but also knew him well enough to understand there were reasons behind his propensity for violence. Elliot knew Michael had tried without success to come to terms with whatever they were but as deep-rooted as they were meant that was always going to have been a painful process. If he received a custodial sentence Elliot didn't know if it would help him or make things worse, whether he would emerge from the experience more in control of his feelings or whether it would actually break him. Elliot knew that as a friend he should support him, be there for him (whatever the hell *that* meant, he thought) but he wasn't sure he wanted to. It almost felt as though he could no longer be bothered. We all have to tame the demons inside us, the thought, or learn to live with the consequences and he couldn't tame Michael's any more than he could his own. He thought he *should* be loyal to him (and

Linda) but again questioned why. Linda looked at him, waiting for him to explain but he sensed she knew what he was thinking and that this moment marked some kind of departure for them.

How are the girls? He asked

What do you think?

There was silence again for a few minutes. She had her back to him as she stared out of the patio doors.

Is there anything I can do? he asked. There was further silence.

Just fuck off, she said without turning round.

He moved towards her, arms outstretched as though he was pleading with her. She looked at me in the reflection of the doors.

Just go, she said.

He didn't move even though the message was clear. He searched for a way to bring them back together, these two friends standing in the same space, both part of an event that had changed their lives forever. He hoped they could help one another as they were now the last strands of the ties that bound them all together. She turned away from the door without looking at him, walked to the kitchen sink and started to wash dishes. If he left then he wondered what that would mean? It would be a relief maybe to shake himself free from the last shackle of this friendship. He wouldn't have to witness her suffering any more and he could then just concentrate on putting his life back together. But he also felt a love for Linda and wanted to reach through her grief to comfort her, help her navigate through the eye of this storm. She threw the scouring pad into the bowl. Soapy water splashed up. Her shoulders started to shake and she sobbed in convulsions. He went to her and put his arms on her shoulders. She turned and let him hold her, leaving her arms at her sides. She cried loudly with deep gutteral yowls. Then she lifted her hand to wipe her nose, looked up at him and he brushed back her hair that was now stuck to her cheeks and forehead. They looked into each other's eyes for a moment. She put her arms around him.

You're all I've got, she said before crying again.

They stayed like that for what felt like a long time, locked into an intimacy they had never physically shared before but neither of them knowing what to do next. He remembered he had to have a chest X-ray and some bloods taken at the hospital and so he prised himself away with awkwardness and apology, explaining how the GP wanted to check some things out after he had complained of a night time cough. The GP had also asked about drinking and one of the tests was for liver function but he didn't tell Linda that.

He walked down to the hospital in the rain thinking he should have stayed with her. The phlebotomist was Eastern European. His eyes were dark, the bags beneath them darker still, his hair black and shiny-slick. He had a side parting and wisps of fringe dropped down over his eyes. His lower lip protruded as he blew the hair away. Elliot watched him work his arm and he filled six test-tubes with Elliot's blood, sticking a printed label with his name and number onto each one. He worked quickly and Elliot felt no pain. Elliot pressed his finger onto the cotton wool and thanked the phlebotomist who stuck a piece of micropore across it.

Have a good day, he said without emotion, turning away from Elliot as he spoke.

He walked to X-ray, handed in the referral form to a smiling receptionist and took a seat. Within minutes he was ushered into the room by an African woman in a blue uniform, called Blessing and who was taller than him smiled as she spoke to him. A small Asian woman in a white coat, presumably the radiologist, without looking up from whatever she was doing, instructed Elliot to strip to his waist and rest his chin on the frame in front of him. He was then told to hold his breath, stand still and look ahead. He obeyed. He felt his breasts press against the cold plate. Seconds later the Asian woman told him he could get dressed and go. He had been there for no more than twenty minutes and he wondered if they had seen or taken anything from him in that short time that would one day reveal any secrets or resolve any mysteries as to the workings of his body and mind.

CHAPTER 10

Despite working with colour for most of his life he had never grown bored of it and when he let himself consider its infinite variations and moods it aroused in him undeniable wonder and exhilaration. He felt like an alchemist in thrall to the universe, seeking to unlock its mysteries as they remained tantalisingly just beyond his reach. To behold an empty palette and to then start setting colours upon it remained a mysterious and magical process to him. As he mixed the paint, his sense of anticipation would intensify and even if he had a plan, a concept, he loved the fact that if his unconscious mind was allowed to guide him then he would have no idea as to where it might lead him.

He was listening to some be-bop, the trumpet was making swirling bubbling sounds like a curlew invisible on some misty salt-marsh. He could see shades of grey and green in that landscape and started to make up his palette, starting with the blues - cerulean, ultramarine and cobalt. Then the yellows - ochre, lemon and cadmium. He knew he would want gradations of both purple and blue so he added two reds - alzarin crimson and cadmium. Last of all he added titanium white and a small squeeze of ivory black. He poured some turps into an old jam jar and had a clean rag at the ready. He then he selected the brushes - two flats, both one-inch wide, two three-quarter-inch rounds and a filbert just in case his mood required it at some stage. He wanted to keep it simple.

That morning he had stretched a four by three foot canvas and had added a small bit of black powder paint to the white emulsion primer so he didn't feel intimidated by an empty white space in front of him. Also the landscape he had in mind would be mostly dark in tone, so the now light grey primer would enhance the process of his achieving the tones he wanted. Like those Dutch landscapes of the eighteenth century, he thought. He tried to concentrate his mind on an image of the Solway at Knockbreck and the way the colours of the sky, sea and land would bleed into one another at all times of day but especially as the sun began to set. He could hear the calls of wading birds eerie in the void. Even though the dominant colours he envisaged were greys and purples the first colour he mixed was a dirty olive green made up of ultramarine, ochre and a touch of white. He dipped one of the flats into it and painted a horizontal line about two inches long in the centre of the canvas two-thirds of the way down from the top. And there it was, his first creative act in he didn't know how long. A wet line of paint catching the light on its ridges and as significant or insignificant as any other life form in his world. He sat back to look at it. His instinct was for a bolder colour next, maybe a purple, but his mind started to look for reasons to confirm that choice, casting doubt on what he should do next. He froze in an unnatural stasis. A recurrent memory came to mind of an eleven year-old full-back going to trap a ball and with the eyes of the world upon him he allowed it to pass unhindered beneath his left foot which remained hanging in the air as the opposition's winger ran past, took control of the ball and headed for goal. The headmaster yelled at him.

Longman you're like an old man on the edge of the bath. Get stuck in lad for pity's sake.

He hesitated further, trying to force himself into the disciplined action he needed to continue. If he acted - mixed a colour then applied it – then there would be a reaction both on the canvas and in his head which would then require yet further action and the whole process would gain impetus and momentum. He felt suddenly afraid of it all. Familiar mocking voices vied for attention in his head and he felt once more as far removed from any creative zone as he could possibly be. Was this how it all ended? he wondered. At least Rothko when turning to his razor blade over the kitchen sink had by then created a legacy of masterpieces. How the fuck does anyone reconcile with mediocrity?

After about an hour of just sitting there he needed to piss so he headed for the dimly-lit white-tiled toilet on the landing. There was no hot water tap and the sink was stained shit-brown. He lifted the black plastic seat and started but had no control over the direction of the flow and as he looked down a thin jet, like fat escaping from a sausage, shot off at a right angle, clearing the toilet bowl and spattering onto the floor below. This always happened when the pain was there nagging away at him like an embittered spouse too long in his company to have any capacity for pity. He had been told the cause was either the pudendal nerve in malfunction mode having a knock-on effect to the down-below functioning or it was the result of scarring to his urethra, itself the result of numerous probes, scrapes and scopes. He realised it probably meant he should sit down to piss and thus avoid having to wipe the floor and the rim of the toilet bowl as he was now doing. He remained defiant of such a solution, believing it only accelerated him on his journey down the road that led to his eventual emasculation.

He returned to the studio and sat at his desk. It was covered with the paraphenalia of a disordered mind - postcards of photographed landscapes or of favourite works of art, phone chargers, laptop charger, envelopes, notebooks, glue sticks, ink bottles, staplers and boxes of staples, paper clips, a desk-tidy in which were straws, felt pens, pencils, scissors, biros and fountain pens. There were also photos of his daughters at various ages, USB sticks, harmonicas, a dictionary, poetry books, CDs without cases, glass jars, sticky tape, masking tape, a can of fixative spray and post-it notes stuck randomly across the desk's surface and sides containing reminders to ideas he had long forgotten about. He opened the drawer, took out some tinfoil and then tore off a piece about six inches square. He cut one of the straws in half and rummaged in his pocket for the skag. He folded the foil in the middle, opened it up again and sprinkled some of the dirty-looking powder in the crease. He couldn't find his lighter. Straw in his mouth he looked through the drawers, across the desk's surface and in his jacket pockets. He would have to go out and buy one. He looked back at the canvass and his line of dirty olive-green.

Fuck this, he said to himself out loud and put on his coat.

The door opened and in walked Brendan. Elliot was aware he still had the straw in his mouth, so he removed it and said *hi* before walking back to his desk and covering the skag with a postcard so Brendan didn't see it. He knew he was acting weirdly and Brendan was frowning at him, asking him if he was okay.

Fine, he replied.

Brendan picked up the postcard and saw what Elliot had been preparing.

Really? Are you mad?

I haven't used it yet. Honestly.

But you were about to, Brendan said not as a question but a statement of fact.

Yes. Maybe. I don't know…look I can't fucking work Brendan.

And *that's* going to help you? I see you made a start, he said looking over at the canvass.

Elliot had to get out, unable to take Brendan's stare which was straight into his eyes, unblinking and unavoidable, stronger than Elliot's will or inclination to look away and pretend nothing had happened. He wanted to demonstrate the situation was normal and that he was in control but he could find neither the actions nor the words to do so. He felt his anxiety rise – a spurting and stuttering fountain of fear coming to life somewhere inside him. The tell-tale cramp in his bowel threatened to embarrass him so he told Brendan he needed the toilet and headed back to the landing. It was occupied and he could hear someone in there unravelling toilet paper from the holder. It rattled and squeaked. He hurried upstairs to the next landing where there was another toilet and hurriedly locked the cubicle door behind him as though he was being pursued by the devil. He let the voiding begin. Someone had stuck a card on the door at eye level that read *Something wonderful is about to happen*. He let it all go.

There was another card above the toilet roll holder - a print of an ink drawing depicting a cockerel biting the tail of a pig who in turn was biting the tail of a snake who completed the cycle by biting the cockerel's tail feathers. They encircled a tree in abundant leaf. Beneath the image was some text -*This bad action which is yours was not done by your mother or your father or by anyone else. You alone have done this bad action and you alone will reap its fruit. Only by overcoming craving, hatred and delusion can one achieve Enlightenment.* Elliot wondered who on that floor wanted fellow users to ponder these things when taking a crap.

There was no soap in the dispenser above the sink nor was there any hot water. The hand dryer emitted a weak stream of air like an elderly person trying to blow out a birthday candle. He thought about the last part of the message on the card. *Craving* – what do I crave? Oblivion? Or just something to numb me. I long for Amelia. Or do I? I want to be in her arms. Or do I want to be in just anyone's arms? I'm not *craving* alcohol or drugs or sex but I am in a constant state of dissatisfaction. Then what? *Hatred* - what do I hate? Who do I hate? I don't think I hate anyone or anything anymore. There were times recently when I wanted to exact revenge and given the word I don't doubt Biscuit or Brendan would have obliged but I pulled back from that. I wanted a solution. Hurting Lennie would have solved but one part of it all, closing one door only to open another and on and on I would have gone, opening the next one and never able to get back to where I started from or find again where I wanted to be even if I knew where that was. That's craving and hatred sorted. What's next? *Delusion* - now what am I deluded about? Oh, fuck this, I can't be bothered.

He met Brendan back on the landing who again looked at him in earnest.

You okay? he asked.

Not really.

Let's go out. You hungry?

Not really. I'll eat if you want to.

They walked down Borough Road, a thoroughfare through the part of town where the majority of shops and cafes were either Pakistani or West Indian. They stopped at a bench outside Doubles, their favourite Caribbean food outlet and Brendan went in. It was run by an old Rasta from Trinidad named Ford who made a mean roti and some of the best fried chicken even though sometimes he made you wait for an eternity while he went about his preparation and cooking.

Elliot was sitting on the bench and two women walked by dressed in summer clothes, one looking old enough to be the mother. The younger one spoke.

He's waiting for my teeth to move.

Well, that's probably sensible, replied the older woman.

A chubby white girl with red hair and rosy cheeks sat down next to him. She looked about sixteen and was wearing a brown fast-food restaurant uniform he noticed looked at least one size too small for her. A round badge was pinned to her breast. Elliot read it - *Hi, I'm Constance, try my pulled pork now!* She pulled out a pack of Regals and sparked one up. Elliot was wearing a leather jacket and felt hot in the sun. He wanted to take it off but worried if he folded it over his arm his wallet would fall out of the inside pocket because the button had come off it months previously and he had never sewn it back on. Amelia had said she would do it for him. He felt an upsurge of grief and the onset of tears but swallowed it all back down because he didn't want to fall apart there, not in front of Constance.

Brendan came out of Doubles and stared at him again in that same penetrating way.

Chicken, he said, and some plantain.

He passed Elliot a brown paper bag which was shiny with oil from the food. They walked on to the park. The grass looked parched. A man was throwing a rubber bone for a springer spaniel. A young woman sat on a rug and encouraged her chubby-legged infant to walk towards her – they were both giggling. Two young men threw an American football to each other - one running ahead of the thrower and turning around as he gauged his run in order to make the catch. They seemed practiced at it. Two large women ate ice-creams as they walked past. Brendan and Elliot sat on a bench and ate the chicken and plantain, sharing a silence as they did so. Brendan was the first to break it.

You know when you're stuck you need to move man. Anywhere...just take a step out. Then come back if you want to.

Elliot didn't reply and took off his jacket.

Man you look a state, continued Brendan.

Elliot looked down at his shirt which was stained and creased. He remembered he had slept in it and had gone out that morning without showering. Brendan carried on speaking to him

Come and stay by we if you like. Rita won't mind...you know she likes you.

Elliot thought of Rita – warm-hearted, kind and bosomy. Homely and wholesome. Cooked real food. Laughed easily and genuinely in a flash of gold and white and pink as she hustled about her kitchen-diner, fixing him a drink, getting him another plate of food. She and Brendan sucked their teeth at each other a lot of the time, sometimes in anger but mostly in mock admonition. They had five kids, ranging from seventeen to seven, the eldest being from Brendan's previous marriage. His first wife had died young of a brain aneurysm and he got together with Rita a year or so later and they worked it all out without drama. It was a house full of life and Elliot tried to imagine how he would feel staying there.

Thanks mate. But no thanks. I can sort this.

Just don't use that shit man. Promise me.

I promise.

So you know where she is?

Scotland I think. Last I heard.

Want me to call her?

To have someone else do for him what he wouldn't do for himself was an attractive option. How would she take that though, he asked himself?

No, he replied.

What about Spain? You were going to go to that place.

Elliot looked at him and frowned in recognition of a long-lost idea.

That was ages ago.

So? What was the place you wanted to paint? You went there with Amelia.

She came to mind, her hair in a messy bun, the wind blowing through it as they stood there looking out to sea.

Finisterre, he said, the end of the Earth.

Brendan grinned and slapped him on the shoulder.

That was a good idea..real good. You should go man.

They were silent for a few minutes before Brendan continued.

Or you could go to see Paul. Yeah man…go to Trinidad…see some light…see some colour…drink some rum. Paul is doing good now.

Elliot thought of Paul whom he had known since art school days and who was now a successful painter of some renown. He had moved to Trinidad where his wife, Vernita, a childhood friend of Elliot's, lived. Paul had set up his studio there and it had changed not only his pallette but his whole approach to painting. He had asked Elliot to go out there a few times but had stopped asking a year or so before when Elliot had come up with yet another excuse not to go.

I'm done though, Bren. I can't paint. So I'm not going out there to just…

For fuck's sake man. You *can* paint. Of course you can fucking paint. Go back to the beginnings…chalk and charcoal, pencils, pastels…just do it. You've just covered it all up with shit these last couple of years. You're like an athlete who's let himself get out of shape and flabby. That's all it is…get fit and lean and mean again man. You can do it. Of course you can.

Elliot looked at his old friend whose dark pupils had blue-grey coronas around them,the whites yellowing in the corners. The hair on his beard was mostly grey, the veins proud on his muscular forearms. Brendan got up and put their bag of chicken bones in a rubbish bin. He walked back, smiling at Elliot who stood up. They gave each other a prolonged hug. They were embracing the constancy and familiarity of their friendship as well as their history together – one that was full of music, laughter, creativity, milestones both good, bad, easy and sad.

What the fuck have I been doing? he asked, looking up at the sky.

Getting flabby, replied Brendan, poking Elliot's belly and then his chest, laughing, Flabby all over man.

Elliot hugged him again and also laughed, tears of both grief and releief running down his cheeks, feeling as though a damn had burst. Brendan suggested they went for a coffee and they walked a few minutes to Keith's Kitchen on the Park, an upmarket greasy spoon, the kind of place where speciality teas could be served alongside the all-day English breakfast. A middle-aged couple were sitting on the next table opposite a younger overweight man whose mouth was wide open and with white saliva concentrated at the corners of his lips. He ordered a diet coke from the waitress who returned a couple of minutes later with a can and a glass. The young man pointed out to her that it was a regular coke and he had wanted a diet one. She apologised and took it away soon returning with the right one.

Elliot ordered a Swedish tea without knowing what it was and Brendan ordered a black coffee into which he added six lumps of sugar. They sat there mostly in silence and both listening to to the conversation at the

the next table. The overweight younger man was speaking slowly and deliberately as though he was under sedation.

I've been living here for eight years now…I just think it's time to move on.

The middle-aged couple took it in turns to encourage him to take the steps necessary to get his life back on track. They weren't behaving as though they were his parents but obviously knew him well. The older man asked him if he had made any friends.

No not really. I don't really get on with the others.

If you get a job you could be more independent.

There was a silence before the older man continued.

Doesn't matter what it is…just something. Then if you show you're committed and don't go off sick you'll get on well and progress…earn a bit of money and be more independent.

Like how?

Start doing things you want to do instead of waiting to be told what to do.

I'm thirty now. I need to move on.

The younger man was perspiring, beads of sweat dotted his forehead and wet patches formed under his arms and across his chest. Their food arrived. The woman was having the vegetarian full-English, the older man the full-English without tomatoes. The younger man had two baguettes, both with sausage and egg in them. He poured salt and ketchup onto them before tucking his napkin into the front of his sweat-soaked polo shirt. They ate mostly in silence. Occasionally the older man repeated his opinion that the the younger man needed to get a job and some independence. When they got up to leave, the older man went to pay at the counter and the younger man embraced the woman awkwardly. He left a hand on her shoulder as he spoke to her.

Thanks for saving my life, he said.

CHAPTER 11

Two days later and he was tidying the house. Dishes first then vacuum cleaning then changing bedclothes then making up the spare beds. By early afternoon he was finished and he watched the road from the kitchen window in expectation. It was one of those hot days when old people died, dogs asphyxiated in cars, babies turned pink as young mothers fussed over parasols attached to pushchairs, women showed too much cleavage and men showed too much abdominal flab. A lassitude would weigh everyone down until later in the day when tempers would flare, train tracks would buckle and an oasis-like vapour would rise from vehicles throbbing in traffic jams on the A-roads to Hell. Doors banged at random throughout the house.

He wondered if they were stuck in traffic somewhere and was about to phone when Isabel's beat-up old Escort pulled onto the gravel. It took them an age to get out of the car as phones were checked for messages or hand-held conversations were brought to a close, handbags were gathered and the iPod switched off and detached. He saw Mark, Isabel's boyfriend, in the front seat and this irritated him as he wanted to see the girls on their own. Iris stepped out of the back, sunglasses on top of her head, fanning her face, puffing out her cheeks and blowing as though she had stepped out of a sauna. Elliot waited in the doorway and she smiled and waved at him. Isabel and Mark emerged next. She carried a handbag the size of an ocean liner over her shoulder.

I and I, said Elliot with his arms outstretched.

Jah! shouted Iris in tune with their time-honoured family joke.

Rasta Far I! added a grinning Isabel.

The three of them embraced as one as Mark stood back (rightly so, thought Elliot) respectfully waiting his turn. He hugged Elliot awkwardly and then shook his hand holding onto it and looking meaningfully into his eyes the way a priest might have done. Elliot noticed Mark had grown a beard. His thick long hair was swept back behind his ears and he was wearing an unbuttoned waistcoat over a white collarless shirt, hipster-fashion. Son, thought Elliot, you have *no* idea about hipsterdom, you look more like an extra from a low-budget western. In fact Elliot didn't really mind Mark at all and had developed a fondness for him, he just hadn't been expecting to to see him there so tried to temper his obvious lack of enthusiasm, telling him it was good to see him. Mark and Izzy had been together for a couple of years so and Elliot had come to accept they were serious about each other. Mark treated her well and they often laughed a lot together so maybe that was all a father could hope for. He also appeared gentle and humble, characteristics fine by Elliot, even though he would have preferred Mark to have had a regular income that would allow the two of them some more security. He scolded himself for thinking so prosaically because Mark was an artist of sorts himself. He was a musician (guitar, singer-songwriter), played in a duo with a violinist and they seemed to get regular gigs and some sort of income from them but Elliot could never see Mark earning enough to secure a mortgage – that (if it's what they wanted and ever got round to it) would be down to Izzy. She seemed happy with the set-up and if she was happy then Elliot knew he had to just let go. Having had some bastard boyfriends in her time who ranged from just hopeless puff-heads through to possessive narcissists, Izzy appeared to be in control and in charge of who wore the trousers in their relationship, which again was mostly okay by Elliot. He just hoped Mark would be strong enough for her when any of life's more serious problems came along.

Izzy was twenty-eight now, established in her career as an events organiser, working for some US firm who put on everything from awaydays for corporate teams to talk bullshit at one another through to conferences, exhibitions and classical concerts in country houses. She had been a happy child who from her earliest years had been inquisitive, funny and creative. Her teenage years had been the usual thing – that whole hormonal hotchpotch of rebelliousness and dependency – that taxed Elliot and her mother from time to time but not to any extremes. Although she got the grades at school she opted for work and cash over university, a decision her parents were happy with.

Apart from the dodgy behaviour of a couple of her boyfriends, all had gone well, the usual ups and downs of life dealt with easily and with confidence. When Elliot and her mother had decided to split up she took it in her stride, even once asserting she wasn't surprised and that she couldn't understand how two such opposites had ever got together in the first place.

Iris, with her dreadlocked hair (now luxuriant and well-established) and hippy clothes was the younger by two years. In another one of their family reggae-puns they had called her Irie from a young age and she still signed off that way in emails to Elliot and her mother. Slighter in build and quieter in nature when compared to her sister, she had always been the more self-contained of the two. Some guys hung around for a while but she shooed them away before things got too serious and she remained single, a state of being she described as being preferable. A first class degree in French Studies led (according to her) nowhere. She now worked as a student counsellor in a university that had faculties spread all over West London. She could speed-read novels in French and English and she also wrote poetry, some of which she performed to genuine, albeit limited, acclaim. She was more affected by the break-up of her parents' marriage and tried in her problem-solving way to get them to reconsider. That she failed didn't affect her default attitude of non-judgementalism. If anyone, it was Iris who facilitated their mother and Elliot remaining friendly and caring towards one another. The two sisters had stayed close at heart, lived near to each other in East London and despite the differences in how they approached life they always looked out for one another. They dumped their bags onto armchairs and then took it in turns to hug their father again.

How's your mother? he asked and they all looked to Iris for the answer.

She's good. Usual. Says to say hi.

No worries then?

No. I don't think so. I told her we were coming up. She asked after you.

And?

And nothing. We haven't seen you in ages. Hardly spoken either so there wasn't anything to tell her.

I know love. There's a lot to catch up on. To tell you.

Where's Amelia? Working? asked Izzy.

Scotland. Knockbreck. That's part of what I've got to tell you.

They both look concerned and he held his hands up in a gesture of reassurance. Nothing to worry about, he added, but it is a bit complicated I guess.

Mark was looking ill at ease so Elliot patted his shoulder as a way of telling him and all three of them not to worry. He gestured them towards the dining table and suggested a pot of tea.

Too hot, said Izzy, I'd prefer a cold beer please.

Mark nodded as a way of telling Elliot he would like the same.

That's my girl, said Elliot, sounding too enthused like the father of a toddler approving of their successful use of the potty. He looked at Iris who rolled her eyes before speaking.

Ohhh okay then.

Over a few rounds of beer (and Mark going out to get some more) Elliot told them the story of the last couple of months. Shock and anger were expressed to varying degrees and Elliot became tearful at one point which started Izzy off and provoked Iris to move her seat next to him so she could hold his hand. He concluded the tale.

So Michael's in prison and Amelia may have left me and I can't just wait around to save my life.

He paused for a few seconds before continuing.

I need to take some sort of positive action.

He went on to explain the choices he believed he had. He could stay put, go to Scotland to find Amelia, or go away for a month or so.

I was thinking of going to see Paul in Trinidad, he said.

Iris homed in on a rationale for a resolution to the dilemma.

Well you can't stay put. If you're stuck you're stuck so you have to move. Agreed?'

Agreed, said Elliot and Izzy and Mark nodded.

You and Amelia need some time apart or at least that's what Amelia has asked for. Yes? But Trinidad is a journey in more ways than one…it will inevitably evoke memories of the past you know. There will be lots of memories of Granny and Grandad and your childhood so you will have to handle all of that.

Images of people and places long displaced in his memory came to mind.

You're right, he said.

But by going to see Paul, she continued, well it's something new. The present instead of or as well as the past. Also he's a good friend and he has family there. You won't drink yourself to death in his company. So you either stay stagnant or you go forwards is what I think.

Elliot once more thought of Paul. Tall, big and gentle. Yes, they had done a lot of drinking and drugs together over the years but Paul had now quit and declared he was dry and clean and how this was a big part of his being able to paint the way he did and with an unprecedented level of energy. There was a silence which Elliot eventually broke.

Going back isn't always the easiest thing…you have to be feeling strong and up for it…be clear about the reasons for going…I used to think revisiting was a way of coming to terms with the past but I'm not so sure now. It can just stir things up. Trinidad was important to me as a kid. A lot happened but a lot happens in any life. To keep on going back to places…I do question the point of it. But then again...

Izzy picked up the empty bottles.

But you like it there, she said, and you haven't seen Paul's set up. It might help.

Elliot recognised that he was perhaps envious of Paul's success. It confirmed to him the persistent notion that he was burdened with a mediocre talent, one he hadn't been able to ignore but one which had condemned him to being an also-ran when in contrast Paul had gone on to flourish. Had his decision to work as an art therapist for all those years been a way of avoiding that truth? Then again, his early-retirement pension now afforded him a freedom to try anything he wanted within reason. Would he be able to handle seeing Paul now he was successful? Why not? He was happy for his friend. It was his self he wasn't happy with. The light and colours in Trinidad were different, more vivid in the tropical light. He could just do some simple colour fields to start with. See where they might lead. No pressure, he could just clean the decks and start again.

You are still an artist Dad, said Iris, just take your paints and go and do it. You never know you might enjoy yourself. Why the hesitation?

Elliot thought of the headmaster shouting at him during the football match.

It feels like a big step. It seems so far away and a long way to go to make a mistake.

You're just a plane ride away, said Izzy.

CHAPTER 12

Michael had a cut lip and smiled when he saw Elliot approach the table and extend his hand. Michael took it and half rose from his chair as Elliot leaned across towards him. They embraced. When they sat down again Elliot left his hand on Michael's forearm and looked him in the eyes. They held each other's gaze as a prison officer walked towards them. Michael quickly withdrew his arm and nodded in obeisance towards the officer. Elliot took in the way Michael was looking. His shirt was creased as though it had just been shaken loose after being in a spin cycle. He was wearing jeans and trainers and had a yellow sash around his shoulder and upper body as though he had won a beauty contest or was a member of some marching band. His smile was crooked. Maybe the cut hurt.

Elliot's decision to travel to Trinidad had concentrated his thoughts as regards seeing Michael, not just because he felt duty-bound to do so or guilty that he hadn't made the effort thus far but also because he needed to know Michael's decisions regarding the court case. Linda had told Elliot that he was planning to plead guilty in the hope of leniency when it came to the sentencing. Whatever happened Michael knew there was a good chance he would be sent down so a guilty plea could mean at best a supervision order with a tag and at worst a custodial sentence of fewer years that could be halved if he kept his head down. Looking at the cut lip Elliot wondered if Michael would be able be able to do that. A guilty plea would make it easier for everyone else in terms of their not having to appear as witnesses. Linda wanted to avoid that and Elliot now felt the same.

He had last visited a prison (Brixton) about forty years previously when a squatter he knew had been charged with and later convicted of the murder of a young woman who was one of Elliot's fellow students at art school. In those days you just turned up, told them who you wanted to visit and waited. He remembered he had queued in the rain with several others people, most of whom were black. There were sad-eyed women with headscarves, some holding hands with kids who looked about themselves with indifference and feigned toughness, young men smoking and avoiding eye-contact, a couple of Rastas with locks bulging in their rasta caps who made defiant eye-contact as they all shuffled towards the door of a small office. Inside there was a desk behind which sat a pink-faced prison officer with long sideburns and a moustache and tattooed arms bulging from his short sleeved shirt to whom they gave their name and the number of the prisoner they were visiting. No one said good morning or thanks or any other platitude. Then they passed through another door to a cold waiting room with plastic seats and grey walls, the paint pock-marked and blistered from damp and with the graffiti of decades and a million life stories scrawled all over it. He had sat down and looked about him in wonder at it all, clutching a form with his prisoner's name and number written on it. Someone told him he had to take the form to the air-lock door. He approached the door aware of everyone (it seemed) looking at him. He saw through the glass that a prison officer was at the other end of a corridor locking or unlocking a similar door. The officer saw him and motioned with a downward sweep of his hand which Elliot had taken to mean he should post the form through the slot below the glass. He did so and returned to his seat. A goup of four or five Rastas stood up and formed a circle, palms open in front of them, closing their eyes as one led them in a chant that was some sort of prayer. At the end they all shouted *Jah! Rasta Far I* a couple of times before sitting down again, the whole weight of Babylon upon their shoulders as they defied its burden with a solemn dignity.

After a long wait the number and name of the prisoner was called. Elliot had walked to the air-lock door and waited while the same prison officer he had seen earlier approached to unlock it. Once he was inside the air-lock he heard the door close behind him and the turning of a key. He stood aside so the officer could lead the way. Instead the officer turned to Elliot and pushed him against the wall, placing his fingers around Elliot's throat. His breath smelled of cigarettes.

Next time I tell you to wait you cunt you wait, he said, his eyes staring into Elliot's.
Elliot had no idea what he meant. The officer continued, speaking like an angry school teacher.

You wait for me to collect your form. Get it? Don't just drop it onto the floor like I'm your fucking servant.

He released his grip. Elliot was shaking.

I'm sorry, he said, I haven't been here before.

Well, now you know.

Elliot hadn't realised there was now a more complicated procedure for arranging a prison visit, most of it carried out online at the GOV.UK website's *Prison Visits* page, where he had had to give Michael's details including his number and the prison in which he now resided. Once he had supplied all of this, the relevant information as to arrival time, the ID he would be required to show, what he was and wasn't permitted to bring in with him and how long he might have to wait before he was allotted a time and date, was sent to him. Impersonal and efficient, he thought, but somehow still intimidating.

He arrived a half-hour early and reported to the Prisoners Visitors Centre, a prefab hut with metal steps leading up to the door. He showed his ID and confirmed Michael's name and number. From behind a misty and scarred glass screen a prison officer, courteous in a disinterested kind of way, pointed to a sign on the wall advising him of the contraband items he was not allowed to bring into the prison. These included mobile phones, keys, lighters, matches, drugs, guns and explosives to name but a few. He was then directed to some lockers whereupon choosing one of them he could deposit any such items.

You'll need a pound coin, said the officer, like at the swimming baths.

Elliot told him he didn't have one and asked the officer for change.

Sorry mate, he said, can't do that.

So what do I do then?

Don't go in.

Look I've come a long way and…

Not my problem mate. I'm not allowed to give change. Even if I had any.

Elliot's irritation was evident. Then he heard a voice from behind him.

Here love, said an elderly woman in a raincoat despite it being a hot day.

She was looking in her purse. They exchanged coins and he thanked her. The officer then asked Elliot to stand to the side of the window where a small camera on a bracket was angled towards him.

Look straight into the camera and don't blink please sir. Thank you. That's you now and if you will just accompany my colleague he will take you for your fingerprints.

Another prison officer appeared and led Elliot into a side room and explained to him the procedure for finger-print taking, assuring him they would be used for no other purpose other than to verify who he was every time he visited the prison. He was then led out of the room and asked to walk through a metal detector after which he was frisked by a female officer who then waved him through to the Prisoners Visitors Waiting Room where he waited to be called.

Elliot and Michael continued to look at each other without speaking, the silence confirming both the enormity of and the mundane nature of the situation they found themselves in. Elliot asked him how he was.

I'm good, he said.

Elliot asked about the cut lip by gesturing towards Michael's face with a jerk of his head.

Nothing. A little…what shall we say? Contretemps.

Michael then laughed but without conviction. Elliot told him about Amelia leaving. Michael stayed silent for a few moments before replying.

I'm so sorry. That's awful. My fault I guess. So sorry man. I really…fucked up.

No Michael don't.

Elliot wanted to reassure him but wondered if Michael could tell he was actually thinking *yes you did fuck up, Michael, and fucked us all up with it.*

It's not worth wasting your energy on that. Amelia and me were fucked up anyway and something had to give. What happened just brought things to a head so it wasn't you, mate. It was me and her.

Michael told Elliot he was going to plead guilty and that there was a provisional date for the trial in four weeks time. Elliot told him he was planning the trip to Trinidad but that he would stay in touch with him and Linda when away.

No need, said Michael, it'll be fine. Things are kind of wrapped up. Once I know the sentence we can start to plan. Things'll sort themselves out.

Anything I can do?

Michael shook his head and looked down at the table top.

Nope. Just let me know if Linda or the kids need anything she isn't telling me about. Other than that nothing. When are you going?

Soon enough. You want me to be in court?

No need. But if you're still here.

It was time to say goodbye. They hugged and Elliot watched him walk to the door where a prison officer awaited, his key attached to a leather cord. There was the sound of a key turning in a lock (the sound you hear the most, Michael had said) and without a glance back he walked back through into whatever world lay beyond.

Elliot's journey home necessitated a wait of forty minutes for a connection at some non-descript town in the middle of middle England. From the platform he could see a bar called *The Under Graduate* and he headed straight for it. Next door to the bar was a mini-cab office and in its doorway about eight young men, all dressed in bunny rabbit costumes, were trying to cram themselves into the confined space, climbing on top of one another, laughing and swearing as they did so. Then as though responding to some signal they gave up and went running off down the street. The bar was empty apart from a woman who was asking one of the two barmen to borrow a mobile phone. Elliot sat on a stool and ordered a beer and a large whisky. It was served wordlessly by the barman who took Elliot's ten pound note and then brought him the change without ever saying how much the drinks had cost. The woman went outside to make her call. Elliot ordered the same again, drank it quickly and left. The woman was shouting at whoever it was on the other end of the phone.

Once on the train he sat at a table seat and noticed a blonde teenage girl with earphones in her ears sitting at a table on the other side of the aisle. Two men (he guessed students) got on and sat behind her. They were speaking in loud public schoolboy accents and swearing at every opportunity. One was carrying an open half bottle of vodka and the other a bottle of coke. There was an announcement from the train manager apologising for the fact that none of the toilets on the train were functioning.

Anthony you little wanker, said one of the students in an exaggerated aristocratic tone, we're fucking going out and I haven't got any fucking money.

Well you can fuck right off, said Anthony, because you're nothing but a dick you dick.

They then noticed the blonde girl in front of them and started to make comments about her body, becoming more and more crude and sexually threatening as they warmed to their fun. She moved to sit directly opposite Elliot, looking frightened. He nodded to her by way of reassurance but was uncertain as to what grounds he had to be reassuring her at all. Anthony and his pal then moved to the seat she had vacated and continued with their abuse. Elliot felt his heart quicken as he asked them to stop. The one carrying the vodka stood up and leaned over Elliot, one arm on the back of his seat. He threatened Elliot, called him an old cunt and told him to fuck off several times otherwise he was going to *fuck him right up*.

He was now pointing the bottle towards Elliot, his spittle landing on Elliot's face and shoulder. Elliot looked away from his assailant and towards the girl. As he did so he started to stand and then forcefully swung his arm, sending the bottle of vodka flying down the aisle. The young man looked startled but had no chance to react as Elliot punched him on the side of the face with as much strength as he could muster. He connected with the young man's nose and blood spurted from it as he fell to the floor. Elliot turned to Anthony and looked at him with what he hoped was an expression full of fearlessness and a propensity to unguarded violence before moving towards the alarm. Anthony begged him not to pull the alarm, saying they were getting off at the next stop. The train slowed as it reached the next station and Anthony helped his bloodied friend up off the carriage floor.

Fuck off the pair of you, said Elliot as they stumbled out of the carriage.

He sat down again and the girl thanked him. He told her he had never hit anyone before.

Really? she said, as though she had never before met anyone like him.

Elliot felt tremulous and an urge to use the toilet before remembering that none of the toilets on board were working. He willed himself to stay in control and succeeded in doing so. Passing through the next couple of stops he noticed how nearly everyone waiting to get on the train was young and drunk. He pointed this out to the girl who looked surprised that he was surprised.

It's Saturday night, she said.

Two men (he guessed in their fifties) got on. Both had shaved heads and were dressed in Harrington jackets, jeans and Doc Martin boots. They had been to a football match. One of them spoke to the other as he tried to read something on his phone.

It's like I've got a spider's web over my eyes. I just don't see the way I used to.

Cataracts maybe, said the other one, my nan had them. Anyway what's he saying?

He can't fucking spell.

He's never been able to fucking spell. He spells like he fucking speaks.

The girl left the train at the next stop after thanking Elliot again and saying goodbye. A young couple then sat opposite him. He guessed they were Japanese. They appeared happy together, giggling and holding hands, speaking excitedly to one another. They then began a game of stone paper scissors, laughing in loud high-pitched tones at the end of each round. When they stopped playing she sounded as though she was scolding him for something. Her companion looked adoringly into her eyes, put his arm around her and she then laid her head on his chest, her long hair falling down over his waist and resting on his thigh.

They closed their eyes. Elliot glanced over at the two skinheads who also appeared to be asleep but one of them kept opening an eye and checking out his friend as though he didn't trust him. The train reached Elliot's stop and the untrusting one got off with without saying anything to his companion. It was half past ten and Elliot headed to the pub opposite the station for a few night caps, knowing he wouldn't remember how he later got home.

CHAPTER 13

A week after his visit to Michael and nothing could have brought home to him more that he was now in a foreign land than the flamboyant trees in bloom. They lined a stretch of the Solomon Hochoy Highway - that bumpy four lanes of frequent madness heading south in pretty much a straight line where signs advising drivers to stay left unless overtaking were ignored as cars, trucks, taxis, maxi-taxis, lorries, motorbikes, vans, jeeps and police-cars managed their journeys in a chaotic harmony, criss-crossing at speed from lane to lane, going past unfinished buildings, hard-shoulder hitchhikers, slip-road bars, randomly placed dwellings of every shape, size and social status and billboards announcing political slogans or advertising beer and different brands of rum. The flowers of the trees vivid in crimson as their branches spread outwards like the hands of the condemned reaching for the sky. To Elliot the trees were so exotic as to be incongruous to the scene but for those who lived there they were commonplace and would hardly be worthy of comment or description.

Everything about the journey had felt wrong to him from the start. First the gridlocked crawl down the M25 to Gatwick, then the tearful farewell and hug with Izzy and a bear hug from Brendan, then the rising sense of anxiety as he walked to the departure gate and a recurring urge to turn back, provoking breathlessness and panic and a sense he was in peril and about to drown as he swam against the tide. Then he found it difficult to handle the unnaturalness of sitting in a confined space next to a stranger for eleven hours as the noises of undercarriage, engines and circulating air competed with announcements, children crying and muffled human discourse. His left testicle throbbed as it played an inharmonius duet with a pain in his left big toe and he shuffled and squirmed in his seat, trying in vain to find a comfortable position. At several junctures he wished he had never started out on the journey. He missed the security of the dysfunctional discomfort zone he had become so familiar with in England and as he now traversed the vortex that was trans-Atlantic travel he felt stateless and vulnerable as though he had cut all the ties holding him to the planet. He stepped out of the airport and into a wall of heat and humidity where a sweet smell in the air of fruit on the turn emanated from the luxuriance of the surrounding flora. This land had been baked under a brutal sun and soaked by torrents of rain for millennia. Touts vied for passengers, loved ones were greeted and car horns sounded, all in a cacophony of chaos and unreined intention.

The journey down the highway was an unavoidable hell. Elliot's driver, Mr. Ramsawak (a man with a belly so large it pressed against his steering wheel) was the personificiation of impassivity. He answered any query with as few words as possible, sometimes no words at all, preferring just a shrug of his shoulders or a nod of his head. If Elliot spoke Ramsawak either ignored him or answered with such an economy of language it became pointless to even try starting a conversation. Elliot gave up, leaned back and told himself to relax. The silence within the car allowed him time to reflect as he orientated himself to where he now was and where he'd come from and the events that had precipitated his flight.

His last journey of any note had been the train ride across country to visit Michael. How tame in comparison to this had been the view from his window that day as he looked out upon the British countryside and glimpsed gentler lives being lived. The flooded fields, ploughed or still bearing crops, wildlife (two hares sprinting from one hedgerow to the next) and the ubiquitous farm stock of cows and sheep, all interrupted by provincial towns with their identikit high streets and suburbs. He also thought of Knockbreck. How he loved to walk the mudflats at low tide with the wind and the calls of oystercatchers and curlews the only sounds beneath the purple sky as great shafts of sunlight broke through the clouds to stripe the horizon with silver. All too enormous and other worldy to ever comprehend. And Amelia there. That beautiful lost love of his. He pictured her making coffee in the morning, putting on her boots, closing the gate as she stepped out onto the beach. He noticed a sign for La Romaine (straight on), San Fernando and Dumfries (right turn). He felt so far away. Ramsawak turned off the highway and slowed down. He cleared his throat, lowered his window and spat as he negotiated what Elliot guessed was meant to be a roundabout, so complicated and signless only locals could know which way they were meant to turn.

He thought of Michael now a couple of weeks into his four year sentence, sitting in his cell with whoever he was sharing it with. Then his thoughts turned to Linda. Their farewell had been perfunctory for the most part as they acknowledged how difficult it was to say goodbye. As they hugged Elliot wondered if he was doing the right thing in leaving her but he knew it was essential for him to escape the cloud of negativity that had engulfed them both those past few months. In truth it hadn't been so hard to leave her behind.

He had sent several texts to Amelia, asking her to call him. The evening before he had left, she phoned. She wished him a pleasant journey and asked what was happening with the house as she wasn't sure when she was coming back. He told her Tom and Jerry had taken a set of keys and were happy to keep an eye on things, pick up mail and tend the garden if necessary until either of them returned. He also told her they had both hugged him and how he was surprised by but grateful for the extent of their warmth. He had hoped that by telling her this it would somehow demonstrate to her what he had been going through and thereby prick her conscience. Instead she had sounded cool and aloof as she asked him if he thought running away was a good idea. Her aim was true, striking its intended target with force. He had started to rationalise his decision to her but didn't have the strength to persist.

Yeah yeah I'm running away…like you did, he said before putting the phone down.

He knew this would have angered her and hoped she would call back but (typically, he thought) she didn't. He resisted the temptation to call again but couldn't get off to sleep until the early hours.

During the previous week Brendan had helped Elliot to tidy his half of the studio, stacking canvasses, moving furniture and cramming paints, brushes, palettes, and boxes of magazines, photos and notebooks into the cupboard. All this was done with humour, enthusiasm and an energy only Brendan could have conveyed as Elliot dithered, prevaricated and pondered the wisdom of it all. Brendan warned Elliot to avoid the weed in Trinidad and advised he stayed as long as he wanted and that he would know when the time was right to return. Biscuit had called him a *jammy wee cunt* and threatened to come out and visit him as they drank a couple of pints at the brewery. Elliot told him he wouldn't be there longer than a month.

Why? asked Biscuit, This country's a shitehole. Full of losers and racists who blame immigrants for everything and who think this is the best fucking country in the fucking world when it's one of the shittiest. No one would want to be here for fuck's sake...it's cold and wet...the food we eat is shite...our transport system's shite...and the government are a bunch of fucking posh boys who havnae got a fucking clue about the rest of us. UKIP supporters fucking everywhere. If we wantae have a holiday here our beaches are shite...the summer lasts for about two days and the motorways are chocker anyway. On top of that nobody can afford to rent a flat...let alone buy a hoose...naebody qualifies for benefits even if they've got nae legs and are blind deaf and dumb and meanwhile everyone is more concerned about strictly come fucking dancing than they are about their neighbour or their community. Nah fuck it man...I'd come with you if she'd give me a pass. You're doing the right thing.

Elliot had popped his head round the door to the brewery's office. Carol was there alone.

You're really going then? she asked.

Yeah...give my best to Jonny.

I'll miss seeing you.

You too.

They held each other's look. He moved closer to her and they embraced, holding on for what felt to be a long time. She pulled back and holding his shoulders looked him in the eyes and kissed him on the lips.

Do you think you and me...?

Yep, she replied.

CHAPTER 14

Once through San Fernando the road took them past Mosquito Creek on the south-western bend of the bay as the sky darkened and the fishing boats bobbed in shadows on the water. In front of the Hindu crematorium a few stall holders were still out on the roadside selling fish and crab even though dusk was fast turning into nightfall. Ramsawak took the the turning that led them through Dow Village and Rousillac and on to La Brea where the traffic slowed to a near standstill.

One of de wonders of de world, volunteered Ramsawak, and dey cahn make road fit for purpose.

Elliot remembered La Brea, a ramshackle village inhabited mainly by poor blacks. It was where the Pitch Lake was situated and from where asphalt had risen up for centuries from somewhere way below the Earth's surface, providing the village and the country with not only a claim to fame (and an eco-tourist destination) but also the largest natural deposit of asphalt in the world. Sir Walter Raleigh had been the first to exploit the lake some four hundred years before when the native Amerindians showed him how to caulk his ship with the pitch. In seemingly endless supply it had ever since been exported to every continent and provided employment for generations of Trinidadians. Ramsawak was right about the road. It undulated and moved in an ever-changing relief of bumps, potholes and cambers as the pitch oozed and shifted of its own accord underneath the surface in an unstoppable force of nature. What Trinidadians referred to as board houses (those built with wooden planks and galvanised iron roofs, usually raised from the ground on stilts) provided homes for most of La Brea's population but the houses also moved with the subterranean forces beneath them and most leaned at angles so extreme that they looked like they could topple over any day. Elliot could see some had actually collapsed. No one built a concrete house there.

Brake lights and indicators marked the way ahead like red and yellow sweets scattered across the road. Their windows were down and the street vendors (coconut, pakchoy, mango, pawpaw and channet) shouted and waved for their attention. Elliot adopted Ramsawak's inscrutability so as to reduce his appearance of being a stranger unfamilar of his surrounds.

Wind up de glass, said Ramsawak, til we reach past La Brea.
Why?
Somebody might think yuh have money. Rich white man.

Once through the village they passed the beach at Vessigny where Elliot had often bathed as a child. He remembered its murky brown waters and the sensation of small fish swimming around his ankles. Then on to Point Fortin where he knew he was close at last to Paul's house and the village where he had spent much of his childhood and teenage holidays. Point Fortin the oil town, known just as Point, was where his father had worked throughout the late fifties and sixties until sometime in the seventies when the foreign-owned company he was employed by was acquired by the national government. He had had no choice but to return to the UK. The silhouettes of rigs and the eternal flame of the refinery gave the town a strange atmosphere - untamed and industrial at the same time. They passed a field of pumping-jacks in perpetual motion looking like giant hunchbacked slaves from a futuristic age who were condemned to pound the earth until eternity. The lights of a tanker flickered on the horizon. Within a distance of about two hundred yards they passed a mosque, a Hindu temple, a Presbyterian church and a Rasta place of worship, the latter bedecked in red, green, gold and black stripes with a wooden sign fixed to it's small turret saying *His Highness the Emperor Haille Selassie-I Church of Ethiopia*. They then passed through Fanny Village on the outskirts of town and Elliot felt a sense of both calm and homecoming. Muga Village was just down the road. A man with waist-length dreadlocks was standing alone on the side of the road shouting to no one in particular, cursing and shaking his fists at the passing cars.

Look at dat crazy niggah, said Ramsawak, laughing.

The last time Elliot had visited Trinidad Paul had traveled with him. During their flight, as Elliot recalled, they drank a crazy amount of rum and beers and Paul expressed excitement at his first ever trip to the West Indies. It had soon became clear Paul was anticipating something that was far removed from reality, the stereotypical vision most non-West Indians have - that of white sands, turquoise waters and coconut palms swaying gently in a breeze as Bob Marley played in the background, spliffs were shared and rum cocktails downed in an atmosphere of harmony, laid-backness and friendliness. Elliot had to disavow his friend of this without disappointing him, explaining how the infrastructure was more third-world than first and that poverty, violence and corruption were more apparent there than anywhere he had experienced before. He explained the racial divide that existed – how ninety-five percent of the poulation was split between near equal numbers of people of either Indian or African descent and that enmity between the two groups, by no means universal, still remained, manifesting itself in racial stereotyping and discrimination. Trinidadians mostly referred to black people as Africans, an acknowledgement of their slave ancestry, whereas Indians, whose ancestors had been indentured labour shipped over from the sub-continent by sugar barons (and so considered by themselves to be a more priveleged group even though they were effectively enslaved themselves) were mostly referred to as Indians. Michael was shocked when Elliot told him Africans were still called *niggers* by a minority of Indian people and that some Africans used the descriptor *coolie* as a derogatory term for an Indian. Anyone of mixed descent, a sizeable proportion of the population, could be referred to by the term *dougla* which was not necessarily an insult. Elliot explained that despite all this there was significant social and physical integration between the races and that this had led to an island unlike, in terms of race, most others in the Caribbean. It was a country where the people lived harmoniously for the most part but also where the lure of drug money and the subsequent crime and gang cultures in the larger towns had led to a crime rate disproportionate to the size of the island's population, especially relating to murder. Elliot didn't want to frighten him so he assured Paul that where they were going to stay was generally a quiet crime-free village but that he needed to be careful all the same.

Elliot's arrival this time was announced by Ramsawak sounding his horn. A pick-up truck with trumpet-shaped speakers on its roof drove past them and Indian wedding music blasted its way into Elliot's consciousness for a few seconds before fading quickly into the distance. Dogs barked and ran to the gate. An old man who Elliot recognised after a few seconds as Vernita's father came to unlock it and as he swung it open he shouted at the dogs, aiming kicks in their direction. He beckoned the car in with an air of importance, sweeping his arms as though directing traffic onto a ferry and jerked his chin upwards in acknowledgement of Elliot's waving to him. People appeared on the gallery. The air was sticky and thick. He felt beads of sweat fall from his armpits, cold against his skin. He heard the croaking of what sounded like hundreds of frogs somewhere nearby in the darkness.

The first person he recognisde among the throng on the gallery was Johnson Carter, the fast bowler. He was a tall lithe African, now in his forties, who was a friend of Vernita's family and with whom Elliot had struck up a relationship the last time he was there, one based on laughter at the ridiculousness of life and the intricacies of field placements, two subjects that overlapped often. They shook hands brother-style and Johnson pulled him close for a hug.

Looong*man*! he shouted, following it up with a prolonged *wheeeey*.

The surroundings provoked memories Elliot found difficult to focus upon. At the same time it felt unfamiliar and foreign and confirmed to him on the one hand his outsider status and on the other his being an integral part of this family and community. Like a returning exile he recognised the sounds and smells that weren't normal to him anymore but once had been. This sense of paradox receded as he climbed the steps to the gallery. Paul stood behind a group of people, all of whom Elliot knew and who were smiling at him with excitement, warmth and genuineness. A flurry of handshakes and kisses before Paul pushed his way through and took Elliot in his arms, squeezed him and kissed his cheeks, his tall broad figure enveloping Elliot's body like a blanket.

They released their grips and holding eachother's forearms looked to one another grinning.

Fantastic, said Paul, arm now around Elliot's shoulders,.

He led him through the doorway and into the house where the sounds of whirring fans and a television filled the air. He could smell curry. Two young Indian children with matchstick limbs averted their gaze from the screen and stared at him with wide dark eyes.

Say hello to Uncle, said Paul.

The children looked at eachother and giggled. Vernita walked from the kitchen area, rubbing her hands on a tea-towel as she greeted him, her smile broad, her hug warm and strong.

Good to see you, she said and added, patting his stomach, you put on a little.

They both laughed. Johnson carried the bags upstairs and Elliot took a few seconds to look around him, not knowing what to do next. He looked to Paul who was still grinning.

Come downstairs, he said.

He walked Elliot to the back door where a stairwell from a small gallery led to a large open space beneath the house and where a few friends and family were gathered. More hand-shakes, kisses and hugs. Paul brought two beers from a fridge and they touched bottles. They were dripping with condensation, the beer the slightest of degrees higher than freezing point. Elliot took a few gulps and then realised Paul was drinking.

I thought you stopped.

I did. Mostly beers now. Rarely anything stronger. You know it's impossible not to drink here though.

I know. For breakfast sometimes.

Elliot saw Ramsawak sitting in a corner next to Vernita's brother Anil. He was holding a glass of rum, talking loudly and laughing.

I would never have known he could talk so much, said Elliot.

You didn't meet him last time? Vernita's uncle. Married her aunt. Fucking know-it-all but he's all right.

They laughed again and Elliot leaned back in his chair, beginning to feel more relaxed. He heard a voice behind him.

Next beer Uncle?

He turned around to see a smiling dark-skinned Indian with a Mohican haircut, sleeveless shirt and tatooed biceps and who was holding two beers. Elliot looked non-plussed at first and it took him a few seconds before he recognised the young man in front of him.

Sachin! he said, rising from his chair and reaching out to to take him in his arms before saying, you've grown man, look at you.

It's been a while Uncle. How many years?

Twelve man. Too long.

Yeah too long. But yuh reach now. It's good to see yuh.

You too. How old are you now?

Twenty-six.

Working? Married?

Yeah. Pitch Lake. And I marry Isis. Remember she?

Johnson's daughter?

Yeah.

Where she?

Home with de kids.

Wheey. Kids too?

Two. Adrienne and Adrian. Tree and one.

Congratulations. You still playing cricket?

Yeah. I ain't gonna stop that.

Good to see you man.

You too Uncle. How long you staying?

Four weeks or so.

Plenty time for we to catch up some more.

Although people had come there to see him there was no drama. Once the hugs, kisses and handshakes were out of the way people quickly resumed their regular demeanours as though saying to any onlooker that life goes on, this is the way things are and this is how we are regardless of where *you've* come from and whoever the hell *you* are. Some were playing cards, others watching television, others just talking. Elliot felt an unfamiliar sense of contentment and confidence and relief at being far away from England, the house, the street, the studio, the brewery and Amelia.

Sounds like you were having some difficult times, said Paul.

Yeah. I needed some time away from it all and thought here as good as anywhere.

You okay?

Yep. Just recognising what I'm leaving behind. Working out what I want to see again. And who. What I want to do next.

The girls?

Oh of course. They've been great. We're good.

So what *are* you leaving behind?

Elliot pondered the question for a few moments.

Sadness I guess. Unhealthy living. Self-destructiveness. To name but three.

They looked at eachother with expressions congruent with the seriousness of the conversation. Then they laughed. Much of their friendship since schooldays had been based on their being able to laugh together at their own insecurities and foibles, from when they were teenagers trying to deal with school, sex, drugs and their own creative impulses to when as older men they would drink and walk together, sharing thoughts and ideas, often arguing, often drunk or under the influence of some chemical but always close enough to be able to be themselves with each other.

So you're still a cunt then, said Paul and they both laughed again.

Vernita came over to them.

You two should eat. Channa and curry duck.

Elliot stood and put his arm around her.

You've been busy then?

Yuh know.

CHAPTER 15

It was 6.30 on his first morning in Muga Village. The temperature had already reached 28 degrees and a white sun was rising slowly as he sat on the small gallery at the back of the house. He looked out towards the untamed bush. A solitary coconut palm swayed in the centre of the scene and he started to construct in his mind a composition based on what he was looking at. Randomly placed houses, some at different stages of being built, some board, some concrete, some a mix of the two but none built to any uniform design, size or colour, the most impressive of which was a large concrete structure of three levels, several galleries, a multitude of windows and the exterior walls painted a cotton-candy pink. Then there were all the add-ons dispersed haphazardly around the houses - black plastic water tanks, chicken coops, strutting cocks chasing hens, a tethered cow, a tethered goat, dog kennels, the rusted shells of cars, disused air-con units, a small gazebo consisting of four uprights and a tarpaulin top standing on a potholed driveway at an angle steep enough to be defying gravity, plastic piping, bricks, sheets of galvanised iron, barbecue pits, styrofoam coolers and crates of empty beer bottles. All around it and within it and in defiance of it all, nature had risen up with an unstoppable momentum – coconut palms, avocado trees, banana trees, plantain trees, lemon trees, lime trees, mango trees, guava trees, pawpaw trees and any number of other trees bearing fruits he didn't recognise or know the names of. And animals – lizards and iguanas fluorescent in green, weird and evil-looking insects and arachnids, birds of all sizes and colours from vultures and hawks to hummingbirds and the tiny Johnny Jump-Up, a black bird who sat on a stem of long grass and jumped vertically into the air to catch flies. It was as though the human race had crash-landed in paradise ten thousand years before and still hadn't got a clue how to live in it. A squadron of eight blue, yellow and white macaws flew past announcing themselves with their harsh call sign. A kiskadee, a species of flycatcher with an onomatopoeic call everpresent during the daytimes, sat on the garage roof. Elliot looked at the bird, its yellow breast as bright as a Lakeland daffodil and its black and white striped head cocked towards him as if he was a curiosity. He saw the next door neighbour, Krishna, stand topless at a sink underneath his wooden house and brush his teeth. Krishna let out a burp that sounded across the neighbourhood (he was nicknamed Goatman) before he put on a ragged t-shirt, picked up a stick and walked towards the tethered cow. Before he had gone far his wife Steebeth called out to him, provoking an exchange of insults.

Krishna ya lazy mothercunt! Lord! Yuh duckin me? Yuh dead boy. Clean the damn pakchoy before yuh see to de damn cow.

Doh make joke, he shouted back at her, Jagabat! Is affair you!

Yuh lazy ass.

You de lazy ass.

Krishna looked at the cow and cursed it before whacking it across its bony back and pulling it towards a small patch of grass behind one of the mango trees. He looked up and smiled and waved when he saw Elliot.

Yuh reach?

Yesterday.

Okay. Why you gone so long?

Elliot shrugged his shoulders as if to say who knows. Krishna laughed before disappearing from view into the undergrowth pulling the cow along behind him. Elliot sat back and wondered why it had taken him so long to return there. When he had come back twelve years previously, bringing Paul for his first visit there, he hadn't been there for about twenty years but he had fallen into step with the way of life more easily than he had expected to. Everything had been familiar and it felt as though he was returning to his real home even though he suppressed that thought, scared of where it might lead him. The two had brought with them, along with as much drawing and painting paraphenalia as possible, a resolve to reignite their potential as artists to be reckoned with. They had planned to stay for six weeks but Paul never returned to England, not to live anyway. While Elliot renewed acquaintances, drank beers and rum, played pool, lusted after barmaids and lay on hammocks for large parts of the day, Paul set about the colours and the light. While Elliot's eyes clouded over with familiarity and the effects of over-proof spirits and weed, Paul's eyes had widened as soon as the plane's wheels hit the runway at Piarco. Elliot had since rationalised his own behaviour as being an understandable and predictable way of coping with a wave of emotion that was capable of drowning him. Coming *home* to a place he didn't live in anymore and to people he didn't live with anymore made him feel a depth of yearning only an exile could appreciate. So many ghosts came back to life and despite having gained much life experience in the years gone by and learning how to bear numerous battle scars, he allowed himself to dissociate by numbing his senses and intellect with the temporary balm of drink, drugs and seductive friends. Within the alcoholic haze of those six weeks some deep friendships and family ties were nevertheless both discovered and rediscovered. He had promised to return soon after.

Paul, meanwhile, despite partying with the rest of them, had started to produce work of real quality – dream-like images of local people set within distorted local scenes of village life or the bush and the rainforest, his changing pallette inspired and given force by the culture, climate and accompanying flora and fauna, all of which was so new to him. The vivid green vegetation, the blue of the sky and its dramatic cloud formations, the colours of the birds, the way people dressed and spoke, all of it sharpened his perception like never before. Elliot could only look on with a combination of admiration and envy and tried to justify his inactivity as being the result of his having to spend most of his time there meeting the expectations of the people he knew. The eyes of someone beholding it all for the first time were bound to see things differently from him, he told himself. After all, he knew it so well, it was already inside him and he could call upon that knowledge whenever he chose to do so.

It was during this time Paul had got to know Vernita and Elliot wasn't surprised when Paul told him he would be staying for a while longer. Vernita and Elliot had known each other since they were children, his father's house a five minute walk away from hers along the road to Point. Her mother, Shivana, used to help his father with cleaning and washing for which he paid her a small retainer. Vernita, a couple of years younger than Elliot, was the youngest of thirteen children (seven of whom were now dead) and she, along with her two nearest siblings, Naren and Mishra, were Elliot's playmates and companions for much of his youth. Naren was the same age give or take a few weeks and Mishra two years older. She had a lighter skin tone than her siblings and was a gentle friend to Elliotin those days, one whose company he preferred to the rougher more boisterous Naren, who nevertheless had taught him many things about life there. Elliot remembered with fondness Naren showing him how to pick a coconut and open it with a cutlass, making a little spoon from its skin so as to scoop up the jelly inside. Naren had taught him how to fire a slingshot (he used to hunt iguana this way) and how to hold a crab without getting nipped. He had explained the whole concept of liming - making a lime, enjoying the lime or going for a lime. Elliot had thought Naren was talking about the fruit until he explained, laughing at Elliot's ignorance, that to lime meant to hang out with any number of people just for the sake of hanging out. It could mean going for a drink, preparing something to eat in order to share it (making a cook) or just standing on the street chatting. Vernita, being the youngest, used to tag along with them for the lime and was always tolerated and looked after. She had a mouth on her too, he remembered, often cursing them with adult swear words if she felt she was being left behind or excluded and they never tired of provoking her into doing so.

Paul had been back to the UK only once, to coordinate and oversee the hanging of his paintings for an exhibition in Liverpool. He had stayed for a few days and Elliot made the trip up there to see him during which time they drank, laughed and hugged a lot. That Paul had never been back since wasn't a surprise to Elliot who could see his best friend had found somewhere and someone that suited him. His demeanour had changed – he was calmer and more confident and his work had correspondingly, or perhaps causatively, taken on a whole new forcefulness. It was brash and bright and full of vivid colour. Elliot couldn't help but feel Paul was succeeding where he could and should have done but had chosen not to. And that had made all the difference, thought Elliot, to both their lives. Then again, maybe that's the difference between those who succeed and those who don't, even when they start from the same place in terms of talent, intent and opportunity. Maybe that's what talent was – having the presence of mind to seize an opportunity and then become focussed enough, to draw on the necessary will power to commit and not be distracted or dissuaded. He had always had the talent but rebelled against the structure required to realise it. He could see as well as the rest of them, he just didn't stand up long enough to sustain the vision.

Elliot sensed he had also come back to Muga to make amends with those who were closest to him. No one had understood why he had stayed away for so long. He wasn't sure either and asked himself what it was that kept him away. There had been work, family, relationships, illness – the usual things that constitute a life, but there was more to it – what he now saw was avoidance behaviour manifesting itself in morbid fantasy (it was dangerous out there), morbid fear (of pain and ill-health) and just plain denial that anyone he knew there gave a damn. All were rationalisations with some elements of truth underpinning them but he chose to amplify them until he convinced himself to not make the journey.

He stayed in touch with Paul by letter and the occasional phone-call and then it petered out until social media allowed them such easy ways to access one another they couldn't avoid it. Paul often reassured him he would be fine there and that he should just come over and bring Amelia with him, Iris and Izzy if he wanted to. Elliot had discussed it a few times with Amelia who said he should go without her. He thought maybe she sensed he needed to make the trip alone but he allowed the inconclusivity of their discussions to help him defer making a decision. That characteristic tendency to prevarication had stopped him doing so much in his life– the image of the old man hesitating on the edge of the bath had never left him. Vernita's father appeared at the top of the steps with an avocado the size of a rugby ball in his hand.

Yuh get up? he asked Elliot.
Yeah long time.
Makin hot boy.
Yeah real hot.
Yuh get a nice breeze in de gallery.

Yeah that's why I'm sitting here.

Heh heh, laughed the old man, putting the avocado down on the table.

It have plenty avocado in de tree...more in de garden. Boy you should see de garden...it have plenty bodi and packchoy...lettuce too...but it need rain.

You not getting rain?

Boy...dis is de rainy season and we ain't getting *no* rain...no rain at *all*.

Climate change?

Eh?

The climate change.

The old man shrugged.

So what we gonna do...I tellin yuh...I go to de mosque morning and say me prayers and I listen to de man preaching his words then I go to de garden and I do a little work and when it get hot I rest in de hammock...boy yuh *know* I at peace with de world...nobody gonna tell me what to do and nuttin I can do about de climate changin...for sure...so what we gonna do...heh heh...nuttin is all we can do...say we prayers...look after we family and trust in de man but maybe even de man don't know what to do...heh heh...what we gonna do?

He slapped Elliot on the shoulder and walked through to the kitchen.

CHAPTER 16

He didn't leave the house during his first four days there, choosing to spend most of his time either on the back gallery looking at the ever-shifting tones and colours of the view or at the front of the house from where he watched the road and all manner of village life passing by. It had been hot every day, always mid-thirties by noon. When he had ventured out into the sun the harshness of the glare and the intensity of the heat soon drove him back inside. If he stood still in the sun for a minute or so he could feel his skin starting to burn. Everyone who passed or stopped by commented on the weather. So many people in the village worked the land for their living and he wondered how they could cope and whether crops were failing. Every morning about eleven he saw a tall African woman walk past the house. She had a wicker basket containing pakchoy balanced upon her head, alternating her arms to steady it. Her clothes were ragged and she walked barefoot with slow deliberate strides, mud caked all over her feet and lower legs. She would always look towards him but never acknowledge his smile or wave.

Despite his apparent inactivity he didn't feel he had been idle. It would have been justifiable to be so as he acclimatised but his mind had been active even his body hadn't. He had been making notes and drawings in a small sketch book, using a soft pencil to make thick lines and arcs, then rubbing over the lines with an eraser to give the sketches more texture. He had made several sketches of different aspects of the view from the back gallery, writing thoughts and reminders alongside them. He could sense he was getting close to painting again.

Immediately below the gallery was the galvanised iron roof of a car port and various birds would come to stand on it and he would try to incorporate them into his drawings or at least the notes he was writing. He needed to introduce colour soon. Senses other than sight were being invigorated by the stimuli abundant there, whether it was the taste of fresh food, the smells of spices or flowers, the sounds of cockerels, frogs and various wild animals, some of whom were unrecognisable even to the locals, or the itching prickly skin that came with heat rash and mosquito bites in a mean combination. The sensory impetus was high. Ideas were numerous, partially formed but flowing and he struggled to articulate them all whether in images or words. His inclination was to just sit back and let it happen and such an approach was already proving more effective than trying to force it to fruition all at once. He was trying not to be influenced by his memory of how vigourously Paul had worked when he had first come there. In the past this memory would have pressurised and distracted Elliot as though he was in competition with Paul but he now realised if he was ever going to work again, whatever came out of him had to be the result of a natural process that was his and his alone. Yes, he would have to work with diligence and discipline but so long as he was being truthful and honest he didn't mind the prospect. At the back of his sketch book he had taped a printed message written to himself a few years previously.

To be in denial of your creativity will never result in your feeling better about yourself or the world around you. Such denial will in fact compound and deepen your negativity. On the other hand, if you accept your creativity and continue to create, these very acts will have a restorative and life-affirming effect. Go to it. be comfortable with it. You have work to do.

During the daytimes he had hardly seen Paul who stuck pretty much to the same routine of rising at dawn and heading for his workspace, sometimes coming home around midday for something to eat before going back to work. He had told Elliot to drop in at the studio whenever he wanted to but Elliot had been hesitant. Paul rented a space below Neighbour's bar, a small rum shop a couple of minutes walk away and behind which was Neighbour's house where she lived with her husband Alan and a seemingly ever-changing family group consisting of daughters, sons-in-law and grandchildren. He would normally have called in to see Neighbour by now. Her bar had been the scene of many a drunken lime in the past and her dining table the source of many a comforting meal.

Wheey boy. When you goin to do de tour? said Vernita, standing at the back door, referring to the necessary walk down the road to say hello to everyone he knew.

He knew *de tour* would take up most of the day as people would offer food and drink wherever he went and he would have to call in on them all lest he offended anybody.

I guess I should go soon, he replied.

Go to de studio now man. He would like you to.

She joined him at the small round table on the gallery having brought a freshly-picked mango for him.

You been dreaming out here?

Kind of, he laughed, this is a starch mango, right?

No julie. Is a julie mango tree we have. One julie and one long.

Long mango. I remember.

Yeah but de long mangoes not so long anymore. Dey *short* long mangoes.

They both laughed and then sat in silence as he peeled half of the mango skin before immersing his face into the flesh, slowly slurping, licking and sucking his way through it before peeling the other half and doing the same, his hands dripping with juice, the stringy fibres sticking between his teeth. His mouth, much to Vernita's amusement was now encircled by a sticky orange stain.

Wheey boy. Look like you been givin dat mango some real lovin, she said.

He went to wash in the kitchen sink. A neighbour, Joy, arrived and walked out onto the gallery.

Mornin mornin, she said, wheeey boy it makin hot.

She fanned her face with a newspaper.

Yeah boy, said Vernita.

I ain't seen Mishra yet you know, said Elliot.

Look she home, said Vernita, pointing across the rooftops to a large white house with a blue roof about a hundred yards away.

The door to its back gallery was open and he could just make out someone moving inside.

Call she, said Joy, yuh have big mout.

She have big mout.

You both have big mouth, said Elliot.

Oy! Mishra!

He saw her appear in the doorway. She waved. They all waved back. He stood up and waved again feeling excited at seeing her. She beckoned and shouted.

Come!

He got up and went to take a shower.

People didn't usually knock on doors there, they either walked straight in or shouted from outside. If in a car they would just sound the horn and wait. Elliot felt a frisson of anticipation as he decided to knock, not wanting to be over familiar too soon. Mishra shouted for him to go in. They met in the semi-darkness of her sitting room and embraced, holding eachother for a few seconds, then, holding hands looked into each other's eyes.

Why so long boy?

Well it's a long way to come and…

Not from England stupid. Why so long yuh here and not come by me? Yuh don't like me or what?

Of course I do. I thought you would come by Vernita. Thought I was bound to just see you sometime…and I've been tired you know…jet lag. I'm sorry.

I'm only kidding yuh. I've been with some family in de north.

They sat down, still holding hands.

How are you Mish?

Okay boy.

She paused, looked away from him for a few seconds before turning to face him again. Her eyes were wide, dark rings underneath them.

But I've been a little sick you know, she said, with de sugar. Blood pressure too. Dey tink I had a little stroke maybe. So I get a little tired but I'm good overall.

The news she had diabetes (like so many there) and that she may have had a stroke came as a shock to him and reminded him of how much time had passed since he had last seen her. It was impossible not to expect people to look and be the same as when he had been with them the last time but inevitably the years would have taken their toll to varying degrees. She was still slight in build and had the same familiar complexion and hazel eyes. She bore a mournful countenance that even when she was laughing or telling him she was feeling good made it appear as though something else of consequence was going on in her life and that she would never tell anyone what it was. Ageing had not affected her beauty, he thought, if anything the lines and colours of life had enhanced it even more. He wanted to respond appropriately to the news of her ill-health but was struck dumb as if by being in her presence and having to acknowledge the enormity of his love for her he was rendered unable to formulate words. His defences were down and he let the feelings flow unhindered. Her hair still black, now with flecks of grey at her temples, was pulled back tightly from her face and fixed in a bun on her crown.

You cut your hair? he asked.

A little, she laughed.

She then reached behind her head to unravel the bun. It fell down her back in luxuriant shiny waves and she stood to spin round and show him its length. It reached past her waist. He shook his head in admiration and wonder as she turned back round smiling at him.

So tell me the story, he said.

She fetched two glasses of water before sitting back down.

Nothing to say really.

Then she proceeded to tell him a potted history of her life over the previous twelve years. Her husband Nigel (someone he remembered feeling indifferent towards and for whom, no doubt, the feeling was mutual) had been knocked down and killed by a drunk driver yards from their front door ten years ago and since then she had lived in the same house with her two sons, Peter and Christopher. She gave up her job in the bank in Point two years ago because her health had started to, as she described it with a minimum amount of detail, cause her some problems and she now led a mostly solitary life, albeit one where she responded to the demands of parenthood even though her boys were now adults. The stroke had left no lasting damage (probably a transient-ischaemic attack, he suggested), but it had scared the hell out of her. He put his arm around her and she momentarily relaxed into him, resting her head on his shoulder before sitting up again and brushing her skirt as though she was getting ready to do something else. He asked after her mother whom, he thought, must have been into her eighties now.

She's okay mostly. Living with Naren and Dollo still in Guapo. She doesn't see so good but dey make sure she want for nothing. She want to see yuh.

She knows I'm here?

What yuh think? News travel yuh know. Yuh think yuh could just reach here in secret?

I guess not.

Yuh gonna do de tour?

Yeah. Why not? You coming?

Sure. Let me just go and bathe first. I been washing de floor and I get hot.

He watched her walk through a curtained partition and then heard the roar of a shower pump being switched on. He imagined her bathing - her long hair against her skin and her washing those long delicate arms. He wanted to go to her and wondered what she would do if he did but he resisted and waited for her, distracting himself by looking at all the photographs she had placed around the living room. There was one of them standing with Naren and Vernita outside his father's house when he must have been about nine years old. He and Naren had their arms around each other and were grinning while Mishra looked at them in disapproval and Vernita stood in front of them looking uncertain and sucking on one of her fingers. They were all barefoot.

CHAPTER 17

They strolled through the village and down the hill towards the old house. A few people waved but for the most part this was an insignificant event to them. Elliot had built it up into something much bigger than it actually was, fearing the focus of attention on him, his instinct to remain inconspicuous. In fact, he realised, it was more like returning to an institution after being years away. Some people had probably not even noticed his absence and others didn't really care if he had returned. Life had just gone on, any change so gradual as to have not really been noticed by anyone who had remained there. People died, others were born, some moved away, some of them moved back again but the majority stayed.

As he looked upon his father's house many memories competed for his focus but he was disinclined to spend any time on them. Instead he just took it in - how it looked, its familiar character and what it was saying to him now. A board house secured on top of a series of concrete pillars, thus creating a large space underneath where most activity took place, it looked like a house with a story to tell. Two hammocks were slung between pillars the way they were years ago. The gallery steps were now concrete where they had once been wooden and the driveway had been relaid with asphalt where once it had been a dirt track flanked by uncultivated bushes and banana trees, none of which remained. A tall coconut palm, bent in its middle at right angles, reached out from the back of the house, swaying in the breeze the way it always used to. Sometimes when the rains came, usually accompanied by high winds, Elliot had feared for that tree's survival but there it was, standing the test of time and having outlived his childhood and many of the other lives that used to grace the land beneath it. The driveway was now gated and a dog walked towards them from under the house, barking in a half-hearted kind of way. It stopped at a bowl of food and sniffed at it, hesitated and then returned without eating to where it had been lying. It scratched behind its ear with one of its hind legs, stretched its body out on the ground and shut its eyes, around which a small cloud of flies gathered.

The house next door had gone, replaced by a large orange and white concrete house which looked gaudy and ostentatious as though the owners by building it were trying to show the neighbourhood how rich they had become. It used to be a board house where Moncho and Asunción Salcedo and their children Vicente, Tono, Conchita and Sabela lived. Moncho had also worked for the oil company and became a good friend of Elliot's father. The families would often get together for long Sunday lunches where the women cooked and washed wares and the men would drink rum and talk. Elliot's mother and Asunción were friendly without being close, neither speaking eachother's language enough to facilitate confidence, even if there had been a willing on his mother's part which was never likely. The Salcedo family also had to leave Trinidad when the national government took over the company. They went back to Venezuela about the same time Elliot's father had returned to England and they never heard from each other again. He had often thought about Conchita. She had been a few years older than him and he had watched with an aching desire her development from child to woman over the years the families were neighbours. She had long black hair, green eyes, a Roman nose and a robust body with large breasts and wide hips supported by strong thick thighs. At the time he had absorbed every detail of her to the point that even now he could conjure up a vivid image of her.

It was during his last summer holiday there that she had showed him some of the ways of the world. He was sixteen and early one morning the two of them went to the beach at Los Iros to bathe before the sun reached its peak. The beach was empty but the sea too rough for swimming. They stood in the water up to their waists for a while before giving up on the idea, instead opting to walk along the narrow shoreline. They sat on a bank of sand and threw stones into the water. Conchita was seemingly unconcerned about sitting there in a bikini while a virginal teenager clumsily admired her form. He told her he thought she was beautiful and she laughed.

Come on let's walk, she said, taking his hand and pulling him up.

They walked past an outcrop of cliff to some rocks where she stopped and removed her top. He looked at her, noticing that even with her brown skin, her breasts were paler than the rest of her. She then removed her bikini bottoms and stood in front of him, arms stretched out wide and smiling, flecks of sand on the tuft of hair between her thighs. She turned around to show him her back, her buttocks also pale. Then she walked towards him and took his head in her hands, pulling it towards her breasts which he kissed as she reached down and stroked the bulge in his shorts. As he gently sucked on her she directed his hand between her legs where she was wet with her own arousal and she pushed his fingers inside her.

That's nice, she said and he felt as though he was gasping for air.

She pushed his hand away, knelt on the sand and pulled down his shorts, taking him in her mouth as he exploded, unable to contain himself any longer. Weak-kneed and helpless, he nearly fell. She laughed, pulled his shorts up, cupped her hand around his balls and pulled him towards her before kissing him and inserting her tongue in his mouth. She then turned away and bent over to pick up her bikini, looking back at him from between her legs. His heart now pounded with the memory, the way it had then as two of them had walked back holding hands. It was the first of many such encounters that summer, all of which convinced him that they were in love. She was able to act normally if they were in the company of others whereas he was always trying to find reasons to be alone with her, such as an innocent meeting outside the bathroom or on the back stairwell. He always tried to contrive sitting next to her at meal times, relishing the touch of their bare legs brushing together. She always kept her cool, even when surreptitiously stroking his cock under the table. However, when opportunities arose for them to be alone together she became energised, seductive and forceful. The amount of time he spent with Conchita that summer meant he spent less time with his other friends and Mishra, for one, had been annoyed about this.

Yuh don want to spend time wid we no more now yuh have big woman to play wid, she said one morning as Elliot helped her to pick chataigne from his father's garden.

What could he say? Nothing could deflect him off the path that led him to Conchita and the way only she could quench his thirsting for her. Then one day he wandered round to her house on a false errand and asked her if she was going to be free at all. She was distracted and evasive, looking towards the road whenever a car slowed. She told him that it wasn't a good day to see him. He sensed something was up but hung around all the same. She was dressed smartly and was wearing red lipstick.

Go now man, she said.

As he stood a car pulled up and the driver sounded the horn. An African man with short locks and shades wound down his window and shouted for her. She left Elliot standing there in his shorts feeling like a child. She got into the car without a look back and it drove away at speed. At the time he couldn't understand how two people could be so close and intimate and then it could all just end suddenly, never to happen again. How a lover could just turn their back and walk away, inflicting such pain on the one left behind. He knew better now.

You remember the Salcedo family? he asked Mishra.

Huh. You remember she.

They walked on to where Saul, one of Mishra's cousins, lived with his wife Karishma. Another house that had changed, this time from a large board house to a modest concrete bungalow with purple exterior walls. Mishra and Elliot stood on the road and called out. A large black dog with protruding ribs ran barking to the gate and jumped up at it. Elliot remembered Marley and Smokey and the old woman picking up excreta behind Easy End and thought how even a dog's life was completely different here.

His car's not here, said Mishra.

A pick-up truck pulled into the driveway of a small board house over the road and a bald pot-bellied Indian man stepped out of the cab and hurled a couple of large wicker baskets onto the ground from the back of the truck.

Look. Ruben reach, she said and they walked across the road to where they were greeted with laughter and hugs.

Ruben's wife Rebecca stepped out from the house, wiping her hands on her apron and squealing in delight.

I didn't know yuh here, said Ruben, glancing at Mishra with an exaggerated scowl, no one tells we anything.

They went into their living room which had just about enough space for a settee, a televison and a small dining table. On the wall was a small three-dimensional portrait of a white blue-eyed Christ looking serene and holding up his right hand as though he was stopping traffic. Underneath the image was the inscription *Wake up to Jesus your Saviour*. A calendar for the previous year advertising Ramsingh's supermarket in Arima completed the decorations. Ruben produced a bottle of white rum and two glasses while Rebecca and Mishra went through to the kitchen.

Hmm. Not plenty left, said Ruben, laughing.

It's only noon, protested Elliot but he was already succumbing to the inevitable.

Rebecca! Bring some ice nah. And water from de fridge.

Rebecca brought a bowl of ice and some water in a plastic jug.

Yuh'll take something wid we? she asked

She mean food, laughed Mishra, seeing Elliot's confused expression.

Nooo, he said, you don't have to…

Yes man…same and peas is all it is, said Ruben.

Without waiting for Elliot's assent Rebecca went back into the kitchen where Mishra helped her to make roti and heat up the curry. Ruben and Elliot touched glasses, downed the rum in one and then chased it with the water. Ruben was a few years younger than Elliot but someone whose company he had always enjoyed. Full of jokes and laughter, Ruben had always been something of a free spirit, albeit one who had been troubled by his inability to be successful at much more than growing vegetables to sell at market. He had once tried a driving job with the oil company but left after a few weeks following a row with his boss. He tried for a longer period working as a crew member on the car decks for the ferries running between Port of Spain and

Scarborough in Tobago but he hated having to spend so much time away from home. He tried smuggling cornmeal, clothes and even guns from Venezuela, taking a small motorboat back and forth across the sea each time but was threatened once too often by local gangsters. So he had settled for the quiet life but retained his dreams of an easier life, coming up every now and again with grandiose schemes to make easy money only to have them dispelled by his more level-headed wife. He had been with Rebecca for over twenty years now and they still led a basic existence that was always subject to the vagaries of climate and the market forces of the time. He showed Elliot the shell of a house next door which he was building in stages dependent on cash flow. He said the market trade was good, that pakchoy especially was selling well but working the garden in the heat was killing him and that of late he had been experiencing chest pains. They went back inside to where Rebecca and Mishra were sitting. They killed the bottle before eating.

You see Saul? asked Rubin.

Saul's not in, replied Elliot.

He not in? asked Rebecca, looking puzzled.

No de car not dey, said Mishra.

He not in? asked Ruben.

When we pass de car not dey, said Mishra.

No he's not in, said Elliot.

Karishma dey? asked Ruben.

Nobody dey, said Mishra.

So nobody dey, said Rebecca.

There was silence for a few moments before she spoke again.

Maybe they go out.

The same and peas tasted fresh and were hot with pepper. They ate in silence and Elliot appreciated the simplicity of the scene as it typified to him a way of life to which he was once again finding himself drawn, albeit in a diffferent and more judicious way than the last time he had been there. He tried to conceal the fact the pepper was too hot for him but it became obvious to everyone's amusement.

Tomorrow maybe, said Ruben, because I have to go to market tonight for de wholesaler so I can't really lime but tomorrow may be free.

By the time Elliot and Mishra returned to her house his shirt was soaked and his left testicle ached with a persistence he couldn't ignore or rise above. She saw he was distracted and asked him what was wrong. He told her it was back pain brought on by the flight as it felt easier to say just say that rather than go into the details of his condition. They parted with a kiss and a promise to talk again soon.

Back at Paul's house he went straight to his bedroom, turned on the air-conditioning and sat on the bed. He checked his phone and saw a text from Amelia saying *use whatsapp to speak or text its free you know x*. He lay back and stared at the styrofoam ceiling tiles and started to count them, noticing how some were discoloured and displaced. He remembered Paul saying the roof had been damaged during a storm and rain had come through the bedroom's ceiling. The curtains were drawn in order to limit access for insects but a thin shaft of light penetrated enough to make a mottled pattern on the wardrobe door. A kiskadee called from what sounded like a position directly above his window. He texted *ok* and switched off the phone. Her kiss at the end of the message was her first demonstrable show of affection towards him since she had left for Knockbreck.

CHAPTER 18

Early Saturday morning and outside it was black as pitch. A cock crowed nearby. There was silence for a few minutes before it crowed again, this time longer and louder. From somewhere in the distance there was a reply, then another from elsewhere, then another before the nearest one crowed again. Elliot had turned off the air-conditioning earlier in the night when he had got up to piss and now he could hear the whine of a mosquito somewhere near his head. The cocks crowed on. The night was still and sticky, beads of sweat on the back of his neck as he pulled the sheet over his head.

He lay there trying to get back to sleep and remembered a similar early morning from years before. He had traveled with Esther, his ex-wife, on a trip which proved to be her first and last visit to Trinidad. Izzy was a year old and Esther was three months pregnant with Iris. The house was a board house in those days and any sound, wherever or whoever it came from, intimate or not, could be heard through the thin wooden walls. It was one of their first nights there and they were woken by a cock crowing beneath the house and then, just like now, the calls and answers from its neighbours. No air-conditioning back then, their sheet was soaked and they struggled to get back to sleep. Izzy woke up and cried. Elliot got up and she calmed as he took her in his arms and walked through the living room and onto the gallery. All he could see were the vague forms of coconut palms that lined the road in those days, all gone now. Dark clouds moved quickly across the sky as a wind picked up and the constellations shone more clearly than he'd ever seen before. There was a short and sudden cloudburst lasting no more than a minute but it was savage, sounding as though a group of angry gods were hurling thousands upon thousands of stones onto the galvanised iron roofs in a brutal display of their power. The whole house woke up with the noise and Izzy cried again. In one of the rooms a radio was switched on. Between the sponsored news bulletin and the sponsored weather report Elliot listened to the announcer offering a thought for the day - good car hygiene was an esential component of life and a clean *in*terior was as important as a shiny *ex*terior because anything less may lead to the car owner becoming depressed. Show the world you're clean inside and out and you will be at peace. He finished by telling his listeners that if their car was looking good they could take pride in themselves and be able to *look de world in de eye*. Elliot heard Saul come out of the bathroom and go downstairs underneath the house to where his car was parked. He filled a bucket and started to wash it. Someone stirred on the gallery of the house on the other side of the road. It was Naren. Elliot shouted across to him.

You going to work?

Where yuh think I going? Naren replied, pulling on a pair of boots.

He had then heard Vernita's grandfather clearing his throat before shuffling out from his room.

You get up? said the old man.

Roosters, replied Elliot.

Baby not sleeping.

The old man chuckled as he walked out through the gallery door.

Baby not sleeping, he said again.

Recalling all this Elliot momentarily focussed on the transience of his existence. Life had flashed by, always one step ahead of him as he had tried and failed to hold on to any precious moments. Why hadn't those fleeting experiences of contentment and understanding had a lasting effect? Happiness always seemed to him to be just out of reach, like an attractive stranger he had started to get to know but who then disappeared around a corner. If he followed they were nowhere to be seen. He remembered how a Buddhist monk, a therapist on a drug rehab programme he was attending, had tried to explain how all suffering was born from desire and that the self driving that desire didn't actually exist. The key to happiness was to let go of the self and with it all the negative states of mind that made it dissatisfied – self-righteousness, hatred, jealousy and pride. At the time his mind had been too chaotic to allow him to understand but it was now beginning to make sense. For now though he had to give up on that train of thought, unable to sustain the required level of concentration in his early morning state of mind.

As first light reached around the curtain's edge he got out of bed and made his way to the bathroom. He had stomach cramps and knew he needed to shit with some urgency. He sat there as waves of pain traveled the length of his bowel before a watery stool gushed out of him with such force he worried the whole house could hear. Sweat broke out all over his body and mosquitoes raided his flesh as he, desperate to conclude this episode but as of yet unable to do so, looked up at the only window which was propped open high above the shower and was serving as the entry point for flying insects. He dared not leave his seat to close it. Rum and hot pepper was once more proving to be too potent a mixture for him and his sytem was now in serious revolt.

By the time he went downstairs Paul was already dressed and drinking coffee while Vernita was making dahlpourri. They all laughed about the state of his bowels. Again a sense of calm came over him. He didn't feel he had to try or pretend. He could just be himself. Vernita put some channa aloo in the dahlpourri, rolling it in such a way it was sealed at both ends and then wrapped it in tin foil. Paul put it into a bag along with a flask of coffee and a bottle of water.

Okay if I pop over later? asked Elliot.

Of course, Paul replied, rubbing Elliot's upper arm and patting his shoulder.

He stopped on the threshold of the front door and looked back.

You should. Also I meant to say last night…I've got to go to Tobago in a few days to deliver some work. I'll be staying overnight but thought you might like to come along for the ride.

Elliot told him he would think about it but didn't really feel like going anywhere just yet. After Paul left he and Vernita sat on the back gallery. There wasn't a cloud to be seen, the temperature slowly rising.

He would like you to go visit where he work yuh know. And go to Tobago wid him. Get some time together.

I'll go today.

She smiled at him as though he had just given her a gift.

We having prayers tonight for Joy's birthday and barbecue after.

Okay. What time?

Six or so. Six-thirty for de prayers.

Within an hour he was walking down the road towards Neighbour's bar. On arrival he walked down the side of the house to where Paul had his studio. Paul wasn't there. Elliot looked into a large space behind an open electronic roller door. Colour was the first thing to strike him. Everywhere he turned - on the walls, on a door, on a fridge, on canvassses and on drawing boards perched upon easels or leaning up against walls and furniture. Colour in all its vibrant animate glory. Primary colours were in profusion as well as mixes of primary colours – purples, pinks, greens and oranges in all shades imaginable - shining, light-reflecting and bedazzling not only in their brilliance but also in their impossible-to-ignore power. Elliot was taken aback and wide-eyed. A roll of paper had been pinned to the top of a wall, the paper allowed to fall to the floor and on it there was a frenzied drawing in chalk and charcoal of what appeared to be the rain forest - coconut palms, banana trees and large leaved plants bending over each other in a chaos of arcs and lines, criss-crossing so much that the image had become multi-dimensional. He moved towards it and peered at the lines from a few inches away. There were hundreds of them, every one a portrayal of a microsecond of perception, some drawn with fingers, others with an eraser and some scratched onto the surface – it was full of energy and life and was, Elliot believed, wonderful. Across the room a large canvass was resting on a series of paint-splattered brackets fixed to the wall, upon which the first tentative lines of a new work had been drawn. He could see branches of coconut palms and the figure of a man or woman just off the centre of the scene.

He hadn't known what to expect other than an ordinary studio space full of the usual paraphenalia and evidence of someone struggling to find their own unique formula so that they might access a higher plain of thought that in turn would trigger some kind of creative action. But this was far from a struggle – Paul was working without inhibition and at a level far deeper or a plain far higher and more evolved than Elliot had ever imagined he was capable of. He felt pleased for his friend but at the same time intimidated by the forcefulness of whatever it was pouring out of him. Amazed, he sat down on an old settee to take it all in.

He heard a toilet flush and Paul entered through a door at the back of the room and gave him a suspicious look, pointing at him as though Elliot had been caught secretly doing something he shouldn't. Paul laughed like a gleeful child. He was wearing a white vest covered in streaks of charcoal, his hands and forearms black and with smudges on his forehead and nose. He looked as happy as Elliot had ever seen him and Elliot grinned at him in recognition of where he was at with his work and his life. They embraced.

Congratulations…it's brilliant…all of it…amazing, said Elliot.
Paul walked to the fridge, took out a couple of ice-cold beers and they sat down together, chinked bottles and started to talk.

It's so good to see you here.
I'm not interrupting you?
Paul spoke in slow measured phrases.

Not at all…not everyone gets this…what I'm doing…how I'm living…it makes me doubt myself sometimes…so…you're my…reference point…my constant…I've needed you to see it.

But you're doing so well. You don't need me.
I do you know…affirmation…can't live without it.

But surely…the exhibition and the commissions…all of this. He gestured around the studio.

Sure…they're nice…they help…but you know it's a weird space we get into…like… how the fuck do I know it's any good?

Because people are buying it.
Elliot wondered what Amelia the aestheticist would have thought as Paul continued.

Some of it is being bought and…the commissions can feel…restricting…but…they pay…they pay well…but most people don't know what the fuck they're buying…most of them see it as…talk of it as…an investment. It's all very well but I don't know if any of it's any good…has any real merit…you know?

But it allows you to work how you want. Surely that's great?

Yes...it...is...but...you...know...an...artist's...work...being... *popular*...doesn't mean it's important or good...you know...suddenly you're significant then just as suddenly you're not. I don't get...affirmation...from the public...or critics...liking my work because that's based on something that's in the past...something I've done a while ago...and I'm just wanting to get on with the next one...I just want someone else around who sees things the way I do... someone who gets it.

There was a long pause.

Like I think *you* do, he added.

Elliot felt a tentative sense of pride that Paul still saw him in that way way, it was something he hadn't been expecting. He had thought that Paul's invitation for his visit was either for him to show off to Elliot how well he was doing or he was acting out of charity, knowing Elliot had a chronic health condition, drank too much and was a self-pitying, self-destructive wanker. To hear Paul wanted him around again as a friend, confidante and fellow artist stirred something in him – a feeling he had sensed a few times since he had arrived there and which was hard to home in on or describe but self-worth was a descriptor of sorts, albeit an inadequate one.

Public recognition the seductive beast, said Elliot.

The siren...calling you to make another one like the last one...so people buy into it.

Or just buy it.

I hate those generalist painters...dealing in generalisations and clichés...using their trickery so their mass-produced prints appear on birthday cards and suburban hallways... and people think as they hang up their coats and take off their boots it's art they're looking at rather than see it for what it is...formulaic...shallow...pointless. They see subject matter as sentimental...and that's all they want...they don't see art as the stimulus to feed...something new...the electricity that can bring a new monster to life.

Do you mean the artist or the consumer?

Both...but the artist is mostly to blame...them and the whole fucking miserable corporate bollocks of a world.

So there is a point to it all then?

Paul laughed, gripped his head in mock anguish and opened his mouth wide in a silent scream.

Yes! There's a bloody point to it. I just wish people didn't just seek validation from a crap picture on a wall in their hallway.

They don't mostly…it's just decoration I guess.

They were silent for a while before Paul spoke again.

Why did you do that job?

Elliot was surprised by the question and paused for a while before answering.   Security I suppose. It gave me a mortgage and a pension.

But why did you do it originally?

As Elliot sought to measure his response the faces and voices of countless patients came readily to his mind before he replied.

I know I didn't do it for vocational or altruistic reasons although that was part of it…especially as time went on…it was more something about me…about what I was looking for…the new, the edge, all that stuff. I knew I would see things I wouldn't normally see. A job like that puts you at the edge of existence. No corporate security, no mindlessness, just life…and death…and madness…in a very raw manifestation. Nothing else can teach you or show you what that's like.

And since you left?

Elliot saw where Paul was going and smiled in appreciation of his friend's insightfulness.

No edge…unless illness and addiction are the edge.

Nothing chronic has an edge. Nothing. I remember you when you were full of a kind of manic glee…full of life…feeling free to create whatever you wanted…and not giving a damn about what people thought of you, whether you made mistakes or not. You were driven.

I've become cautious.

Do you know what are you afraid of?

Failure I suppose…or worse than that…mediocrity. Finding out for myself I'm mediocre and having it confirmed by others.

Did carrying on with that job affect you? You know…get you down? Send *you* crazy?

Not in terms of the experience...of the human...condition shall we say? But yes in terms of it sucking the life out of me...injuring me...helping me to avoid creative thought...yes it affected me.

And now?

It's time to make a leap forward. I realise I can't just expect to pick up my brushes again and it all fall into place but...looking at your work I do realise something.

What?

Well...painting a picture is the result of so many different actions...it involves looking, seeing, thinking, feeling and then making it all concrete. Gathering it all together. A collection of details...formed into something...original...unique. But most of all it requires being able to see...beyond what is immediately apprent...then making something new...capturing an instance of perception. Like walking through a forest...pushing aside the branches and and cutting a pathway through the undergrowth until you reach a clearing...and the light shines down and you see it there...it's clear and pure...and then it's gone. Time to move on.

Yes...it's a way of *not* seeing something...and then not being sure of what it is that you *do* see until in that unconscious way when your brain and hands are working independently of your will...you describe it...and it appears in front of you.

Slipping off the chains...that bind us to a conventional perception...yes I understand that...the need to free yourself from the constraints of habit, conditioning, brain-washing...often self-inflcted...I need to do that and take the leap...defy the tyrant that has usurped my conscious mind and all my decision-making processes...keeping me away from the unconscious or not allowing there to be some kind of resonance between the two...like it's holding me hostage. It's almost as though it warns me off from being creative again...truly creative...unshackled...wagging its finger at me...tellling me *you know what will happen if you go in there my boy...you may never come out*...as I cower in the corner with my bottle of whisky.

But you know it's the only way to go...if you want to stop the torture...you know you've got to just do it.

Or give it all up as a bad idea.

You won't be able to…try to enjoy the journey again. Ride the fucking wave. What colour do you think of when you think of here?

Where?

Here…this country. Don't think about it just answer.

Pink strangely enough…and red…the red of the flowers on the flamboyant tree.

How do you see it? What's it doing?

Broad-brush arcs overlapping.

What size canvass?

Again strangely…very large.

Elliot pointed at one of the walls.

You'll need some space then. Easily arranged.

Not really. No one has that space.

Of course they do. Anything can happen here.

Maybe I need to think about it. Anyway…I'm due home in three weeks so there's no point in starting something now.

You're putting up barriers and I appreciate and respect why you're doing that but don't…you don't need to…just go with it. There's space beneath Mishra's house and she won't mind…in fact she'll love having you around. Even if you do it for three weeks and then go back just do it.

Elliot imagined going to work every day and being near to Mishra. He smiled at the thought.

Really?

All of it…as you know…can be…taken care of. It's easy to make things happen here. Have you brought a camera?

Just my phone.

Then use my SLR…it's digital and synced to a printer.

For what?

To start making notes…I use photos all the time…they're like…visual memos. Not for what they represent but to…remind me…of whatever it is I've perceived when looking at the subject. It's like a trigger.

Elliot imagined putting a gun barrel to the roof of his mouth and pulling the trigger. It would end all this.

Okay then, he said but not entirely convinced he had it in him or could be arsed to do all the necessaries to make it happen.

For now, if only to placate Paul, he was agreeing.

I'll need some big brushes. Like decorating brushes…the ones you paint walls with.

Then he glanced down at a scrubbing brush leaning against a wall and pictured the strokes the brush would make on a canvass, the textures it could create. He would need a sizeable surface like a table to mix paint on.

Paul was staring at the charcoal drawing pinned to the wall.

You need to get on, said Elliot.

Paul nodded. Then as Elliot started to leave, he spoke without looking up.

Come to Tobago. It will give us a chance to talk. Also I have to pick up some materials on the way back in Port of Spain. You could get some too.

Elliot once again heard the voice of resistance shouting at him from somewhere way down inside. The voice was getting weaker though.

CHAPTER 19

Back at the house Elliot was sitting outisde on the front porch eating a doubles with *slight pepper* and reading the Trinidad Star. Under the headline *Man Chopped Woman After Argument* he read the story of how a forty-six year old man, Roberto Cuffie, had killed his fifty-one year old wife with a cutlass *dealing several chops and stabs to her body following an altercation* that had taken place the previous year. When asked why he had attacked her so Cuffie had replied *man, she vex me.*

He turned the page and started to read the *Women Section,* settling on the column of an agony aunt named Kimberley who was guiding readers uncertain of their, as the strapline read, *lifestyle etiquette.* Someone whose signatory was *A Shy Hostess* had asked Kimberley whether she should dispense with a tablecloth - *I really don't like them* - for a forthcoming dinner party and just use placemats instead. Kimberley's answer was printed beneath a colour photograph of herself dressed to the nines, sporting a pearl necklace with matching earrings and her finger placed in front of her pursed lipstick-laden lips in a *shhh* pose, presumably to assure the Shy Hostess she wouldn't tell anyone about this. Her reply started empathically - *I know how one can feel with tablecloths* - and she went on to encourage Shy Hostess to be creative and instead use a curtain because, once draped over the table, it would look *exotic.*

The next one to seek Kimberley's advice described herself as *A Wine and Cheese Romantic* and she asked Kimberley to give her details of how *to properly present a wine and cheese party.* This time Kimberley's photograph showed her still dressed to the nines but in a different dress and pointing towards the reader with a smiley know-it-all, smug expression. She advised a wooden board for the cheese although a breadfruit leaf could also *pleasantly surprise* the guests. As for the wine she suggested *red, white or rosé* to be served in glasses and opened with corkscrews unless her correspondent had bought wine in screwtop bottles.

Ruben pulled up in his pick-up and sounded the horn. He leaned out of the window and shouted to Elliot.

Yuh ready?

Elliot had forgotten Ruben had said he might call round.

Where we going?

I have a little ting to do in Sando. Come for de ride.

San Fernando?

Yeah come nah.

There was an enormous wicker-basket in the back of the truck filled with pakchoy. Elliot guessed Ruben was going to the market.

You going to market?

Yeah just to drop off.

Elliot knew San Fernando was at least a half-hour's drive away on a good day and that it would most likely take longer and all those bumpy roads and stop-starting in the traffic jams by the creek would play havoc with his back and balls. He got in. Ruben was listening to a CD of country and western standards all played in a reggae-lite style and sung with Jamaican accents. He was leaning forward, his chin resting on the steering wheel as he drove with one hand, his other arm draped out of the window. Elliot related the story about the man who had chopped his wife with a cutlass and Ruben laughed as though *the man, she vex me* explanation was the punchline to a joke.

By the time they reached the main road running along Mosquito Creek the traffic had slowed to a crawl, the cause a long stretch of road works attempting to turn two lanes into six and which Elliot remembered from his journey with Ramsawak the night he had arrived. So quickly had he seemed to acclimatise that the memory of his journey, even the state of mind he had been in, had receded to somewhere nearly distant. It was as though the person who had arrived that night fronting a jagged and exhausted persona had suddenly relaxed allowing a destructive burden to have been been lifted. It's still early days, he thought, but the signs are good.

Still a few miles from San Fernando there was a wide unmade section between the operant lanes where Elliot noticed a car and a lorry parked facing each other. Across the windscreen of the lorry was a banner reading *Big Man Ting*. A young-looking African man was standing in front of the car with one arm around a young Indian woman. He held an iron bar in his other hand. Facing the couple and standing in front of the lorry were an Indian man waving a cutlass and two women screaming abuse in high-pitched voices and gesturing angrily towards the African man.

Wheeey! Bachannal boy, laughed Ruben.

They reached the centre of town after another half hour or so and Ruben pulled up outside the market place. They stepped out of the truck and Elliot saw a tall African man without a shirt walking with purpose towards them from a bar across the street, waving his arms and shouting.

Raaaaassss! What de fuck time is dis bamba claat? Fuckin coolie boss keeping me de fuck waiting all de damn day for yuh!

The whites of his eyes were a deep red. Elliot felt alarm and looked to Ruben who was walking towards the man with his arms outstretched, fists clenched and shouting back at him.

Come on then mothercunt come on niggah!

They were nearly touching, staring into eachother's eyes with equal menace and people walking past stopped in anticipation of the fight that seemed bound to follow. Suddenly the two protagonists hugged. They were laughing and slapping backs before high-fiving and then leaning into the back of the truck to haul out the wicker basket in a smooth practised movement.

Who he? said the African, jerking his head towards Elliot.

Friend from England.

Friend? Huh – yuh have friend?

Old friend.

Old? Maybe he don' know yuh like me.

Elliot pretended to laugh in an attempt to demonstrate he was at ease with the situation. Ruben and the African man carried the basket down the road a little way and threw it onto the ground next to a woman sitting by a small table upon which were some mangoes and avocadoes. More shouting and abuse ensued, this time between the woman and

Ruben, the difference being Elliot now realised it was in good humour. Within minutes Ruben returned and motioned for Elliot to get back in the truck. As he started to drive Ruben put a roll of money in the compartment between the seats. Elliot could tell it was more than a basket of pakchoy would sell for. Ruben winked at him.

Let's go baby!' he shouted.

He drove around a few corners taking them away from the town centre and completely disorienting Elliot in the process. He pulled up again, this time outside a rum shop. He indicated for Elliot to stay in the truck and then went inside the bar, returning seconds later with two beers and flicking the top off his with his thumb before he downed most of it in a few gulps. Then he drove on.

Where we going? asked Elliot.

Don' worry *maaan*. Somewhere wid food… a little bit of piggy…maybe some ducky but if it have nuttin else we'll have some chicky.

Ruben laughed again as he took a narrow corner at speed before suddenly parking with a jerk of the brakes outside another rum shop. On the outside wall someone had painted in precise calligraphic letters *No Peeing Against D Wall.*

They stepped into one of the most run down bars Elliot had ever seen. The paint on the grille was flaking, the door to the ladies hanging off it's hinges (not that there were any women there) and the beer adverts on the wall, all depicting semi-naked women, were tattered or defaced with crude graffiti. The floor was littered with napkins, styrofoam containers and cigarette butts. There was a group of African and Indian men sitting at a table playing cards and drinking rum. An old Chinese man with thick spectacles emerged from a door behind the grille and jerked his head towards them.

Yuh frying pork? asked Ruben.

Pork finish only chicken…wings.

Ten wings and two Carib.

They sat at the bar drinking before the proprietor returned with a styrofoam container full of wings. He handed it over through the gap in the grille followed by napkins and a bottle of pepper sauce. They shared a few unremarkable minutes, concentrating on the food and washing it down with a second round of beers. The men playing cards all turned to stare at Elliot when he went to wash his hands. The sink outside the toilets was cracked and stained and Elliot wiped his hands on his jeans.

I have to go Avocat on de way back, said Ruben.

No worries.

Yuh bound to get back?

When?

Today tonight.

Prayers for Joy later.

We could play some pool.

Sure.

Elliot was reminded how a simple plan with Ruben could easily end up becoming messy as the day went on and the beers went down. The last time Elliot had been there the two of them frequently played long sessions of pool in a variety of bars, Ruben always driving them home drunk.

Maybe I'll beat you this time, said Elliot.

Ruben laughed.

Let's go baby, he shouted as he ordered two more beers to take with them, throwing some dollar bills through the grille as payment.

The route to Avocat took them on back roads through villages all looking much the same – the mix of board and concrete houses, rum shops, raggedy kids, women walking underneath umbrellas, coconut palms, mango trees, banana trees and telegraph poles with flyers stapled to them advertising the next fete or a DJ sound system or random religious messages - *Does the Lord know YOU?* - and as they headed down a steep hill Elliot read a continuous message placed in installments from one telegraph pole to the next - *UNTO THEE O GOD...DO WE GIVE THANKS...UNTO THEE...DO WE GIVE THANKS...FOR THAT THY NAME...IS NEAR...THY WONDROUS WORKS DECLARE.*

They stopped outside a concrete house, the underneath of which was full of wrecked cars, tyres, wheels, doors, tools, welding torches and gas barrels, all scattered and piled there in a chaos of metal and rust. Ruben sounded his horn. No one came out. He sounded it again, this time for longer and then sucked his teeth in annoyance.

Stay here, he said.

Ruben got out of the truck and walked up the steps to the gallery, shouting a name Elliot couldn't make out. Before he reached the top of the steps a slight young Indian man without a shirt and holding a little girl in his arms came out and jerked his head in acknowledgement of Ruben who had stopped a few steps away. They argued, shouting at one another. Elliot realised this wasn't banter, it was serious. The girl started to cry. Ruben, still a few steps below the gallery, was pointing his finger at the man and nodding his head emphatically, making an expression that looked as though he has just worked out the answer to a conundrum. The man shouted at Ruben.

So what you gonna do?

Ruben walked up the last steps and eyeballed the man as he spoke to him. Elliot couldn't make out what he was saying. After a few seconds Ruben ruffled the girl's hair and walked back down the steps.

Problem? asked Elliot as Ruben got back into the truck.

Nah. Business. That is all. Business. Money business.

He laughed again as he drove over the road and parked up outside a rum shop called *Uncles* where an empty pool table stood in front of an empty bar. To Elliot the heat felt like some kind of malign force-field that burned into him as he tried to walk through it. Sweat stained his shirt. The beers and chicken wings had given him heart burn and he felt as though a hot stone was caught somewhere in his throat. They ordered more beers and a petit-quart of rum with a bowl of ice, two glasses of water and a bottle of soda. The proprietor, an elderly Indian man in shorts and a stained vest - presumably Uncle - came out from behind his bar to watch them play. Elliot took the first frame and Ruben congratulated him for his first ever victory over him as he racked up for the next one. Elliot played Uncle and noticed, despite his engaging in the conversation, that Ruben kept looking back over to the house where he had just been discussing his money business. They played a few more frames with Ruben winning them all, then drank some beers and finished the rum. Uncle went to get another petit-quart and while he was away Ruben's business associate walked languidly across the road towards them, still topless, affecting an air of nonchalance and confidence that Elliot could see was hiding his fear. He handed Ruben a roll of banknotes and Ruben patted him playfully on the cheek.

Take a drink nah man, Ruben said to the him, more as an order than an invitation.
When the rum arrived the young man sat down and poured himself a shot, then downed it in one, chasing it with one of the glasses of water. Ruben introduced him to Elliot as Fez and they shook hands without speaking. Then Fez went back across the road.

They played another frame but Elliot started to feel concerned as to what people would think if he arrived back back later than expected, especially if he was drunk and missed the prayers. He told Ruben he didn't want to offend anyone. Ruben told him not to worry but Elliot realised he didn't really want to be with Ruben anymore and that in fact he hadn't really wanted to be with him at all. He had just gone along for the sake of friendship and an unwillingness to confront this particular truth. Last time he was there they had spent whole days liming - eating, drinking, hanging out in rum shops, playing pool and gambling. Ruben's expectations were that they would do this again. Elliot's expectations were different now as he felt a sense of balance and calm returning to his life, even that he wanted to avoid drinking too much. He wished he could explain to Ruben that his body couldn't take it anymore, that he wanted to paint again, that he wanted to put an end to all the self-destructive behaviour he had practised for most of his life, that he needed peace and calm after the traumatic events back in England but he feared Ruben wouldn't understand and the particular tie that bound the two of them together could slacken to a point where it might eventually unravel. Ruben meant something to Elliot that was meaningful and deep but as he began to see the choice he had to make about how to live his life, Elliot understood he may have to jettison certain friendships or at least avoid aspects of them. The positive way forward was one where he commited himself to his work, his health and the relationships he saw as having a good influence but he was only too aware of the voices calling him out to play, telling him not to worry, that there was still plenty of time for the serious things so they could still go out, get wrecked and laugh at the world. Ruben's was one such voice.

By the time he was dropped back it was dark and he had missed the prayers. The first thing he did was apologise to Vernita who just smiled her smile and told him it was *no problem*. Paul was busy behind the barbecue pit as about forty people, including numerous children, ate, drank, danced, played cards, watched television and talked loudly while soca music blared from a pair of outsize speakers. Elliot piled potato salad onto his plate and went over to get some chicken from Paul. The sense of calmness returned, managing to penetrate his drunkenness and consequent anxiety.

How was your day? asked Paul, sweat dripping from his brow onto the cooking chicken.

Long. Drunk.

You don't look drunk.

Practice, he sighed.

You okay?

Just sorry I was late and missed the prayers.

No one minds. Don't worry…this is Trinidad. People don't really give a fuck…not about shit like that anyway. You're not beholden to anyone here mate…you don't have to do anything you don't want to do…just be you…there's so much scope for that.

Elliot could see Mishra sitting on a settee full of children who were fighting and shouting as she looked towards a wall-mounted television showing an American soap opera. He pushed her elbow off the arm of the settee, making her jump. After an exchange of smiles and a gentle touching of hands he sat down next to her and she leaned her head against his arm as he ate. There was an intimacy about this which felt both innocent and knowing at the same time. He welcomed it and felt as comfortable sitting there with her amidst the sensory overload and chaos of people, noise and music, as he felt anywhere. He felt something akin to being at home. Amelia came to mind and with a familiar sense of guilt he realised she could never share that feeling or feel the same way as him and he was glad she wasn't there. He would have to face the meaning of that at some point but for now he was happy to go with the flow of feeling at ease in familiar surroundings with people who accepted him for who he was.

CHAPTER 20

He awoke from a dream and as he lay damp with sweat in the half-light of dawn he was able to recall all its detail. He had been in a bare box-like room without doors or windows and standing side-on in front of him was a giant herring gull. It was looking at him, opening and shutting its one visible eye. He dared not move and instead focussed on the red spot at the end of its lower bill. The colour of the spot started to intensify before it turned to liquid and dripped like blood onto the floor. Beyond the walls he could hear other gulls calling – the way they did outside seaside hotels - and he was aware of someone speaking but all sounds were muffled. Then he realised it was Amelia's voice. It sounded as though she was speaking on the telephone but he couldn't make out what she was saying, only that she wasn't speaking to him. He wasn't sure if she knew he was in there or not. The floor was filling with what he now understood was blood as it gushed from the gull's bill. He was telling himself amid a rising panic that it wasn't the end of his life and if he waited he would be able to leave the room and all would be calm once he stepped outside. He understood there was no point in calling for help as no one would hear him, including Amelia, but the waiting felt impossible to bear, the sense of impending death too frightening to withstand.

The dream reminded him of when he and Amelia took their first trip away together and went to the city of Porto. They had stayed in a two-star guest house overlooking the Douro not far from the cafés and bars of the Cais da Ribeira. One afternoon they made love in their room beneath a giant crucifix nailed to the wall above the bed. The gulls were calling loudly outside their window and Amelia, in the throes of their love-making, told him how much she loved the sound. They had drawn the curtains and the blue light of a flickering neon sign sporadically lit up the room like lightning.
A memory such as this inevitably stirred his soul and brought Amelia to life again, to the fore of his conscious mind as though she was suddenly present in the room. He could sense her – how she moved, how she smelled and tasted. He could envisage her in that world they

shared – talking, reading, writing, doing a crossword with a thesaurus by her side and chewing her pen. He could picture her sitting next to him watching television as they ate, trays perched on their laps, two glasses of wine on the coffee table. He could see her eyes looking back across a table at him as they drank coffee in some European café. The way she could sashay onto a dance floor. He remembered every part of her body, starting with her hair and working down to her toes. How he would lay his head beneath her navel, stroking the soft down of her legs, the hair of her pubis, and feel so at peace with the world. They had been so close, so terribly close and in love.

He heard a radio come on downstairs. The house was coming to life but he didn't want to let go of Amelia as a sadness engulfed him. He had an urge to speak with her and looked at his watch. It was about one in the morning in Knockbreck and even if she was awake she wouldn't have a signal. Maybe she was in bed with Elvis Ewood. He thought about the kiss at the end of her last text. When was that? Two days before or three? He hadn't replied yet and he felt a sense of panic arise in his stomach when he thought he had let her down by not doing so. What would she be thinking of him? Had he angered her? If he was to WhatsApp her now she could read it when she was awake or in signal. He reached for his phone and when trying to switch it on saw it was dead. He got out of bed and looked for the charger which he found on a shelf in the wardrobe. Now he needed the adaptor which was charging his toothbrush on the landing outside the bathroom. He wrapped a towel around himself. As he walked along the landing he looked down into the kitchen where Vernita was already cooking, the smell of pepper and garlic reaching up towards him. She looked up and waved with her customary warm smile. He knew he must look rough, hungover and flabby – the complete opposite of her in fact - and he waved self-consciously back to her, smiling with just half of his mouth so he imagined it looked more likea grimace than a smile and that he probably appeared half-crazed. He returned to his bedroom and lay on the bed having plugged in the phone and adaptor. The charger lead was so short that by pulling the phone closer to him the phone detached from the lead and fell behind the bedside table. He had to sit up again and position himself on the side of the bed in order to retrieve it. In doing so he knocked over his glass of water onto his passport which he had wanted to keep by his side as though he might have to suddenly take flight. He took the dripping passport to the window where he had hung his towel and wiped off some of the drips before propping it against the windowpane, hoping the morning sun would dry it out. He returned to the bedside and re-attached the charger lead to his phone. He opened FaceTime by mistake and then struggled to close the app, opening up Siri instead who spoke to him saying *I'm sorry I am not sure what you are asking for*. He said *fuck off* out loud and mused that she was actually speaking to him so he replied *neither am I* to which she then repeated her apology. His sweaty fingers eventually regained control of the phone and he opened WhatsApp, found Amelia's miniature photo in the contacts list and texted *sorry 4 l8 reply-when is good 4 U? thinking of U x'* and pressed send. He then touched the photo of her in order to enlarge it. There she was sitting on a wall in front of a blue sea beneath a blue sky. She was wearing a white singlet and white cycling shorts with her legs crossed. She had sunglasses on and was smiling but looking away from the camera in that way she always did, believing she wasn't photogenic. She looked beautiful to him. He remembered taking the photo. They were in Whitstable and had just eaten a seafood and white wine lunch before walking back to their hotel along the front. More seagulls.

He heard the phone ringing downstairs and Vernita saying *oh lord* a few times before laughing.

Well yuh know, she continued, he wanted to go to de ting…yes yes but dat is a woman ting…yuh know? To get there?…oh shucks let me think…once yuh pass all them place…no yuh understand…when yuh reach so and yuh see so yuh go *so*…okay?…once yuh reach call we…wait nah…he up…yuh want me to call he?…okay okay…I tell he…when yuh say Bigfoot comin?…okay no problem…later…bye.

As he walked towards the bathroom for a shower she shouted up to him.

Bigfoot comin late morning to Mishra with de boys to help clear de space.

What space?

The garage space beneath de house.

Sorry I'm not with you.

The space for *you*. To work! and she laughed.

He stood under the shower, the water at its coldest that time in the morning, and pondered this latest development. Things had moved quickly. It seemed that without his knowing Paul had asked Mishra if Elliot could use the space beneath her house to paint. She had obviously agreed but Elliot didn't now know how he felt about that. Was this Paul encouraging him or suggesting he was in need of some structure and organisation? He started to feel irritated and hemmed in and wished there was somewhere to go where he could be alone, where he wasn't dependent on anyone or beholden to them. Where no one knew his business. He understood village life was like this but didn't like his affairs becoming everyone else's, however well-meaning they were. He stayed under the shower for longer than he needed to, trying to work out why this had got under his skin. Why had no one mentioned it the previous night? The fact that he was in doubt about his worth as an artist meant that beneath an exterior of apparent self-containment he was a bubbling pot of procrastination, prevarication and self-consciousness. However close people were to him, surely he was entitled not to expose such a weakness of resolve and spirit? Some things, surely, he was entitled to keep to himself. Or could they see through his smokescreen? Maybe his defences weren't so robust.

He went back into his bedroom again, switched on the air-conditioning and lay on the bed. People were trying to structure him, he thought, and he had never been able to handle that. Or were they? Maybe they were just being genuinely helpful but usually whenever someone had told him what they think he should do in any given circumstance he tended to do the opposite or at the very least ignore them. Is this what they were all doing? Telling him to get back to work? Didn't they appreciate he might not be ready? He put on his iPod on and pressed the shuffle command.

He heard U Brown singing *get on the board my brother, the train is coming, get on the board, my sister, train to Zion is coming, don't want no man to miss it, train to Zion is coming, we don't want no one to miss it, it's the Black Star Liner, it's going to Zion...*
The peaceful easy rhythms and lyrics calmed him. He remembered Amelia at the blues and how she loved reggae music and how they had danced together that night. He loved the way she had put her hands around his neck and pulled him towards her for a kiss.
Rub it on the Black star Liner, dub it on the Black Star Liner...
His mind was full of her. He felt as though he was now reaching a critical point, about to enter a vortex without knowing how he would emerge on the other side, if at all. He was *here* but he was also *there*. *Here* was like being with family, people who accepted him and didn't want him to prove anything. *Here* was Paul. *Here* was his childhood, the nearest thing to roots he had. *Here* was where everyone minded his business. *Here* was sunlight and colour. *Here* there was no pretence. Or pretension. *Here* was Mishra. More positives than negatives. *There* was his studio. *There* was London and all its power, stimuli and anonymity. Brendan and Biscuit. Michael and Linda. Carol at the brewery in her jeans and fleece. Izzy and Iris. The house. Amelia. Life would be simpler *here* if he could just let go of some of the ties that bound him to *there*. He missed the girls but they could and would come over and he could always go to stay with them. They might even have a better time together that way. And if he really worked again *here* and produced something real again, it would be worth it. Or would it? Should everything be secondary to the work? He believed most artists would say the answer to that is always *yes* but does that make it right? Art above all else? Above everyone else? Maybe it didn't have to be that way. Paul had found a balance. Vernita demanded nothing from him and he demanded nothing of her. That was the secret. The solution. How had he and Amelia become so *demanding* of one another?

And Mishra - what was he thinking of there? Would that really work? He could see no reason why not other than that they were a long way from even acknowledging what their feelings for each other were. He didn't know what her feelings for him were. Maybe he was imagining something that didn't exist. He thought of her leaning against him last night. We are so close, he thought, and she is beautiful and I love her and she has no one else…and she's happy for me to work underneath her house. If Amelia wasn't part of the equation she would be the perfect person to talk to about it. She could be cold and objective and abrupt, especially when she saw the truth and he hadn't. She could bypass all the stages in a problem-solving process because she had the ability to quickly understand and see how it must conclude and would get frustrated when others were still working their way through all the options. He wondered what she was thinking at that moment. He checked his watch. It was still too early over there wherever she was but he messaged her all the same - *Am, what are we going to do? X*

The peace he had felt since coming to Trinidad was in danger of disappearing and being replaced with anxiety, irritation and petulant denial. A therapist would tell him him he needed to refind his centre. A Buddhist would tell him to lose his desire because desire was the root of all his suffering. They would both be right. Fuck, he thought, what do I *want*? The old man was still standing on the edge of the bath. Maybe he should go over to Mishra's and talk to her before Bigfoot and the boys arrived. He dressed quickly and headed downstairs for a mango breakfast.

CHAPTER 21

Mishra's cousin Bigfoot had two sons - Shortman (so named for obvious reasons) and Google whom Elliot had always known as Ferguson and who had, since Trinidad went online, developed a propensity for internet searching, particularly as regards matters of health and well-being. For any required answer, diagnosis or remedy Ferguson could apparently be relied upon to search, find and advise accordingly. *I'm gonna google it* became his mantra, at first encouraged by friends and family, then tolerated and now ridiculed, albeit in good humour and in which he took a sense of pride, making it even more funny to those who knew him. As for Bigfoot, his feet weren't particularly big at all but he was once a footballer of some renown throughout the island, playing centre-back and relied upon to *stick he big foot in* when necessary. Since injury and age stopped his playing he had grown flabby, developing jowls that flapped like the wattles of a turkey. The whites of his eyes were red with rum, the once bright green pupils now grey.

The three of them were already at Mishra's, sitting at the back under the house when Elliot arrived. He was greeted warmly with hugs and brother-shakes before they exchanged the usual round of questions as to how they all were, what they were we doing now and, in Elliot's case, how long it had been since the last time he was there. All this meant any plans he had to speak with Mishra would have to wait. She came down the steps to join them and gave him a smile to melt any resolve he may have had in terms of resisting her.

Wheey boy…you reach?' and without waiting for him to reply, unnecessarily added, Bigfoot and de boys here to help yuh.

Bigfoot was lying in one of the hammocks and waved a hand dismissively, telling them he wouldn't be doing much.

You sure about this? Elliot asked Mishra, realising the question had more than one meaning.

She just looked at him with a mock frown and then turned to Bigfoot who hadn't moved from the hammock.

Will I thank yuh *now* for your help? she asked Bigfoot, narrowing her eyes.

Yuh giving me bad eye or what? he replied.

Boy you so full a rum, any maljo ain't gonna penetrate, she said to laughs all round.

Hey Bigfoot where is Cecil? How he doing?' asked Elliot.

That black man? He in Tobago.

He okay?

Me n know.

Cecil was Bigfoot's brother by another father for a while had been Elliot's closest friend there. A doogla, more African than Indian, who as he got older developed a love for reggae music, herb and Rasta, all of which made him something of an outsider and oddity in the small and (as he had felt) oppressive nature of village life. He had once had what everyone else described as a good job with real prospects working for the Company in Point but as his locks began to grow and timekeeping began to matter less to him he found the increasingly hostile nature of the criticism and carping leveled at him hard to take. He left the job, fell in with a woman called Jemima, whose only flaws were a violent disposition when drunk and a possessive disapproving bully of a father who hated Cecil and set about ensuring that this doogla Rasta and his daughter were never going to be allowed to settle. It got to the point where the old man slit the throats of a couple of chickens over a gravestone as part of an obeah ritual, the aim of which was to put a curse on Cecil. One afternoon Cecil arrived home to see his house had been encircled by a ring of petals - a sign meaning without doubt the obeah man had been engaged and was out to get him. Ignoring the petals, Cecil did exactly what you shouldn't do if you want to avoid the curse - you were meant to get a priest to lift it - and stepped over them to access his house. No sooner had he entered than he stepped barefoot onto a nail protruding upright from a floorboard. The subsequent infection, pain and treatment nearly did for him. At some point during the protracted recovery, in which he thought he was going to have his foot amputated when gangrene set in, Jemima left him. As soon as he could walk again he left for Toronto, worked for eight years as a barman, bellhop and kitchen porter before returning home. Elliot had been hoping to see him and had just presumed he wasn't living in the village anymore but had no idea he'd gone over the water. As teenagers they had spent a lot of time together and shared the milestone experiences of girls, drugs, watching the stars and listening to music, mostly reggae. One night they sat on the sand by Mosquito Creek and smoked weed, watching the moonshine on the water create a thousand steps that glittered all the way to the shore. They slept that night under a coconut palm and thumbed rides back to Muga in the morning. Elliot regretted the years they had been out of touch and now, especially after hearing Bigfoot's mocking tone when talking about Cecil, he had an urge to see him. Maybe he would go to Tobago with Paul after all.

The help he was now deemed to require was to clear the garage space of various household and garden items that had been stored there, to fix the electronic shutter-door - Shortman was an electrician - and to remove the malfunctional television set from the wall. Mishra was helping them and Elliot had to control any urge to touch her or to look at her too obviously. He asked her about rent for the space and she laughed at him, then told him when she saw he wasn't joking he could help out in the garden now and again, especially to harvest the avocado and chataigne, both of which she struggled to reach.

How long you staying? she asked.
He shrugged.

Huh, she snorted, could be in for de long haul…or de short haul…Google that machine of yours answer everything? Find out how long dis boy gonna stay before he run on home to England.
Her tone was derisive, possibly aggressive. Elliot watched her walk back up the stairs and he followed her, looking at her backside. When they were in the kitchen he put his hand on her shoulder and turned her around. She had tears welling up in her eyes and he pulled her towards him. She resisted at first then relaxed into his hold. He kissed the top of her head and she looked up at him, tears now on her cheeks, their faces touching. They kissed with lips barely open, slowly and gently. His hands were on the small of her back and he pulled her into him. She put her head back and looked at him again, then started to gently punch him on the chest with balled fists.

Are yuh serious? she asked, separating herself from him.

Of course I am.

How can yuh be? Yuh live with a woman. Yuh have a home over there…daughters. I can't do this if yuh ain't serious.

I'm serious…I love you Mishra…I just…

Pah to love. What de hell is that?

I just don't know what to do…I don't know if Amelia has left me or not.

You want she?

I don't think so.

There is a but coming.

No…I love being here. If I'm here I want to be with you…I can't stop thinking about you…wanting to be with you.

Me too.

This admission from her made him pull her towards him again and they kissed once more, this time with more urgency. She pushed him away.

I don't want those boys to know, she said, and definitely not Bigfoot…big mouth more like.

Elliot leaned against the sink, trying to calm his desire for her. She walked over to him and jabbed him in the chest with her finger.

Yuh better make up yuh mind soon, she said, meantime maybe I will be able to persuade yuh. Now get back to work.

CHAPTER 22

Back on the Solomon Hochoy Highway, sitting high in the cab of Paul's pick-up truck and it was early morning, coffees in the drink holders as rain began to fall monsoon-style and Damian Marley on the radio was singing *Rasta work a manifest and it a blossom and a bloom, nature always run it course, de tide is rising wit the moon, it only take a spark to put a fire to de tune, what is hidden in the dark shall be revealed so very soon...* and Elliot, despite the weather and traffic, felt safe, tuned in to his surrounds and company.

It was too early for them to be talking so he allowed his mind to drift back to the previous evening when he and Mishra had spent time alone together after Bigfoot, Shortman and Google had left. It had felt gentle and natural to be together and without pressure, despite their approaching what they knew was a threshold from which they couldn't step back whatever happened. They had started kissing again in the kitchen and after a few minutes she had pulled herself away from the embrace and holding his hand had asked him if he was sure about the direction in which they were heading. Without hesitation he had told her he was certain. After so many years they were doing what they had always wanted to do, he said, and she didn't disagree.

They had spent the evening watching an American soap opera on the television, laughing at the plot and the acting, her head sometimes resting on his shoulder as they held hands without saying much. He left early enough so as not to arouse the suspicions of Paula and Vernita but they had parted like lovers do – with tenderness and a reluctance to separate, prolonged goodbye kisses and promises to speak over the next couple of days while he was in Tobago. He wished he hadn't agreed to go with Paul so he could just spend the day with her but also thought the trip would maybe provide a necessary interlude, something to dampen their fervour temporarily in order to allow for some perspective. He broke the silence by asking Paul how much the ferry tickets cost.

A few dollars each. But they're not for today.

Eh?

Chief mate is a friend of mine…I called him. Tickets are for yesterday…I bought them weeks ago…but he said it's no problem. Gonna be rough out there though unless this weather calms down.

How do you know the chief mate?

Actually he's family…Vernita's second cousin or something like that…good bloke…lives in Aripero…by the pond. I was down there hoping to see the scarlet ibis and his house is right there backing onto it. His dogs were barking at me so he came out and we chatted…found out he's related…she likes him just doesn't see much of him as he's at sea a lot of the time.

Elliot hadn't thought about how the weather would affect the crossing and now started to feel nervous. The anxiety spread through him, provoking a rising sense of panic but he realised that it wasn't just about the crossing. The feeling had targeted the most vulnerable point in his defences and in front of the breach sat Amelia, Mishra, Paul, Vernita and, to a lesser degree, Izzy and Iris. They were all looking at him, questions behind their eyes, waiting for an answer. Or maybe Amelia had already answered one herself, he thought. He needed to speak to her. Why does it feel as though I am doing something wrong? he asked himself. Being with Mishra felt right and life-affirming – how could that be wrong? Why did he fear the judgement of others? Two consenting adults were choosing to be together so why should anyone judge that? Why did he care what others thought? Because they don't see me as a single man, he thought, and they will think I'm leading Mishra astray, making promises I cannot keep…they will think I'm abandoning Amelia, being unfaithful to her even though she was the one who left me…left me to deal with all the shit in the aftermath of Michael's arrest…left me alone to cope with only thought for herself.

He started to feel angry towards Amelia and this came as something of a revelation. He hadn't felt like that before but he felt justified in doing so now. He had been so caught up in evading danger and resolving the situation in England that he'd never taken any time to reflect on why he carried so much guilt for it happening. He hadn't asked Michael to lose control, or for that little toe-rag and his pals to start their hideous campaign, or for Linda to want to start using heroin again. He didn't ask Amelia to leave for fuck's sake. She abandoned him. Selfishly left him to get on with it. Judged him to have somehow caused it all because of his relationship with Michael. What about *her* relationship with him? He was angry at her for getting angry with him when she had found out he wasn't going to his studio when he said he had been. He was angry at her for not being more understanding as to the reasons why and for not being helpful or supportive. He was angry at her for not showing *any* fucking emotion towards him other than anger.

As the internal dialogue continued Elliot conceded that some of what she had said about his life was right. That he couldn't hide behind the diagnostics of chronic pain and addiction. That he couldn't use them as excuses to self-destruct and drag her or anyone else who cared down with him. He accepted that - but if she loved him she would have stayed. If she loved him enough she wouldn't have run off to Scotland. They may well have eventually worked out that they should break up but she was the one who had walked away, doing the whole I-want-to-be-alone thing. And then being *in*communicado at a time she needed to be communicado. Fuck that, he concluded.

He recognised the voice of Dennis Brown singing a song he and Paul had known for years. He sang along to it out loud - *live up roots children, live up Rasta children, my head is annointed and my cup runneth over, surely goodness and mercy shall follow I all the days of I life...* and he had an urge to hug his old friend.

Love you mate, he said.

Hee hee! shouted Paul with that familiar manic joy Elliot had witnessed so many times in the past.

Paul started to bang the steering wheel and nod his head exaggeratedly in time to the beat as he sang along to the next track by the Abyssinians and Elliot joined in - *there is a land far far awayay, where there's no night, there's only dayay, look into the book of life and you will see...*

At the end of the track Paul shouted *yeeeeessss* at the top of his voice and turned off the highway to head into Port of Spain. He pulled into the car park at the ferry terminal as the rain let up and patches of blue appeared through the black clouds. It was a humid day already even though still early. He told Elliot to wait in the standby queue which had already formed with about thirty people in front of him. An old African woman in a floral dress, sunhat and thick glasses was tapping her walking stick against the glass of the ticket office. A younger woman was with her and shouting into the empty space where a member of staff should have been sitting. Eventually an obese doogla woman in a blue uniform sat down and attended to them. She looked languid, with sweat on her brow and an expression suggesting she would rather be anywhere else but there. She was the only staff member serving the standby queue and Elliot figured he could be there for a while. The man in front of him sucked his teeth and lit a cigarette. A policeman told the man it was a no smoking area so the man pinched it out while sucking his teeth again before putting the half-smoked stub into the breast pocket of his polo shirt. They shuffled slowly towards their objective as more joined the queue behind them.

After about twenty minutes Paul came over accompanied by a tall Indian man in an all-white uniform with gold-coloured stripes around his cuffs. He shook Elliot's hand as they were introduced.

This is Vin, said Paul, sorry it's taken so long.

Everything okay? asked Elliot.

Vin spoke in a baritone.

Yeah no problem but I had to clear it with de harbourmaster first and he wanted to take a little rum with me so it took a while.

Really? This early?

Yuh know.

As a result of Vin receiving the harbourmaster's blessing over a glass of rum they were able to drive on before anyone else. Vin was waiting for them on the car deck and then escorted them up some stairs past a *crew only* sign. As they passed the first level two policeman roughly herded a group of six men handcuffed together.

Criminals, said Vin, to stand trial in Tobago.

Paul asked him if he'd seen a weather forecast.

Rough, he said with a grin.

He wasn't wrong. They had taken seats near to the food bar and the boat had barely left port before the rocking started. Members of staff were handing out sick bags. Paul advised Elliot if he needed to use the toilet to go now as it would soon be awash with vomit. He discovered it already was. He struggled to stay upright and keep a steady aim. A half hour into the journey the boat started the turn northwards between the islands of Monos and Huevos, the tip of Venezuela visible to port. Now they were in the Caribbean Sea and the boat, a catamaran, headed into the waves to begin a roller coaster ride, rising and falling from aft to prow in a manner more likely to be associated with a North Sea trawler in a force ten gale.

This must be normal, said Elliot, I mean the crew must be used to this.

Always rougher on the way out...that being said this is pretty bad. If I've died... then this has to be one of the deeper rings of Hell.

He gestured across a vista of hundreds of people in various stages of panic, illness and prayer. Elliot, hardly reassured, tried to rationalise it all and settle, the sick bag as yet unused on his lap. He looked at his fellow passengers - a mix of Africans, Indians, dooglas, young, old, families, lovers, nuns, priests and a few white tourists. He wondered at their lives - who they were, why they were travelling and where they were going. As a snapshot of humanity, he thought, it was cheerless. He imagined looking down on the scene from high above and saw this little boat leaving one small island, a pinprick on the face of the Earth - which itself was less than a pinprick on the face of the Universe - and heading for an even smaller island whilst carrying a multitude of people, all with their own unique collections of myriad thoughts, memories, emotions, hopes and aspirations. The apparent pointlessness of it all struck Elliot. How we scrabble around, he thought, imposing ourselves on the planet and our fellows with our greed, vanity, arrogance and ignorance of our place in the order of things. If this boat capsized and every one of them travelling on it were to perish what would it matter?

He looked across at Paul - eyes closed, earphones in and tapping his feet in time to whatever he was listening to. Elliot watched him and thought about who he was, what he meant to him, their years of friendship and their intimate knowledge of one another and he became mindful of the fragility of their lives. The ties that bound people together were gossamer thin, yes, easily broken, and yet they were the truth and the only truth, the only tangible things in life. Possessions, careers, social status, even his own art, didn't matter. He concluded there was no mystery to life, no great secret, all that existed was *this* and if there wasn't any secret, any great code to be cracked, and that he was just one of billions of particles moving through the universe, then life was simple. The thought comforted him.

The pain in his lower back, left testicle and left big toe was irritating him to the point that he couldn't ignore it any longer and had to take remedial action. He stood up to stretch and was immediately propelled into the table between him and Paul as the boat hit another wave. His hip took the force and the subsequent pain made him conclude that this was confirmation of life's insignificance and he sat back down again. The pain management group facilitators had placed emphasis on *mindful meditation* as a pain management technique. The cynic in him had at the time had taken this as meaning the group were being told they were fucked and there wasn't anything anyone could do about it. All that was left to them was mindful meditation for fuck's sake. However, he had come to realise it helped, not least as an aid to his relaxation, the key to managing this curse. So he closed his eyes and started to mindfully meditate, at first focussing on his body, starting with his feet, trying to sense each toe and the tension between the soles of his feet and the floor and then he moved through the structure of the boat, descending slowly through all the decks, all the way to the ocean. Then he imagined being beneath the turbulence of the waves, swimming downwards, sensing the daylight above the surface diminish as all around him grew darker. He was alive and alone in a dark fluid space and felt calm, at one with the surrounds that he moved through without any effort or discomfort.

He wasn't aware of how much time had passed when he was brought back to consciousness by the sound of someone throwing up. He opened his eyes and saw a woman lying prone on a seat, leaning over the edge of it and vomitting into a sick bag. The smell wafted over. Her track bottoms had slipped down, revealing the cleft between her buttocks. She was without dignity and Elliot felt compassion for her and wanted to help. Paul was awake and watching the same scene. They looked at eachother and laughed at the ridiculousness of the situation before going to help the woman, sitting her up and offering her water. Elliot took her sick bag and put it into a plastic bag he had with him, tying a knot in it but now not knowing where to put it. The woman's eyes were closed and she was far beyond being able to acknowledge their helping her. People were watching Elliot, wondering what he was going to do with the bag of vomit. He walked to the toilet. The sea was calmer than it had been earlier but it was nevertheless still only possible to stagger in a stuttering movement of two steps sideways before one step forward. He balanced the sick bag on an overflowing rubbish bin before returning to his seat. He could see land on the horizon.

CHAPTER 23

The scene outside the ferry terminal in Scarborough was how Elliot always remembered it - the road jammed with traffic as passengers waited to be picked up and cars stopped and parked anywhere causing a cacophonous flurry of car horns and shouting. This competed with the everpresent noise of sound systems in cars and bars and the general hum of local people, tourists, policemen, stall holders selling everything from fruit, vegetables and fish to t-shirts and bracelets and taxi drivers touting for fares, all of them going about their business in an apparent lack of harmony with one another. The scene was in contrast to much of the rest of the island where it was still possible to find the archetypal Caribbean scenes of tranquility and laidbackness along with the white sands, green seas and coconut palms. But not in Scarborough, a place Elliot had always been glad to leave. Something in the air about the place he couldn't quite put his finger on but he sensed it as though the town sat somewhere on the cusp between the virtuous and the diabolic. Seek either one out and you could no doubt find it.

They were the last off the ferry – apart from the criminals who waited with an increased number of armed guards at the top of the boat's ramp. Paul told Elliot they had to meet his client at a bar somewhere a few minutes drive away and that he would collect her keys so they could deliver the paintings directly to her house. They drove up a narrow road lined with a variety of shops and stalls - the *Soca One-World Record Shop* painted in the red, black and white of the national flag - then a clothes shop outside of which on the pavement stood several half-mannequins dressed in tight, brightly coloured short skirts and in front of whom a monkey sat chained to a shopping trolley, squawking like a parrot with a throat infection - underneath two tattered beach parasols and on top of a tressle table was a pile of bras of numerous colours and sizes and beside which sat a young African woman, bored-looking and barefoot, who was eating crackers and feeding crumbs to a green partially-feathered macaw with a bell around its neck - *The Novelty Store* with a sign reading *birthdays, fetes and celebrations* - *Sonia's Hairdresser* offering *African, Indian and Euro styles 4 U* - a pink building with darker pink window ledges and red curtains which had a sign on its gable-end reading *Come and explore at Edwina's Unique Jeweller and Best Body Therapies* and in front of which a large woman dressed in primary coloured clothes leaned against a lamp post fanning herself with a newspaper, overfilled shopping bags at her feet.

Paul pulled up in front of *Gillian's Variety Store* - a wooden shack painted purple with white polka dots. Next door to it was a narrow passageway leading to a door above which a red light shone underneath a neon sign that flashed *Taylor's Bar*. They stepped through the outer door into a small storm porch where there was another door painted black and above which three pairs of open scissors hung with the blades pointing downwards. Inside the bar the light was dim and coming from the brightness outside it took them a few moments to adjust. Elliot could smell incense and there was music in the background – rhythmic repetitive drumming interspersed with shouts and screams. There was no one behind the ebony-dark wooden bar. Elliot's eyes focussed on a painting hanging on the wall behind it in which under a full moon a large breasted and naked African woman was rising up from the sea. A host of other naked people were emerging from her navel and queuing to up to suckle her. A hand-written note above the painting read *The spirits call, you are entitled to an initiation.* On the shelves and walls there were African tribal masks and carvings of heads with scowling faces and beads hung around their elongated necks. More open scissors hung from above the bar.

A white woman appeared through a beaded curtain and in a whispery voice greeted Paul with a smile. He took her hand over the bar and kissed the back of it before introducing Elliot. She shook his hand so gently he felt it was like being brushed by feathers. Her accent was Tobagonian. She poured them each a beer and took down a bunch of keys from a hook and slid them across the bar to Paul and then without saying another a word disappeared again behind the curtain. They didn't see her again. Beers drunk, they emerged into the light and got back into the pick-up truck.

What the fuck was that? asked Elliot.

Paul laughed.

An obeah bar. She's a priestess.

Whaaaat? Real obeah? *Really*? You serious?

Yeah. She's a good customer.

What are the keys for?

Her house.

She lived in Bacolet, up the hill from the beach in a residentail area of detached villas, a short distance from Scarborough. Paul opened the double gates with a remote control on the key fob and drove the hundred yards or so down a driveway to a carport next to the house. It was a large single-storey property looking more like it belonged in an ex-pat urbanization somewhere in southern Spain. A large crab stood guard and flexing its pincers before the front door, its black eyes fixed upon them from the tips of three-inch stalks. It scuttled sideways as Paul unlocked the door and they stepped inside. The interior was bright and clean, the walls of the open-plan sitting-room, diner and kitchen all painted white. Elliot recognised two of Paul's paintings on one of the walls. There was a locked grille, behind which was a locked glass door leading to a patio and swimming pool. A sign read *don't forget to shower before and after bathing*. An iguana sat in one of the mango trees lining the side of the surrounding lawn. It was fluourescent green and sat stock still as they walked out towards the pool. Paul fetched a couple of beers from the fridge and they sat for a few moments at a small table. Elliot looked all around for more signs of obeah but didn't see any.

I don't think she brings her work home, said Paul with a grin.

A cocrico - Tobago's national bird - was standing on a coconut palm branch, looking like an old man trying to balance on a surfboard. It screeched its high-pitched *ka kra reek ka kra* and Elliot remembered how that sound would wake him in the morning when his parents brought him to Tobago all those moons ago to stay in a house near Charlotteville above Pirate's Bay. There was a small beach there where he used to walk in the early mornings, sometime with his father but mostly alone. He had once watched a fisherman drop anchor a few hundred yards from the shore before diving into the sea fully clothed, including a baseball cap reversed on his head, and swim powerfully to shore, his hands arrowed like seabirds' beaks as they broke the water's surface with sharp chopping strokes. A small boy ran to greet him and when the man reached the shore he lifted the boy up and pressed him to his wet body before spinning him round by his arms and dropping him into the water amidst wails of delight and innocence. Elliot's father had always loved to be there and said more than once it was where he would prefer to end his days. He came to mind easily. His easy smile - all too rare - hair wet from the sea, skin burnished by years in the Tropics. How he had loved to show Elliot the wonders of the natural world, so abundant in Tobago, with an enthusiasm that belied his age but also with what Elliot understood now was a deep sadness, one which emanated from his soul and directed most of what he did and how he behaved. He would always pretend to be energetic and happy around Elliot, especially when Elliot was young, but his melancholy and dissatisfaction with his world was apparent to the boy even at that age. Their early morning walks on the beach at Pirate's Bay were Elliot's favourite times in his father's company, happy just to be holding his hand and witnessing his father at his most carefree.

The cocrico screeched on. They unloaded two large canvasses wrapped in bubble wrap and carried them into the house, leaving them propped against the sitting-room walls. Paul then locked up. They were booked into a hotel somewhere on the road between Scarborough and Crown Point.

   I want to find Cecil, said Elliot.

   You know where he is?

   Mount Irvine I think.

   I can drop you there. I've a potential client to see later - the Chief Secretary and Secretary of Planning, Public Administration, Information, State Lands and Energy Matters no less. I can meet you back at the hotel.

He dropped Elliot in the car park by Mount Irvine beach which was busy with tourists and Elliot walked onto the sand. The sea was calm and green, swelling gently with waves working their way to shore. He took off his sandals and walked in the shallows towards the far end of the beach where there was a bar and restaurant as well as a few stalls displaying souvenirs.

Elliot saw him before he saw Elliot. Tall and muscular, wearing cut-off jeans and a vest, leaning over from behind a table talking to a white man who was with an Indian woman, a mixed-race younger woman and a fair-skinned black guy. Cecil's locks were tied up above his head in a circular heap that looked like a bird's nest on top of a tree trunk. As Elliot approached he heard the white guy speak in a London accent.

Well we all kinda Rasta…this is my family.
The man gestured to his companions.

Nice nice, replied Cecil in a deep melifluous voice, it's not about locks or skin colour yuh know…it's about how yuh live your life.

Elliot waited for the family to buy a couple of bracelets and watched them all shake Cecil's hand and leave before he approached. Over Cecil's shoulder the sea reflected the start of the sun going down and he looked up from tidying the wares on his table. They smiled at one another. Cecil stepped out from behind the table and took Elliot in his arms, lifting him off the ground. They were both speechless, looking at each other with head shakes of disbelief and grins as broad as they could be.

Rasta work a manifest, said Cecil.

CHAPTER 24

They were sitting outside Cecil's two-roomed board house in front of a barbecue pit upon which lay six mullett they had been given by one of Cecil's friends who sold fish and crabs at one end of Mount Irvine bay. The fish were shining fresh in green and grey. Cecil's wife Sandra was breast-feeding their baby boy Saul through multiple folds of her wrap-around dress. She wore her locks high and covered in a long scarf of red, gold, green and black, arranged in an elongated turban. Her green eyes glistened in the light of the flames licking up from the pit.

They had reached Cecil's home just before dark and after they had bathed in the sea directly behind his stall and then stopped for a drink at a nearby bar where Cecil had a ginseng soda and Elliot took a beer. Cecil told Elliot how he hadn't drunk alcohol in eight years and hadn't missed it.

My mind's clearer and I sleep better, he said, my conscience cleaner.

When they arrived Sandra was working a small lawn of coarse grass with a crook stick, bent over as she cut in a rhythmic swinging motion, her sleeping child wrapped in a bundle on her back. She greeted Elliot with a bow of her head and her hands together as though she was in prayer. They kissed cheeks.

Welcome, she said, before turning to Cecil and kissing him, rubbing the small of his back and asking, how was today?

Some nice tourists, he replied, and bracelets selling well.

Elliot took a seat at the side of the house underneath an open but covered area where there was a chicken coop, a plastic water tank, numerous hoses, baskets, metal bowls and an oil drum cut in half in which Sandra soon bathed Saul. Live ducklings swam in his bath water and he squealed with joy as Cecil cleaned the fish and Elliot looked out and down towards the sea and the silhouettes of a few houses scattered across the hillside, their lights coming on as the sky darkened. Mosquitoes whined and attacked. Sandra threw him some repellant spray and lit a couple of coils, the smell acrid against the sweeter smell of night descending. His phone buzzed and he read a message from Iris - *Hi dad. Hope ur havin a gd time. All well here. Did u knwo Am back at the house? Lotsa luv X*. He leaned back with a sigh and tried to picture Amelia. Her features were vague, their house a blur. He tried to force his thoughts away from where he now was to where he had come from - maybe where he should be - but failed. He sent a text back - *Thanks love. I'm good. Love you X*

Before eating Sandra said a prayer.

Princess shall come out of Egypt…Ethiopia shall stretch forth her hand unto God…oh thou God of Ethiopia, thou God of divine Majesty, they spirit come within our hearts to dwell in the parts of righteousness…that the hungry be fed, the sick nourished, the aged protected and the infant cared for…teach us love and loyalty as it is in Zion.

Rasta Far I, said Cecil.

They ate mostly in silence other than Elliot praising the food every so often. Cecil asked him what had brought him back and Elliot told him something of the state of mind he had got into, of the problems in his relationship with Amelia and of his wish to paint again.

I don't know how yuh do it there man, said Cecil, all those people… cars…pollution.

Carnivores too, added Sandra and Elliot wasn't sure if she was joking or not.

Ain't it like a real Babylon? asked Cecil rhetorically.

I guess so, replied Elliot before starting to defend it, it's not all bad you know…there's a lot of culture…stimulus…I have friends and I have the girls…I have my own studio.

He remembered the toilet on the landing there and the Buddhist quotation before adding,

It's different…I don't know if it's better or worse.

It have fresh food there? asked Sandra.

Yes yes. You can get everything…there's lot of choice.

She looked doubtful.

Too much maybe, said Cecil.

Elliot thought how so many of the things that filled his life now appeared to him to be without purpose or meaning. How so much time and energy was spent in pursuit of those same things. What drove that? Ego maybe, the need to cling onto possessions, people, places even, in order to secure him. The need to appear normal and conventional. In control.

Life here is much more..., he struggled for the words, I don't know...stripped down...to the essentials I guess. It's simpler. In a good way no doubt about it.

Food and drink. Love and shelter, said Cecil.

And warmth.

Then after a few moments Elliot continued.

And colour...so much colour.

He pointed at the yellow moon, whisps of silver clouds passing over its face.

As they sat in silence Elliot thought of London. Its busyness. How he relished the in-your-face stimuli as soon as he stepped off the train. How he loved the walk from London Bridge tube station to Tate Modern via Borough Market, having a pint or two in the Market Porter, the view across the river to St. Paul's, then crossing the Millennium Bridge and cutting down to Broken Wharf to that Spanish restaurant where they had celebrated one of Amelia's birthdays. How she had loved it there looking out across the Thames at night, it's banks and bridges alight with life. Or the wander through Green Park up the Mall to Trafalgar Square, the National Gallery and being able to gaze for free upon Pissaro's painting *Fox Hill, Upper Norwood in the Snow* or Caravaggio's *Supper at Emmaus* - two paintings he'd probably stared at more than any others - before moving on to the British Museum and nearby Bradley's Bar or the Euston Tap – all of it teeming with history and humanity. Maybe he did need it after all. He asked Cecil about New York.

It was an adventure...and I enjoyed it...before it turned sour. America...the rich pretty child...full of charisma but such little grace. Yuh know it's as though it did too much too soon...got rich too quick...and now it don't know who is its real friends. And the winters man...cruel.

He didn't offer detail as to how things had gone wrong but the look on his face betrayed enough. Elliot sent a text to Paul to tell him he would see him in the morning.

CHAPTER 25

He slept on their beat-up settee before waking up with a pain in his pelvis radiating malevolence down his left leg. He felt a despondency worm its way into his destiny in its familiar way. After a pre-dawn breakfast of fried plantain and roti he said goodbye to Sandra who told him to come back soon. He wondered about that. They lived idyllically for sure - or so it seemed - but he wasn't convinced he could could live like that. That he didn't belong there came to mind and he wondered when it would be before he returned.

He and Cecil went down to the beach where the dawn light shone on a row of flamboyant trees, turning their flowers a dusty pink and their trunks blue and black. Elliot took photos with his phone, thinking he would use the images in a painting. They swam. The water was as calm and still as a mountain lake and as he floated on his back he saw an osprey flying overhead, low enough for him to see the yellows of its eyes. It circled a couple of times before swooping with its talons outstretched to pluck a fish out of the water no more than twenty yards away from him. A purple and green heron stood on the shore watching the scene. A glass bottom boat, empty of passengers, chugged past on its way, no doubt, to Pigeon Point or Buccoo Bay where tourists - Brits, Americans, Japanese, Germans, Italians and Trinis - would bring the boat owner some much needed custom as he escorted them out to the coral reef and the Nylon Pool, playing out the contradictory and inevitable dynamic where the erosion of the reef caused by tourism would eventually erode the boatman's income when no one wanted to visit anymore. On the bow of the boat was a hand-painted sign - *Powered by God!*

The two of them got out of the water and sat on the rocks, looking out.
      I will die happy here, said Cecil.
      You've a while yet.
      You too brother.
It was time to go. They exchanged hugs and Cecil gave a look that bored into Elliot's eyes.

Elliot and Paul spent the day together drinking cocktails by the pool, eating shark and bake and talking, avoiding the big subjects and laughing as they reminisced, spending easy neutral time together without pressure or expectation. In the evening they walked a few hundred yards to a rum shop which was frequented only by locals and where they drank beers, ate fried chicken wings and got bitten by mosquitoes, some of which, Elliot thought, were the size of aeroplanes and who spurted out globules of fresh blood whenever he managed to swat one of them. A sign above the bar advertised herbal aphrodisiacs - *Charge up de boy!! NO side-effects! Last up to 168 hours! 7 day pill $100 only!* They pondered what it might be like to last for one hundred and sixty-eight hours.

Next morning a little after seven, they were standing in a queue outside the ferry terminal ticket-office. A light rain fell. On Vin's instructions they were waiting with the other standby passengers but there seemed to be an inordinate number of them. Maybe thirty or so in front of Elliot and Paul and at least the same number behind. Vin had assured Paul he would arrive early and arrange their queue-jump and passage. A tall African man with a gaunt face was standing in front of them. He was wearing a faded LA Raiders baseball cap, a red polo shirt ripped across the chest, camouflage shorts - against the law since the attempted coup of 1990 - and flip-flops. He carried a battered suitcase with a BOAC sticker on it and which was secured by a piece of rope wrapped around it several times. He was sucking his teeth and speaking out loud.

Oh man oh man oh Lord.

He turned, eyes red and wild, pointed to Elliot and addressed him.

Are *you* computerised? he asked.

Before Elliot could answer - not that he knew what to say - the man continued in a more urgent voice.

Are *you* computerised? Am *I* computerised? Are all a *dem*?' and he gestured towards the office and the sky.

Elliot smiled briefly and looked away. He had a hangover – he and Paul had drunk a forgotten number of rums for the road before they had left the rum shop and for all he was worth he didn't want to have to engage with this guy.

And what to do when it rains? the man asked.

Take shelter? Elliot responded, provoking the man's mocking laughter.

Shelter? he shouted, Yuh tink dey give a black cent for yuh and me needing shelter? Dey *computerised*! We ain't. Dey coulda open de doors but no no no no…no…dey…it is *dey* who is computerised. Not we man not we.

The queue shuffled forwards. Elliot felt frustrated and ill at ease, the hangover having reduced his capacity for being able to deal with the human race. Surely *all* these people didn't want standby tickets? Paul walked off to look for Vin and Elliot eavesdropped a conversation between two Indian men in suits and learned there had been a cock-up in the issuing of tickets for a later ferry – tickets for the evening ferry had been issued with the time for the morning ferry printed on them. This had resulted in possibly double the usual number of people trying to get on the boat for the morning crossing and others wanting to exchange their misprinted tickets so they could still travel in the evening. There were now over a hundred people in a snake of a queue waiting to reach the check-in desk. A member of the port staff opened up a single booth - there were three more - and she then started to deal with the passengers of whom each one had a tale to tell, a desire to check in or a ticket to exchange. People were getting angry. Their muttering intensified.

A young man with a Jamaican accent walked up to the booth and slammed his fist on the counter, startling the woman behind the glass. He shouted at her.

You a pussy-hole! You a pussy-hole in a pussy-hole factory in a pussy-hole country! You all fuckin pussy-holes.
A policewoman walked towards him, one hand on her baton, the other gesturing at him to calm down.

Mothercunt! he shouted at her, before looking back at the queue and shouting again, Pussy-holes!

He stomped out, waving a hand at them all in dismissal and disgust.

He not computerised, said the gaunt-faced man.

This provoked laughter among the crowd and so encouraged him to continue. We are many dey de few, he said as though he was a priest addressing a congregation, dey have computers so what do we do? Rise up! Rise up! Like the beasts from slumber…children rise up…because dey got your number!

The policewoman warned him to be quiet or she would arrest him. He looked at her as though she had spurned his romantic advances.

Are *you* computerised?' he asked her.

CHAPTER 26

Swinging an axe to split a log. Building a fire. Poaching an egg. Simple tasks done well, he thought, were usually more fulfilling in their completion than the inconclusive pursuits associated with creativity. Engaging in the simple tasks brought refuge, contentment and confirmation of a life lived with purpose and meaning. Stretching a canvass was another one for the list. First learned in week one of art school, he had always taken satisfaction from doing it, seeing the process as an integral part of his painting. He sawed some lengths of two by one for the stretcher bars and cross braces, cut the joints then glued and stapled the corners together before stretching the raw canvass across it mid-point to mid-point on each axis, securing it with staples as he went along, working towards the corners where he folded the material as neatly as the ends of a hospital bed. It was taut like the skin of a drum, unlikely to develop creases beneath the paint's surface. Then he primed it with white emulsion, creating a timbre of an even higher pitch as it tautened even more. There was now before him a space both defined and undefined within which something new and unique could be added to the world.

He had once gone through a stage of buying ready-mades which had been easier, in that it consumed less time and energy, but it had never felt right to him. They were always second-best and it pricked his conscience because it meant second-best was what he was settling for. It felt like compromise - and therefore failure - before he had added even a single brushstroke. Then he had used a picture framer in Commercial Street in the East End to make them for him – a woman from Cyprus with afro hair, swarthy skin and black eyes, who doubled as a shaman and seer and who always wanted him to throw the I-Ching with her whenever he visited her workshop. He never did. She unnerved him with her lack of social grace and the intensity of her gaze, as though she wanted to see him cut up and fried before she devoured him. She prepared good quality canvasses but he still felt he was being lazy by not making his own, that it meant he wasn't committed to what he was doing and that he was still scared of stepping into hot water. The preparation of a virgin canvass, when done properly, was to him a dutiful act, an honourable and meditative process that prepared him for the creative action that was to follow.

He had now stretched four canvasses - the largest a six by four, then two of three by two and one - the least intimidating - of two feet by eighteen inches. Paul had given him an easel and Elliot had constructed a pair of wooden brackets with the offcuts of the two by one. He had then secured them to one of the walls and placed the largest canvass upon them. He was going to add a touch of ground charcoal to the primer to give a tone of grey neutrality and texture to the surface but changed his mind, despite the brilliance of the white, because he wanted the colours he mixed and used to be as clean and full as they could be. There is light in abundance here, he thought, and he wanted to exploit it to its maximum.

His pallette was a piece of chipboard with a white laminated surface that had once been the top of a chest of drawers and that he had found lying at the back of the house. He had painter and decorator brushes of different sizes, rollers, horse grooming brushes, sable paint brushes of different textures, widths and styles, an array of paints, pallette knives and rags as well as an ample amount of white spirit and turpentine. Satisfied everything was prepared, he mixed cadmium red with titanium white and thinned it with the white spirit. He then stood before the large canvass holding a five-inch brush more suited to painting a fence than painting a work of art. He felt like a waiting banderillo, poised to run at the bull and strike. It was sometime after ten in the morning and he'd been up since half past six. He was listening to Thelonius Monk and feeling fine.

The first brush stroke he had made in weeks was an arc somewhere centre left of the blank canvass. He stood back and watched it drip. Too much white spirit and he didn't like the texture of the brush - it wasn't coarse enough for the mark he had in his mind's eye - so he added more paint to the pallette until it was as thick as porridge.

On their way back from Port of Spain, after they had first stopped to buy the materials he wanted, Elliot requested they went to a livery supplies shop where he bought a half dozen grooming brushes. It was one of those he reached for now. It had a strap across its back into which he put his hand, making him feel as though the palm of his hand was itself now bristled, the brush having become a seamless extension of his arm. He made another arc sweep across the first one. The consistency was now right and the brush marks what he was looking for. He was on his way. Amelia came to mind and he wished she was watching so he could prove to her he still had it in him, that he wasn't a loser and his talent was still alive. It was something she had never done. Something he had never invited her to do.

He resisted the urge to text her, it was too early in the day and anyway he wanted to refocus on the painting. He started to feel doubt. He stuck some of the photos of the Tobago dawn onto the wall next to the canvass, then added cobalt blue and some more cadmium red to the mix on his pallette. Satisfied with the colour, he used a roller to make a vertical trunk beneath the arcs. The sky was going to take up about half of the composition and he wanted a row of hills to undulate across the horizon in order to bridge the sky to the foreground. He felt in a hurry to paint it, his thoughts and ideas racing ahead of him, so he mixed some more white with a touch of yellow ochre and then, using another grooming brush, painted horizontal streaks across the upper section of the canvass. He added pale pinks, cadmium yellow straight from the tube and some cerulean blue lightened with a touch of white. The sky looked better than the one he had imagined. It now throbbed with the start of day, having been uniform and opaque before the other colours had brought it to this state of vibrancy. It was a living sky. It shimmered. He then outlined the hilltops with the blunt end of a pencil before sitting down on a stool to stare at it all. I'm doing it, he thought, at last I'm doing it. It was such a natural process to him that he couldn't imagine how he had let himself remain blocked for so long. Twice that morning he had felt the old fear. The profound hesitation. Both times he overrode it. Stormed through it and, as he mixed colours and painted, a state of grace came over him.

Mishra came down from the house and stood behind him, linking her arms around his neck. He leaned back and rested his head against her breasts. He didn't want her to move. She stayed put. His arousal started to override any thoughts he had about the painting. Neither of them spoke. He swallowed with a drying mouth and still sitting turned to face her, put his arms around her waist and his face where the back of his head had been. She held her ground. He brought one of his hands to the front and stroked her thighs, moving it to the join of the seams in the crotch of her jeans. He pressed her there and stroked some more, his other hand holding one of her buttocks. She didn't move. He unbuttoned the waist of her jeans, pulled down the zip and eased them over her hips. She pulled his face tight into her chest. A car horn sounded from the front of the house and they heard the gate being unbolted. She pushed him away, pulled up her jeans, pulled up the zip and rebuttoned as she walked quickly up the steps without looking back.

He moved away from the workspace and headed for underneath the house as though removing himself from the scene would make him less conspicuous. Naren stepped around the corner. He was with one of his cousins, Froggy, whose real name was Mohammed. Froggy was also known as Mo, Dribble or Crapeau – the local name for a giant frog - but for now it was mostly Froggy. This nickname had come about the last time Elliot had been there when a group of them went to Columbus Bay in the back of a pick-up truck, bouncing their way down the road without fear as they drank rum, waved at passers-by and laughed. Mo had then started to experience stomach cramps, saying he needed to shit and didn't know how long he could wait. Holding on until they reached the parking bay at the edge of the beach, he jumped from the back of the pick-up and ran to the facilities, long-abandoned and now reclaimed by the bush as its own. On sitting down upon a seatless toilet bowl and surrounded by spiders webs, wasp nests and grasshoppers, peristalsis kicked in with some urgency as his sphincter reacted autonomously and prepared to relieve him of the force that had been so troubling him. He then peered down between his legs and saw a giant frog sitting in the bowl looking up at him, croaking, opening its lips and blinking its eyes.

He leapt up and in that very instance of sudden movement voided his bowel of a liquid, so malevolent, putrid and foul it made him retch, not least because much of it had landed on the backs of his legs and his shorts. He came out screaming *crapeau! crapeau!* and then ran into the sea as they all applauded him with handclaps and shouts of delight.

The two of them had either just come from or were about to go to the mosque as they were both wearing thawbs and prayer hats. They greeted him by both saying *as salamu alaikum* and he replied *wa alaikum salam* and Froggy shook his hand brother-style, giving him a weak hug. Naren just shook hands.

Ma wants to see yuh all yuh know, he said smiling, wants to make you baigan aloo…same and peas…and curry goat.

Sure great…when? asked Elliot.

Saturday evening…about five. Where she?

Upstairs.

Elliot called Mishra who came down quickly enough to suggest she had been waiting at the top of the stairs. Elliot looked to her for a secret sign, an acknowledgement of what had happened just a few minutes before. He saw none. She was inscrutable. He replayed the scene in his head. She hadn't resisted. She hadn't moved away from him. She held him there. She had been aroused. It's inevitable now, he thought, that they were going to cross that threshold. Froggy lay in the hammock and Naren took a chair and turned it around to sit with his arms resting on its back.

I busy, said Mishra by way of excusing herself as she moved towards the steps.

Yuh all have sweet drink? asked Naren.

Yes.

Bring some nah.

He jerked his head, indicating upstairs.

Yuh know where it is, she said walking away.

Wheeey…happen to she?

Naren looked to Elliot who made an expression of puzzlement and shrugged. Froggy, said Naren, let we go nah. See yuh Saturday brother if not before. Inshah Allah.

They bumped fists by way of saying goodbye and Elliot now didn't know what to do. Follow her upstairs? Is that what she wanted him to do? Go back to work? Maybe she would come back down. His phone vibrated on the table. It was a text from Amelia - *Can u speak?* - she had never used used abbreviations before when texting, he noted. He didn't want to, not now.

What's up? U ok?

Nothing just want to speak

He waited, considering his options. She text again.

I'm home btw

I heard

Minutes passed, his indecisiveness a force-field around him, impenetrable.

She text again.

Well?

He replied *Difficult* and thought please not here, not now.

When then? We need to speak. I need to

He made a decision. *Half an hour?*

Ok don't forget please xx

She wanted to speak. She signed off with kisses. She was back home. He headed for Neighbour's bar, his hands spattered with paint, brush streaks on his trouser legs.

CHAPTER 27

Neighbour passed a beer through the grille. He asked for a petit-quart of rum and some water. She frowned at him.

Yuh in de mood today?

He laughed and gave her a smile as if to say *don't worry everything's normal.*

Something like that Neighbour, he said.

And when yuh in de mood yuh come and see me…ohhh that's *nice.*

He sat at the bar and drank. An Indian guy with a James Brown haircut and wearing overalls sat next to him nodding in acknowledgement of Elliot's presence but nothing more. He ordered Puncheon, the overproof rum they call firewater. Elliot ordered another beer, drained the glass of rum and walked over the road to a bench beneath a mango tree, behind which was a pile of discarded bottles, cans and cigarette packets. He sat down, gulped half the beer, held the cold bottle to his forehead for a few seconds and then called Amelia. She answered with a *hi* that sounded over-enthusiastic. Maybe she's nervous, he thought. The inevitable first question followed.

How are you?

Okay.

This was followed by what felt to Elliot like an uncomfortably long silence.

And how are you? he asked eventually.

Fine.

Another silence before she spoke again.

We've left this too long.

Yes I agree.

I've worked some stuff out. I feel more positive.

That's good.

Positive? *Positive*? he thought, what the fuck does that mean?

And I miss you, she said, I wanted you to know that… but things had got too… much.

When you were in Scotland? he asked accusingly.

Yes of course…but I needed to be away…I needed that time.

More silence.

You sound unhappy, he said.

How do you know? I mean how can you tell?

More silence.

You're so far away, she said.

Are you?

What?

Unhappy.

Yes…but okay. It's just not good being here alone.

Yeah…well…I know that obviously.

What I mean is I miss your being here.

Well…I miss you too. Missed you when you went away…now I'm just trying to get on…you know?

By running away?

His anger stirred and it felt as though his heart was about to burst through his chest.

I'm not running away.

You sound angry.

I have been…I don't know what I'm feeling now.

Let's not…do this…please…I came in peace.'

Really?

Yes. I want to see you. When are you coming back?

I'm working. I've started.

Oh *wow* that's great.

He knew she was being genuine but, he thought, she was trying too hard so he should cut her some slack. He could picture her, sense her, almost touch her. His guard was slipping. She spoke again.

I love you dearly…as in lots…as in abundance…buckets of it. Clear? I want to spend time with you. I don't want to live without you in my life.

Really?

Of course.

Why?

Because I love you for God's sake. I just hated the way things were going…you were drinking so much…then when you told me you weren't working…then Michael and all that nightmare…I just hated your drinking so much…especially in the way you were doing it…so angry…locked down. I understood it but it was hard to watch…hard to live with.'

He felt defiant.

I reserve the right to do that if I have to, he said, I don't enjoy it you know.

Maybe you wouldn't want to be like that if we were…you know…

What?

Together…you know properly together…sharing things…communicating.

How was Elvis?

He felt an usolicited bitterness rising. There was some more silence.

He's well, she said finally.

And?

And what?

Did he look at you the way he normally does?

What do you mean?

Did you sleep with him?

He walked back over the road and signaled for another beer.

No.

Did you want to?

He crossed back over the road to stand underneath the mango tree.

Yes…satisfied? But we didn't. I was alone and felt like shit.

Oh *you* were alone and felt like shit.

Oh come *on*. That's not fair.

How close did you get?

He was aware he was being hypocritical, projecting his guilt onto her but he couldn't stop himself.

We…we...

So rarely did she hesitate he felt like twisting the knife a little more.

…we just talked…he's a good guy…intelligent and wise…helpful. What is this? Why are you doing this, Elliot?'

I bet he was helpful.

Why are you being like this?

Did he want to sleep with you?

I don't know.

She hesitated again before continuing.

It was never mentioned. He's not like that.

Most men are.

Speak for yourself.

All men want sex…they just couch it in the preliminaries in case it puts the woman off. He's no different…all the listening and laughing, the sharing of the stages…it's part of the game. All that I'm-such-a-nice-sensitive-guy shit. Sex is still the driver.

He's honourable.

Honourable men want sex too.

You mean cynical. Not everyone is as twisted as you.

More silence. He reflected on the word *twisted* and his thoughts turned to a corkscrew willow that used to grow in the garden before they had to cut it down to make way for the conservatory. It was beautiful when in leaf and had formed an archway across the lawn. Why did we allow it to be killed like that? he wondered.

Do you remember the corkscrew willow? he asked

Yes, she laughed, why?

That was twisted.

She laughed more.

Are you drunk?

Nope. I'm just…mediocre.

You *are* drunk…I thought you were working.

I am…I was.

Just tell me you're coming home. You don't have to say when…just that you are…that this isn't the end.

There's never an end.

Don't give me that enigmatic bullshit. Just tell me.

You fucking left *me*.

I'm going now…this is pointless.

Fine.

Call me if you want to…preferably when you're sober.

She hung up. Elliot went back to the bar. James Brown was now sitting with a guy called Ratty whom Elliot knew. They called him over. He told them he couldn't stop and that he would see them later. He walked.

The heat throbbed. Sweat stung his eyes. Mishra pulled up with a sound of the horn and leaned out of the window.

Wh'appena yuh?

Just wanted a beer.

You lookin tight.

More than one then. Where you going?

Town. Coming?

No...I'll go back. Later.

She looked at him, screwed up her eyes and frowned in both puzzlement and disapproval.

Okay, she said, looking away before driving off.

He was sitting alone in front of the painting, staring at it, not knowing how long it had been since he had got back. I like it, he thought, even through this fog I like it...don't let the fog win...don't let it swallow you. The voice came from the fog and was telling him it was no good. Invalid. Weak. Mediocre. The voice was getting louder.

Burn it, it told him, take up your scalpel and slash it...it's worthless...you're shit...you know you are.

Elliot sung out loud the old football chant.

You're so shit it's unbelievable.

And then another to the tune of *Knees Up Mother Brown*.

You're not very good, you're not very good, you're not very, you're not very, you're not very good.

But I like it, he thought, and I *can* paint. I *need* to paint...otherwise there's no point in anything, is there?

There is no point, it said, bollocks you *need* to paint. Only if you're any good and *you're* not. Pretentious cunt.

Elliot tried to picture the speaker, the owner of the voice hiding somewhere in the fog.

I won't let you win this, he said out loud.

Already won, it replied.

Elliot pictured a naked, malformed, ugly, barely human figure.

Come out you bastard, he said still out loud.

It laughed. Elliot shouted.

Where do you come from? Who are you?

He took a photo of the painting and sent it to Amelia. She replied immediately, texting *Wow! That's beautiful.* My aestheticist likes it, he thought. He then mixed some paints before applying lines of blue and purple flowing across the centre of the canvass where the mountains would be. He worked on for over an hour before the phone buzzed. It was Amelia again.

Try again?

And they did, he called her back and they spoke at length - both apologising, reassuring, even laughing. He asked after her book. She said she completed it in Knockbreck having turned it upside down and made it less stuck up it's own arse, that she had been making the mistake of doing exactly what she was fighting against – being over-intellectual and precious about the sacred discipline of philosophy. She reminded of the conversation they had had when walking the day it all went wrong and that how talking to him about it had helped her realise where she was going wrong. They agreed that they had been in good form that weekend before it had all gone haywire and that if it hadn't then maybe they would have got themselves back on track.

> You see through me, she said, I need that.
> Not through you…inside you maybe.
> And when you look there do you like what you see?
> Yes…I have always loved what I see there.
> Do you love it now?
> Yes. I do.

She told him about home. New neighbours next door – a young family with two kids and the woman had a loud laugh you could hear through the walls. She had seen Iris once and all was well there. She hadn't had much contact with Linda but what there had been had been friendly enough. No news of Michael. Tom and Jerry brilliant. They had had her over for a meal and too much wine. She said she liked living there.

> By the way, she added, a few messages from the surgery…they want you to call.
> Really?
> Yes. Know why?
> Results maybe.

They signed off with promises to speak soon. She told him not to get distracted or let the flow of his work be interrupted. She was going to be busy revising her manuscript. *Love you*s were exchanged. He went back to work and despite the amount he had drunk, the flow was still there. The fog had receded. If not out of sight, it was far enough away to not distract him. The voice was silent. He mixed some good colours and worked on.

After an hour or so he guessed that Mishra would be back soon and thought it might be better if he was gone before she arrived. He started to clear up and felt an urge to stay, to carry on from where they had left off. It was getting dark as he locked up and headed back to Paul and Vernita's. His phone buzzed with a text from Amelia - *Gd 2 talk. Glad ur working. Dont 4get 2 call GP x.* He couldn't believe she was using abbreviations with such abandon.

CHAPTER 28

He set an alarm for four so he could get through to the surgery in time. He lay in bed listening to the automated reply *all lines are busy...please hold on...you are caller number...seven.* It repeated this for at least another ten minutes until he was number one. The receptionist wouldn't give him the results, telling him he had to speak to a doctor which immediately made him fear something serious was going on. He explained where he was and the time difference and she said she would try to get the doctor to call back.

He was sitting on the back gallery with Vernita when the call came a couple of hours later. A familiar voice was expressing sincerity and integrity. A voice he trusted. He imagined her sitting in her consultation room. She told him one of the blood tests showed a negative result – he now *knew* it was serious and thought she was going to tell him he had cancer. She told him the liver function test showed a raised number of enzymes - called ALTs - in his blood, meaning the liver wasn't functioning properly and was leaking these ALTs when it was meant to hold onto them. The leakage was definite evidence of liver damage. He asked her how bad. She said it was hard to tell other than the levels in his blood were significantly higher than what they were meant to be.

What do I do? he asked.

Well we need to test you again. Until then you have to radically cut down on your drinking, preferably stop it all together...

Really?

Yes. It's serious enough for me to have to tell you that.

Will it get better if I stop?

In time it could...but you're at risk of it turning into something else...if you're not there already.

Like what?

Cirrhosis mainly. Have you noticed any yellowing of your skin or eyes?

He told her hadn't even though he had noticed a yellow tinge to the whites some mornings. She advised him to either get another test done in Trindad or wait until he was home but not to wait more than another four weeks, reiterating the need for his cutting down on booze. He sat back and looked at the view. The sky was cloudless and blue. A black hawk dipped and soared over the rooftops and fields. He told Vernita the news.

Shucks, she said.

The last man standing - the great indestructable, the first to the bar, the night cap champion - had to stop drinking. A chicken he never thought he would see come home to roost was now walking up the driveway. It was tatty and scarred and had seen better days and it brought with it the prospect of a life without booze or the alternative which, in a nutshell, was death. A yellow-skinned death. Nothing like a shot of mortality to spread turmoil through the soul, he thought. All those things put off for another time, he had stuck them in a box he hoped was big enough but evidently wasn't. What about the girls? Should he tell them? Amelia? She would want to know. He could lie. But he *wanted* to tell her. He wanted her wisdom and pragmatism. He would have to tell Mishra. He would have to go back for the next test. Or could he have it done there? He didn't like the idea of that. He was feeling mortal and didn't want to brush with death when in Trinidad.

Please don't tell anyone yet, he said to Vernita.

He called in to see Paul who was in his studio. He was drawing with charcoal. Pages of sketches littered the ground around his chair. Be-bop jazz played in the background. Every now and again he blew an imaginary trumpet, fingers dancing over imaginary valves. He looked over to Elliot and grinned. They hadn't spoken yet and Elliot felt a surge of love for this mad bear of a man. Paul made coffees and took a break from drawing. He stood up, now clicking his fingers in time to the music and pursing his lips as he shook his head, took a slurp of coffee, spun in a pirouette, spilling some onto the floor and the discarded drawings. As the track ended he raised his arms above his head - more spillage - and shouted.

Yes! before giving Elliot a a hug lasting the best part of a minute.

Life was so simple again. They chatted for a while and Elliot decided not to tell him what the GP had said. He then headed to Mishra's and his painting. She was sweeping the front gallery, wearing cut-off denim shorts and an orange singlet. She stood and leaned on the broom with a look of mock disapproval, changing after a few seconds to a smile. Her skin was shining. It glistened. They walked into the house, his hand on the small of her back where she was wet with perspiration. He was instantaneously aroused. It was as though he had no filter system, no way to put this into the abstract, no route to rationalising it all away. He wanted her and if she wanted him now he would accede to her wishes without hesitation.

I'm going to Mum's, she said, see what she needs for Saturday. I'm cooking some for she...the baigan maybe.
The arousal is not mutual, he thought.

I have to work, he said
Eat here later...conks and bhajee.
My favourite food of all.
I know that.
I'll be here...thank you.

She told him her boys would be there too. Maybe a good thing, he thought, even though he wanted the two of them to be alone.
The boys had brought their girlfriends, Charlie and Grace, with them, neither of whom Elliot had met before. Charlie was shy, Grace feisty. Both were thin as rakes. They all ate together and the conks and bhajee were finished in an atmosphere of hilarity and cussing, Elliot feeling at ease and able to join in with the laughter. There were times there when he forget all the dichotomies and contradictions in his life and he was just happy to be in the moment, happy in his own skin, comfortable with the company. Something he rarely, if ever, felt back in England, he thought. He could go back, get his liver seen to, settle things with Amelia, tell her he was leaving, sell the house and then return here to Mishra, Paul and his work.

Charlie asked to see his painting so the two of them went downstairs. When he swithched on the light in the workspace her eyes widened with surprise as she swallowed it all in, the way someone who had never seen something before might have reacted. She walked up to it and stared, not saying a word. Then she put a finger in a coil of paint on the pallette and sniffed it before streaking it onto her forearm. She said she liked the smell. It was as though she had discovered a new dimension to life, one that had been hidden, perhaps forbidden. A sensual delight.

I would like to try this, she said.

He told her she could come by any time. She looked away from him as though she was embarrassed by what she had just felt. Then she said thanks in a voice as soft as a feather falling to the ground. She walked back upstairs. It made him feel like an ancient, that he had just witnessed the alchemy of ages. One of the secrets of the universe. This is the world in which I could live, he thought, if only I could just let go. The streak of ultramarine on her forearm, all the mystery it contained. He hadn't felt such wonder for a long while.

He and Mishra were sitting on the settee watching the news. Her head was on his shoulder, her feet tucked under her. An English couple, long time residents of Bacolet, Tobago, had been murdered in their home. Kenneth and Emily Perkins, sixty-three and sixty-two, were found hacked to death, having suffered slash wounds to their bodies and heads before having their throats cut. The police believed a cutlass or cutlasses were used by one or more assailants. It was the three hundred and fiftieth murder that year in Trinidad and Tobago.

A neighbour was interviewed, a local man.

Every day. Every *day* in we country we have bloodshed, he said, we have more murders than days of de years. Killers roam free. Police incompetent. Wh'appen to the Perkins my neighbours is de final straw. We want dese animals hanged.

A newsreader reported with a photo of the Perkins behind him – white-haired, white skin tanned brown, smiling at the camera, arm in arm - that Emily was found on the stairs in a pool of blood as though she was trying to flee to another room and Kenneth was found in a pool of blood on the kitchen floor. A man and a woman were sought by the police and the Prime Minister warned the country's murder rate was harming tourism. The report closed with the statistic that there were more than one thousand people charged with murder awaiting trial in Trinidad and Tobago.

The reporter moved on to the next item. Residents of Claxton Bay were calling for better recycling practices to be implemented at the Forres Park dump after a fire burned through most of last Saturday and left the area covered in smoke. A spokesperson for the Regional Corporation was interviewed. She said the Corporation was working closely with the waste management company responsible to put in place proper procedures and protocols to ensure this wouldn't happen again. She couldn't say if or when air quality testing would take place but she would do all in her powers to make it happen. Mishra jabbed the remote control towards the television, switching it off. She stroked his leg. She moved as though she was getting up but then manoeuvred herself across him, straddling him, pressing into him, looking down at him, hands at her sides. They heard laughter from downstairs. She unstraddled with a smile that was both playful and flirtatious, then walked over to the sideboard and waved a bottle of rum at him and asked him if he was having one for the road. Was this the time to tell her that he had to go back to England? He decided it wasn't and they hugged and kissed before he headed for the door.

I'll be back in the morning, he said.

I've to take ma to de doctor.

They agreed to lunch together if she was back in time.

Paul was up when he got in, television on, glass of rum and coconut water being poured. Elliot joined him. They talked about the murders. Was anywhere safe these days? Paul said he had heard Costa Rica was meant to be safe. Elliot mentioned Nicaragua as a possibility. He then told Paul he would be going back soon and the reasons why.

Ever to return? asked Paul.

Of course. As soon as I can.

I like having you here.

I work better here.

You have to sort your health. It might be easier to do that over there.

Maybe.

Elliot kept having to remind himself that his condition was real. Not fantasy or exaggeration. Just the truth wrapped up in its mundanity. In a cloak of beige. Forty years drunk and now no more Captain Indestructible. Fate's gnarled finger beckoned. This time back across the ocean.

Time to face the music, he said.

Elliot poured them both another one. They were leaning on the breakfast bar, standing there like outlaws who had just ridden into town - serious faces, grim and dusty from the trail.

What about Mishra?' Paul asked.

What about her? replied Elliot, immediately regretting that he sounded too defensive.

You've got close.

We always were.

You know what I mean.

We haven't…I know yes…I've not told her yet. I've wondered if I could stay but I need to see a hepatologist apparently.

You have to go back for that…but it doesn't mean forever.

No…but for a while I guess.

And Amelia's back.

Yes. Two lives…one here…one there. It's always been like that though. This time it felt like I was really back though. Liver or no liver I've felt so at home at times…and once I started to work…well being here has catalysed that. Less to worry about. Less need to impress. Not feeling judged.

Amelia judges you?

I don't mean that but I sometimes feels she does. Maybe with good reason. No I mean the life there…all the things you get wrapped up in. Most of which just isn't of any note here.

I   know…that's why I stayed.

And it's worked.

It could for you too…once you've sorted things…health, Amelia, the house, your studio. The girls.

I miss them. The daughters are such a force of life for me and I need their energy around me more than anyone else's.

But it could still work..your being here.

He poured another two drinks.

I would miss them.

You go back every three months...they come here...you holiday together.

Yes you're right. It could happen.

Elliot felt drawn to Iris and Isabel more than he had done since his arrival. He wanted to sit with them. Hear their chatter. Be there for them like a father should be.

I don't want to be ill out here.

Then get well. Do what you have to do.

They hugged. Paul lifted him off the ground.

CHAPTER 29

Saturday evening just getting dark and Shivana's house was busy.
Elliot and Mishra were the last to arrive. She had spent most of the day
with her mother, helping to cook and then had gone to collect Elliot. He
was still working when she arrived, paint streaked over his hands, arms,
legs and face. The painting alive and shiny wet. He didn't want to leave
it. By the time he had tidied up, walked to Paul's to shower and
changed, they were running late. Paul and Vernita had left earlier and
Elliot thought it could be the right time to tell Mishra the liver news.
She knew already. Vernita had told her that morning. She said in a
matter-of-fact almost singalong voice that he would have to go to
England to get it sorted, that he couldn't afford to have it all done there
and that she would find it hard to love a man with yellow eyes. Her
ability to immediately see all the way to the end-point of any
conundrum impressed him as did her lack of bullshit or neurosis. She
was selfless and wise, he thought, a pragamatist full of heart and
sagacity. He told her so and that he loved her all the more for it. She
also said that by going back to England he would have to face up to
things, look them in the eye and then make up his mind about where he
wanted to live and work, with whom he wanted to live and why.

If yuh wan my two cents worth, she said, I don think yuh legs
long enough to straddle de Atlantic Ocean....and for now yuh don
know where yuh wanna be.

What do *you* want? he asked.

Me n know...yuh could get real sick if yuh don go back. I know
that means yuh may decide yuh want to be with she. Yuh have Iris and
Isabel too to think about...I understand yuh get torn between we here
and dem there...but only yuh can decide. If yuh do decide to come
back here when yuh well...then that is all well and good. But I ain't
gonna wait for long...hanging my heart out in de breeze and...you
know...we getting old boy.
The kiss that followed was the deepest yet.

She was sitting on his bed when he entered the room wet-haired and
wearing a towel. She stood up.

One more before we go, she said.

They kissed and then touched where they had never touched before. Her shirt unbuttoned. Her shorts undone. She snatched his towel away from his body and threw it to the floor. She leaned back, arching her spine away from him like they were dancers, his hands on her shoulders holding her up. She stood again, eased her shorts over her hips and placed his hand between her legs. She bit his lip. She then pushed him away and said they had to leave. He stood naked before her and nodded. She smiled and held him close again.

Yuh just gonna have to wait boy, she said.

As she drove he wondered whether it mattered they were arriving together. What would people say? Would they suspect? There was no way they could, he thought, neverthless he was circumspect and felt self-conscious and unrelaxed as they pulled up at the gate and then walked up the potholed driveway. There were at least twenty people, maybe more, underneath the house – a wide space lit by bare bulbs and where a couple of trestle tables, numerous chairs and hammocks were randomly placed. Chickens wandered freely among them. Shivana greeted him warmly and scolded him with a wag of her finger for taking so long to visit. She was shorter than he remembered and much thinner, her face drawn tightly across her cheekbones. He put his arm around her and felt her frailty. One of the cousins he recognised, Beharry, a man so thin it looked like his limbs were made from wire coat hangers, beckoned Elliot over to a table to get a drink.

Take a drink with me nah, said Beharry and giving Elliot a high-five, it have whisky or rum…soda…sweet drink or coconut water.

Rum…soda, he replied.

A man with white hair and a solitary tooth was sitting up on the hammock. He waved in recognition of Elliot who had no idea who he was but waved back and smiled like he'd known him all his life. The man gave a one-tooth grin back at him before taking a nasal decongestant stick out of his breast pocket and snorting into each nostril. He then wiped the stick onto his shirt before putting it back in his pocket.

Elliot mingled. He made conversation. He glanced away from whoever he was talking to and looked for Mishra. Sometimes he saw her, sometimes not but whenever he did she was talking, laughing, looking relaxed in the folds of her family, more at home than he had ever felt anywhere or could ever feel. No matter how long I stay, he thought, I will always be an incomer here, however familiar it is, however free I feel here, I could never call it home. It came closer than anywhere though.

He and Paul started talking to Nicholas, an eleven year old boy who was holding a cricket bat and telling them about the runs he had scored that season. Paul asked him to show them his shots and he obliged, miming a forward defensive, a drive, a sweep, a pull, a hook, all of which he carried off with a high backlift and the swagger of an old pro.

What about your square cut? asked Elliot.

Uncle that is de one shot I cannot master…but I will…practice makes perfect yuh know.

Nicholas picked up a wooden box and placed it on the driveway, inviting them to bowl a tennis ball at him. They obliged. He showed off. They all laughed. Paul took a caught and bowled and shouted *yeeesss*. They went back underneath the hose for more rum. Elliot rested his arm on Paul's shoulder as they drank and told him how much he loved it there and that he felt pretty sure he would come back to live.

A few more rums were down before Shivana told them to eat. They obeyed her (like I always did, thought Elliot) and joined the other men who had taken up the seats around the table. No women joined them. Mishra, Vernita and Shivana brought the food - baigan aloo, channa, curry duck and dahlpourri. They stood back and watched the men eat and drink and talk in raised voices. When he finished Elliot took his plate to a sink where Mishra was standing. She took it from him, told him it was okay and that she would do it and he wasn't there to wash wares. He rinsed his hands and mouth. She handed him a towel and they looked at eachother, breaking into smiles after a few seconds.

Could you ever leave here? he asked.

What for?

Nothing…just wondered if you ever wanted to.

Once maybe but not really serious. I been to Toronto…been to New York… Barbados. It's better here than all a them places. Why? Yuh wanna carry me somewhere?

He nodded and stroked her cheek with the back of his hand. She turned back to the sink.

Shivana came over to them and linked her arm through his.

Come, she said, there is something I have to tell yuh.

They strolled down the driveway and onto the road. Crickets and frogs in the darkness. Indian music loud from the neighbour's house. He told her he had to go back to England soon and she asked him why.

Medical reasons, he said, trying to sound light-hearted, nothing serious but I have to see a man about my liver.

How soon?

Next couple of weeks.

So soon?

Then after a few moments she spoke again.

Maybe for de best.

Yes maybe…because I can't afford to see anyone here and I need to see to it as soon as I can.

I don't mean for yuh health. Sorry to hear that all de same.

He started to sense a panic rising.

Why for the best?

That girl and yuh too close.

We've always been…close…you know since we were…

Not like yuh are now though.

She sounded stern and determined. She looked up at him and he wondered how she knew. Her eyes bright and sad, the life she had lived there to see, the struggle evident and set in her lined face. She looked ancient, her jaws tight and her mouth turned downwards as though she was about to cry.

Yuh've always been like a son yuh know. When yuh mother was ill…wasn't able to manage…didn't know how to look after you.

I know Shivana…I've often thought you were more of a mother to me than she.

I made sure yuh eat and made sure yuh bathed...made sure yuh get to school...always let yuh sleep over with we in we house.

I know...you offered me security Shivana at a time I didn't even know I was looking for it.

And when yuh had to go back to England we all sad. Missed yuh. Life is so. It is here at least. It hard boy. Family can leave yuh and yuh never see them again. Some stay...and some go.

You looked after us.

Yuh father was a good man. Worked hard. Lived an honest life. Never complained. Even about she yuh mother. It was a sad day *again* when he had to leave. If de government didn't take over de company he woulda stayed. He was a good man. He was sad too sometimes yuh know? But he *never* complained...not at all.

They walked down the road, her arm through his again. She felt so light and fragile he tightened his arm against her in case she was blown away. She broke the silence.

But yuh can't be with Mishra.

They stopped under a street light. It cast a dim glow over them. She looked up at him.

I love her very much Shivana.

I know. But promise me. Please.

She was earnest, entreating. He felt fearful.

Why?

She is yuh sister.

Yeah...we've always been like that...like...family.

He began to shake, his body knowing the truth before his mind could make it clear.

She is your sister. *Blood.*

He let the words hang in the air between them. They wouldn't go in, he wouldn't let them enter. She continued.

Your father and me...

She left the next words unsaid. He felt calm now. All was clear.

Does she know?

Shivana spoke slowly.

Nobody knows. No*body*. Some maybe suspect over de years and make maco. But she a big woman now...nobody mind she business. So what yuh gonna do? You just get on with *life*. So please...don't tell her. For my sake.

Tears sprang and found their way down her cheeks, negotiating paths over the cracks and crevices of her ancient skin. One lingered on her jawline before it dropped away.

Please don't tell her, she repeated.

CHAPTER 30

It was time to visit the ghosts. Elliot got up before light and Vernita was already busy peeling potatoes. They chatted as she watched him fill a backpack - sketch book, soft pencils, some channa and roti in a tupperware container, a plastic cup, water and a bottle of rum that he added when she wasn't looking. He heard Paul getting up and when he came through to the kitchen he expressed surprised at seeing Elliot who told him he was going to Point Coco for the day. Alone. Paul said he could drop him there and asked how he would get back and to phone him if he wanted to. Elliot said he could thumb a ride back, adding he didn't want to put him out. Paul reassured him that it wasn't a problem and that it was a safer option. He then asked Elliot if he was okay. Elliot told him that all was well. He didn't believe it himself even though he was feeling calm and detached.

They journeyed in silence and Paul dropped him at the end of the track leading down to the sea. Rain forest either side of him. The vultures they call corbeau in flight above him circling something on the ground. He stopped for a piss and looked up to see a dozen or more fork-tailed flycatchers, their heads black and shiny like oil, sun-white throats and grey bodies curving down to their tails which were long and forked like pairs of pincers hanging along the telephone cables. His father used to show him these things, knew the Latin names of plants and birds. Fork-tailed flycatchers were *tyrannus savana*, he remembered. His father used to love Point Coco.

The tide was out (not that it ever went far), the sky was overcast and spatters of rain blew into his face as he walked down the slope to where they used to make camp. His father had fixed four bamboo poles into the sand to support a tarpaulin under which they would cook and eat. Someone else's poles were there now and a mound of discarded plastic and glass bottles lay behind them. He put down his backpack, took off his sandals and walked onto the sand. Coconut palms leaned out bending towards the sea, their roots exposed in nest-like domes dotted randomly along the sand. The land had receded so much it had left the trees behind. He could see the light and flames of the refinery at Point to his right and the rigs of Venezuela out to sea to his left and further away still the outline of the hills that this small island had once been attached to millions of years ago. The sea had eroded the cliff-face, exposing stripes of strata made up of different coloured sand that could have been designed by a meticulous decorator or an abstract expressionist. Some were orange like sandstone, some were different shades of brown or red and near the base a whole layer of black. His father had surmised this was carbon, the residue of fire formed so long ago as to be unimaginable. Elliot had asked him if it meant people had lit the fires. His father said he didn't know but that may have been the case. Caribs or Arawak Indians or their predecessors. Or maybe the earth itself had been aflame for centuries. He looked at the rainforest on the clifftop, imagining it unchanged for millennia. It was as if the gods had just hacked the island away from the land mass of what had become South America, thus allowing the ocean to roar through the channels left behind. It was on the sands of Point Coco that his father had first instilled in him a wonder for the universe.

No omniscient being son. Just nature. Nature did all this.

But why Dad? What *made* it do this?

His father picked up a handful of sand and told him to count the grains.

I can't Dad.

Well when you can son then you'll understand the universe.

Remembering all this, his father's voice and his own childlike tones, Elliot bent down to pick up another handful of sand and started to count. He pictured his father - sunburned brown, wiry and muscular, his crown of uncombed curly hair, a pair of faded red denim shorts, the creases at the side of his mouth when he smiled, the way his eyebrows raised and green eyes widened when he was explaining the wonders of it all. They used to stand for a long time in the sea, casting lines baited with shrimp or sardine. One day they caught a baby shark and threw it back, as well as salmon and grey mullett which they would then season and barbecue.

He was distant most of the time. Undemonstrative and stoical. Elliot now saw him as self-contained and self-sufficient in his withdrawal. Shivana was right, he wasn't happy for much of the time. He hoped he had found some happiness in her arms. He started to speak to him out loud, crying as he faced the waves and the panorama his father had known so well.

Dad don't leave me…hear me…hear me now…I miss you so much Dad.

He could hear his laugh. He laughed too and wished he was still the kid whose hand he'd take as they walked at the water's edge and talked about the birds, the sun, the moon, the ocean, as they cemented their love wordlessly on that wild bit of land on the edge of the world. Meanwhile his mother would stay under the tarpaulin, saying she didn't like to get sand between her toes.

He pictured her in the house. Ethereal dressed in white, moving like a ghost between the rooms. She hated having to live here. Hated the heat. Hated the strange-tasting milk and the bread and the cheese. Hot pepper didn't agree with her. Her bowels never adjusted. The Dutch and Venezuelan ex-pats whom she had nothing in common with. Any natural inclination to motherhood she may have once felt left her sometime when he was a boy and drink became her way to cope with being stuck on what she saw as a backward island thousands of miles away from home. She missed the High Street, a decent butcher and Typhoo tea. He was allowed to become feral and unwashed with a Trini accent. Sometimes she would be the one who put him to bed and if sober would sing a Scottish song or two she said her father used to sing to her. Elliot's favourite had been *Wandering Willie* - the tune and words come back easily, the double-entendre still amusing the way it was then…*here awa', there awa', wandering Willie, here awa', there awa', haud awa' hame; come to my bosom, my ain only dearie, O tell me thou bringst me my Willie the same.*

There were more words coming through the haze, something about *resting wild storms in the cave of your slumbers* and *wafting my dear laddie ance mair to my arms.* The memory made him feel a warmth towards her he'd not felt since those days. An understanding too or at least an appreciation of how she found that life so difficult and alien. So much so that she didn't cope and abandoned the duties of motherhood and gave in to the easy balm of drink. How we could talk together about that now, he mused. He was reconciling with her for the first time and told himself he would go to see her when he got back. His sister too.

Long-suffering Melanie who had married a *nice* man called Leonard and with whom she went to live in the Lakes and run a post office only for him to die too young a few years later. Her guilt at leaving their parents in their dotage then ate away inside her as she carried on as best she could before persuading them to move up to live with her where she could keep an eye on them and care for them in their demise. Their father's Parkinson's Disease became more evident and could no longer be ignored so Elliot helped move them, promising to visit often and managing that only twice before his father died. Melanie was older than him by ten years and they shared next to nothing, only the tie that bound them. And bound them still, just, despite it's fraying and wearing thin. She had voted for UKIP and he had lived with black women. He worked in mental health and painted. She worked like hell - for the most part on her own - to make a living and earn a pension. He consumed drink and drugs as soon as he was able to access them. She became teetotal. Why was that? He must ask her, he thought. Who knows what she had gone through? He realised he had never invited her to share any of her history. He had no knowledge of it. My family, he thought, disparate or dead.

Back in London suburbia his father had never seemed happy in his suit doing the commute each day to Waterloo. Elliot hit teenage years, they clashed too often to maintain the *fun* and his father spent large amounts of his time behind a newspaper, arguing with his mother or odd-jobbing in the garden. Melanie had gone to university in Southampton. Some nights he would hear his parents through the walls, his mother drunk and barbiturate-crazed and his father unable to control his anger. She would hurl abuse at him up to the point where he would either walk out or hit her. The sound of a slap, deadened by the wall between them, was powerful enough to strike fear into Elliot as he sat at a desk listening to Dylan or the Stones, pretending he was doing his homework.

Go on then fucking hit me, she shouted and he did.

One time his father slammed their bedroom door with a bang of such force and violence it made ripples in the glass of water on Elliot's desk. Usually when they fought they would exhaust themselves and it would eventually go quiet. Elliot would wait until then so he could sleep but this time something different had happened. Elliot heard his father's hurried steps on the stairs followed by the front door slamming and the car engine starting up. He looked out of his bedroom window and watched his father drive away. He was left alone with her. He didn't know if his father was ever coming back. However bad it had been before this the fundamentals of family life had carried on. Now the carpet had been pulled from under him. He was fourteen and alone. He was afraid to go into their room, she was silent and he feared what he would find. If she was asleep he didn't want to wake her. If she was dead he didn't want to find her. He waited. His father didn't come home. She called for him. He went to her. She was sitting up in bed. She handed him an empty plastic tumbler and said she needed a drink. He protested, telling her she couldn't ask him to do that and anyway there wasn't any drink in the house. She told him there was and where to find it. She said she needed just one, just one to make her well again. She was shaking. He went into Melanie's room and opened the wardrobe and on the shelf hidden behind piles of jumpers were six gin bottles, five empty, one half-full. He poured half a tumbler and took it to her. She complained it wasn't enough but downed it anyway. Then asked for another. He said no and walked away. He heard her get up and go into Melanie's room.

His father came home in the early hours. Elliot heard the car as he lay on his bed clothed and awake. He never told his father what had happened but the next day he looked in Melanie's wardrobe and the bottles were gone. The following weekend he was kicking a football against a wall in the garden. His father was bent baggy-trousered over the flower bed, pulling at a weed that didn't want to give way. He swore out loud - a rare occurrence - and Elliot went to offer assistance. Without looking up his father gestured him away but not before Elliot had seen the tears trickle down his cheeks.

A pick-up truck pulled up at the end of the unmade road. Two Indian men with weather-black skin and beer bellies were unloading fishing gear from the back of the truck. They waved at him. He didn't recognise them but waved back thinking he should have brought a cutlass with him as their intentions towards him may be the opposite to the friendliness they were showing. Feeling cautious, he sat on the exposed roots of a coconut palm and took a gulp of rum. The two men walked a little way up the beach. One of them spoke.

Boy weather good. We gonna hold some big fish…I can *feeeel* it…in de bones boy …in de *bones*.

They placed a cooler by a coconut palm – Elliot guessed it contained their bait - and secured two tripods in the sand. They baited their hooks and cast, then rested the rods in the tripods. They then returned to the bait box and baited another couple of lines before wading into the waves still wearing their shirts. The water was chest high before they cast again. One of them got a bite immediately, his rod bent nearly double and he slowly waded backwards towards the shore winding the reel, then stopping, then winding again. Ankle deep now and the rod was so bent it's tip was brushing the waves. He jerked the line and pulled a sting ray out of the water. He whooped in triumph and dragged the ray up the sand where it lay thrashing for its life. He needed a hand so Elliot walked over and the man threw him a towel. Elliot knew what to do and knelt with the towel between him and the ray's leathery skin. He held the animal down. The man used pliers to remove the hook, thanked him and then took the ray by the tail and threw it further towards the trees, its shiny skin now covered in sand.

You keeping it? You can eat that? asked Elliot, thinking Trinidadians can eat most things, but not this, surely.

Leave it for de corbeau then they leave alone anything we hold.

He re-baited and headed out to the water again, on his way checking the rods on the tripods and the tension of their lines. Elliot watched them catch more fish over the next hour or so, mostly salmon and grey mullett. Then one of the beach-based rods bent over and was pulled from the tripod. The men hurried back to shore, one of them grabbing the rod before it went into the sea. Something heavy was on the line. He played it well, releasing a little then winding in, gradually pulling it to shore. It broke the surface about twenty feet out. A shark. Not a baby, it was bigger than that but not fully grown either. Heavy though. He pulled it in. Sleek grey-black skin and pure white underparts, it's tail thrashing sideways as it fought for breath and life. Determined not to give in, its every instinct was for survival. Its whole life had been about that moment. This is where it would end.

The shark was about three feet long and Elliot hated to see its struggle, he felt sorry for it but the guys were whooping. One of them pulled a cutlass from a bag, inverted it and wrapped the towel around the blade. He hit the shark between the eyes with the handle. It took a few blows before the thrashing stopped and its eyes glassed over, just its tail continuing to flicker and denote the dying of its light.

The two men had had a good day and they wanted to share their success with Elliot. They were joyous and simple and toasted their success with his rum, drinking it from the neck and passing it round. Not once did they ask him his name or what he was doing there. He asked if they could drop him back to Muga. He had never taken out the sketch book and it didn't matter, he thought, as he had never once felt the urge to draw. They stopped at two bars on the way and regaled their audiences with tales of their day, the ones they had caught and the ones thatgot away. Some people doubted them so they opened up the trunk and showed off the catch. In a rum-fuelled generosity of spirit they proceeded to give away most of the mullet and salmon. An Indian man, tall with a chiselled face, grey swept-back hair and goatee – Elliot thought he looked sad like Don Quixote - and dressed in beige slacks and a white shirt said he would buy the shark off them. They said no but he told them he had a large female iguana in his freezer, that it had eggs and that he would gladly swap it for the shark. It sounded like a good deal to the two men, so all three of them followed Don Quixote back to his place, a large concrete house with lights on in every room. Elliot had no idea where they were. Ragged Hindu flags were flying outside and they sat beneath the house on leather armchairs, bright florescent strip-lights flickered above them as their host served them whisky with ice and coke. He took the iguana, maybe three feet long, stiff and dull-eyed, from out of a chest freezer in the corner and the two fishermen whooped some more. He wrapped it in newspaper and the three of them took their leave with handshakes, backslaps and laughter.

Elliot didn't remember getting back. He guessed they had brought him to the gate but he couldn't recall any detail. Last thing he remembered was leaving Don Quixote's house. He had slept in one of the hammocks. Paul woke him. He had cut open a coconut and he handed it to Elliot, telling him to drink. It slaked his thirst as he felt the first signs of a tyrannical and merciless hangover.

We were worried, said Paul.

Sorry...but you should know better.

Shouldn't *you*?

There was just a hint of disapproval in Paul's tone. Elliot put his legs either side of the hammock and started to haul himself up by gripping the ropes securing it to the pillar.   He felt like hell.

Guess so.

Are you going to see Mishra?

Why?

After last night.

What?

It dawned on them both that Elliot didn't remember. He felt panic and looked to Paul in disbelief.

You went round there.

Fuck, thought Elliot, what did I do? What did I say? He raked his fingers through his hair. It was sticky.

Shit, he said.

What the fuck happened?

236

I met some guys…we drank. They swapped some fish for an iguana.

Who were they?

I don't know…but they were good guys.

You have a black eye and a cut in your head.

Shit.

He went into the washroom and looked in the mirror. He had a purple bruise encircling half of his left eye and dried blood on the top of his forehead. He didn't know how either had got there. He came back out. Paul was standing there, arms folded. He spoke.

You know this has to stop.

Yes I know…but how the hell..? What did I do at Mishra's?

Cried apparently. After you woke her up.

It was all going so well, he said with all the irony he could muster.

Don't do this mate.

Don't do what?

Defiance.

He went upstairs to shower and passed Vernita on the stairs. He told her he was sorry. She nodded in neutral but the fact she wasn't smiling at him the way she usually did told him enough. I'm in the naughty corner, he thought. As he stood with the still cool water pouring over him he tried to reach through the fog blanketing his memory to remember what had happened the previous night. He had no recall beyond getting into the pick-up truck to leave Don Quixote's house. How the fuck did he get back? he wondered. More worrying was what the fuck did he say to Mishra? He dried and dressed and walked round there.

She was sitting looking at his painting. It had been daubed in black paint, the word *cunt* written in large letters with red oil paint across the middle. It had been slashed in several places. He stood before it unable to register or speak but knew he must have done this. Everything was strewn about the floor - paints, brushes, pallette, photos, paper. Her eyes were puffy and red. He went to her, knelt before her, looked her in the eyes and told her he was sorry. She was unyielding. She stood up and started to walk away. He stopped her and held her. She brushed him aside. He still didn't know what he had told her. She gestured at the painting and spoke in a voice barely above a whisper.

How can yuh do this?

He didn't answer.

Tell me, she continued now angrier, how can yuh do this? One thing to come here drunk in de early hours of de morning and wake me up…yuh know…I can take that….even if I don't want to…but then to do this…to destroy something like this…something so much part of yuh…something yuh *create*. Yuh sick boy…yuh have a darkness in yuh I don't know I can handle.

I can't remember doing it.

She cocked her head and looked at him as though asking him if he was for real.

Yuh can't remember huh…yuh remember being here at *all*?

Nope.

Waking de whole house…looking for rum…crying…yuh snot dribbling from yuh nose…falling down de steps. I think yuh were dead boy. Then yuh get up and do this.

She gestured again at the painting. Her voice shook.

What is in yuh boy?

Drink. Drink was in me. It wouldn't have happened if I hadn't drunk so much.   I'm going to stop, Mish…really I am.

Something *in* yuh make you drink so and I don't want *that* in me life.

What was I saying?

All kinda foolishness. Yuh really can't remember? How yuh love me…how yuh love she…how yuh don't wanna leave here…how yuh a failure. I'm telling yuh boy if yuh coming back here make sure yuh sort it out. I can't take this. I love yuh being here but I ain't going to watch *this*. Yuh destroying yuhself…no boy not for me..no way. Yuh think yuh can come back here and yuh and me be together and yuh carry on like this? No man…I ain't going to love a man who wanna kill heself.

All the different ways of saying sorry he tried to form in his mind. He wanted to promise her something but didn't know what. He didn't even see the point. He looked away unable to take her eyes fixed on him as she waited for him to say something. At least now he knew he hadn't betrayed her mother's secret. Eventually he spoke.

I'll clear this up.

She walked away and up the steps into the house.

CHAPTER 31

The last drinks he had were on the plane but they were in addition to the few taken before he had even reached the airport. Ruben had driven him and they had stopped a few times on the way. They did some lines in the car.

Aha, said Elliot, the baskets of pakchoy.

Ruben put his fingers to his lips and with a smile told Elliot to *shh*. Then more beers in the airport bar. Elliot was queuing to check-in when a white man in an open necked shirt, jeans and deck shoes approached. His voice was posh English. A spook wanting to know where he'd been, where he was going and his inside leg measurement. Elliot managed not to speak too fast or too much but was conscious of his drying mouth, hoping the spook wouldn't notice or suspect his level of intoxication. He told Elliot to have a good journey and Elliot thanked him. On board he had six gins and one tonic. Four of those little bottles of red. He had planned to drink right through but fell asleep and woke up dribbling when they were somewhere over the south coast. Iris and Isabel were there to meet him and they took him back to Iris' flat where he drank soup, took valium and slept. But no drink.

He was two months dry now. And clean. He counted the days every day. Little milestones. Apart from a few sweats and night terrors in the first week or so it had been physically easy. Some shakes - enough for him to stay indoors and avoid pouring the kettle. He craved drink but didn't want it and not *wanting* it, in the end was all that mattered. Fuck yoga, fuck mindfulness, fuck AA. This was *his* journey. He was two months dry. And clean. The GP's urgent referral to Mr. Grey the heptologist - name and nature, thought Elliot - had come and gone. The consultation and Mr Grey's monotone statement of fact - *If you pull back now you have every chance, otherwise you will develop cirrhosis.* Amelia's hands-off encouragement and concern. Iris' pragmatism - fruit and veg to juice, turmeric in everything, supplements to swallow and a tablespoonful of apple cider vinegar twice a day - and Isabel's tears and entreaties. Brendan's humour and Biscuit's expletive-laden incredulity which made Elliot laugh loud and deep, Linda's positivity, albeit from a distance as she now attended NA on a regular basis, practised CBT - she swore by it, recommending it to him with the evangelical zeal of a convert - and had adjusted to her life without Michael, helping her kids to do the same. Elliot admired her. All had kept him on track, this new road he was on and from where he was beginning to admire the views and not worry about the destination.

He was sitting in the living room feeling confined. The wood burner emitted enough heat for the whole ground floor but Amelia had a cold so the doors were closed. The heat was stifling. He looked at the garden through the conservatory windows. It needed tending. The lights were on and it was barely afternoon. He longed for sunlight. And space. He missed wearing shorts, a vest and sandals. He spent hours online feeling aimless while he was prolapsed into the settee, spine bent in three or four places and pain through his lower hip and the meatus of his dick as though ground glass had been poured down there.

Two months dry ticked off on the road to recovery, physical wellbeing, emotional wellbeing, even-handedness, even-mindedness, functional relationships and productivity. Two months enduring twice weekly group yoga sessions led by a smug, vain, self-righteous cunt who embellished the teaching of exercise and movement with pseudo-spiritual aphorisms - *even a small star shines in the darkness* – as well as *a squirrel cannot carry forests on its back but the mountain cannot crack a nut* – all designed to transcend the group to a higher plane but mostly show off the fact that he was just so fucking perfect and balanced. He even had the arrogance to show Elliot a couple of his life drawings as though he wanted either to impress him or bond with him or both (look I can draw too!). And they were awful. Technically, conceptually and compositionally awful. But Elliot indulged him with a pained smiled on his face and a few grunts of encouragement.

Amelia told him how much she was looking forward to the forthcoming evening with Brendan and Rita who whom they had invited over for a meal. Elliot was the cook. The healthy, functional, friendly cook. He told her he needed a few things from the shops so he would walk into town. She offered him a lift. He declined.

The walk will do me good, he said.

Promise to call if the rain starts again.

He promised. As he stood to put on his coat she asked if he was okay. He told her yes, he was fine. She kissed his cheek, told him she knew it was hard but she was proud of him and it would get better and easier as time went on. He told her it hadn't really been hard at all. She told him it felt good to have him back. The *real* you, she had said - as though everything before was the *un*real him, he thought.

Not just the physical you standing before me, she elaborated, but the living considerate and sensitive you.

He lifted her hands to his lips and kissed them. It felt good, he conceded, to be feeling how he was feeling even though it was only for some of the time and a significant part of him was hoping it really would get better and become *most* of the time. Two months dry wasn't that long but it had felt longer than War and Peace, Bleak House and the Bible put together.

Two months dry and it was coming on Christmas. Sixty-two days ticked off. Two months back in England. Two months of missing the light. And heat. The lack of neurosis - people in England said sorry all the time - cross someone's path and say sorry, sneeze and say sorry, bump your trolley into someone else's in the supermarket and say sorry, get bundled out of the way as you step on a bus and say sorry, make way for someone walking the other way and say sorry – everyone was so damn sorry. Missing Paul. Missing a cold water shower on a hot afternoon. The food. Missing the feeling of freedom. Away from it all. Away from all this. Missing her and her playful scolding. Missing the way she just folded up onto his shoulder and into his arms. Two months of being back in the house. Hospital appointments. Blood tests. Two months of trying to be back in the studio. Staring at that fucking painting – the replacement, the mark 2 after he had destroyed the prototype. Two months of trying to bring it to life. Postcards, photos on the wall. Playing reggae and soca. It just doesn't breathe here, he thought, the colours don't shine the same way under electric light. The clock going back. Opaque skies the colour of suet pudding every fucking day. Dark at four. Colour didn't pulse. Or was he failing to make them pulse? His new painted sky didn't ache with the heat. Watching it shut down like a flower at dusk. Watching it tire and close it's million pairs of eyes and go to sleep. He had been the lifegiver and now he couldn't give it life.

Two months dry. Amelia had finished her book and got a deal. She was going for the Head of Faculty post. Bushes to cut back in the garden. He planted bulbs for Spring. He felt calm. We have got along well, he thought. She said she preferred him sober and that came as no surprise. It was easier on her. They slept together better. They made love gently and he couldn't keep it hard and she said it didn't matter. But it did. Two months of marvelling at her beauty and African ways. They walked hand in hand and smiled more - across café tables, when grinding coffee beans, across the dining table when friends visited or they visited friends. When she slipped her arm through his he was comforted by the brush of her breast. Two months since Izzy and Iris met him at Gatwick. The warmth and tears of reunion. How they could talk, how they had supported him. Recipes and regimes for regeneration. Family dinners when he drank apple juice with tonic water - *it looks just like champagne, Dad* - and how he would confirm for them how much better he was feeling. More energy. More sleep. And it was all true. He kept a picture in his head of a leaking liver, a porous organ he used as a charm to ward off the evil spirits. It was his totem, he thought. A bloody, leaking liver.

He went to see Michael and told him everything. They looked forward to being sober *together,* laughing at how different it would be. Michael now attended anger management classes and told Elliot of the benefits. How thoughts were just thoughts and not the truth. He had installed an anger management filter in his brain like an app. He was a walking cognitive behavioural therapy success story. He was flabby and his skin was grey.

Two months of fearing fear. Of understanding the nature of fear. Where it rises. Where it goes. Of looking it in the eye and knowing it is illusory, easily challenged but not denied. Fear of failure, of being ordinary, of being disliked, of people's indifference, of dying unacclaimed, of standing denuded after every layer had been stripped away. Fear of losing the last fragile tie that bound him to this godforsaken life. Fear as a shield, a cloak to wrap around him. As a pit, a well-shaft to fall into so he could avoid the light. He had seen the light. It was easy to stand in it. People didn't give a shit though where he was standing. He was standing in the light and feeling fearless. He was without fear. Two months of working this out. Two months dry. Two months avoiding the temptation. Avoiding going into London. More a home than anywhere. London where he used to drink alone. London where he always thought he would die. Avoiding the bars and the carousers. The cripple didn't need his crutches. The blind man could see. Allelujah. This was *it*.

Two months dry and it's coming on Christmas. Plastic trees and fairy lights. Bing Crosby and David Bowie singing *arumpa pum pum*. This was it. Fearless life. Fearless sober life. Sometimes he looked at Amelia and wondered if she realised -as he cooked the meal, did the shopping, planted the bulbs, reassured her everything was, and was going to be, fine - that he was climbing out of his skin craving a drink, craving a hit. Any hit. Any fucking chemical to change *this*. She tidied away the letters he needed to still deal with and he couldn't find them. He eventually found them where she had put them. He didn't know she had put them there. It made him think to himself fuck *this* and made him want to climb out of his skin. Made him push the urge away so he could carry on standing in the light without fear. Made him accept *this* was *it* and it could be so much worse. He could have no legs and three dicks, four noses and rampant fungal infections in the folds of his skin. It could be so much worse. He could be ugly, unintelligent and ill-informed. He could be drunk and lying at the bottom of that deep, dark hole, scrabbling around at the bottom of the well-shaft, festering, stinking and all alone.

Sobriety worked. The mind cleared, the eyes sparkled, the jeans fitted. Joy in the things described as little. Peace reigned in the heart of the nihilist. But he thought men who told you they juiced were cunts. He thought men who were yoga teachers and thought they could draw nudes in their spare time were cunts too. He thought men who wore *Iron-Man Challenge* t-shirts and cycle shorts when travelling by train were probably the biggest cunts of all.

So two months dry and he was not afraid. He was mindful of the benefits. Packs of Christmas cards lay unopened on the conservatory table. Amelia was making plans. Forget about the war in the Middle East, about the threat to their lives from mad dog bombers, forget about his liver, forget about his painting, they were going to have a *good* time. She's right, he thought, and thank God. They had bought a real tree and they were making an effort. He sang out loud.

I'm dreaming of a dry Christmas just like the ones I've never known.

Sunday, middle of the day. He had walked to the supermarket near the football stadium. No waterproof and the rain like the gods were mist-spraying the terraced streets and rooftops of the town in a vain attempt to bring them to life. Decorations were in some of the windows, holly wreaths on front doors. He arrived at the supermarket. They needed a few things. He was cooking a saddle of venison for Brendan and Rita. Sauteed potatoes. A blueberry joue. He needed stock and some vegetables. Cheese for afters. A couple of decent bottles of red. If I die and go to hell, he thought, I will be sent to this supermarket on this day at this very time. Why did whole families go there together? Trolleys full, kids picking up random items and getting shouted at. People were lingering and staring at the shelves, overwhelmed by the choice in front of them or just indecisive or mind-numbed by the blandness of it all. Staff with Santa hats and tinsel around their necks stood at the end of aisles, smiling at customers and offering in voices much too loud a taste of cheese, a tiny cut of mince pie or something that looked like a sample pot with a tot of sloe gin in it. Fairy lights across the deli counter, fake presents piled up beneath a plastic tree next to the booze aisle. All to a soundtrack of Christmas songs.

Just hear those sleigh-bells jingling, ring-ting tingling too, come on it's lovely weather for a sleigh ride together with you...

He had a basket's worth of what he had come for and was standing in the self-check-out queue. An elderly woman was struggling to pay, the machine repeatedly rejecting her card.

Outside the snow is falling and friends are calling yoo-hoo...

She was looking around for someone to help. Her mouth was wide open, she had lost sense of her place in the world, there was nothing or no one to help her find it, her mind was floundering. She was in a world she could not deal with.

Giddy-yap, giddy-yap, giddy-yap, let's go...

He put his basket down, went to her and asked if he could help. She looked at him, searching for something to recognise. He offered to swipe her card for her. She gave it up to him, speechless.

Giddy-yap, giddy-yap, giddy-yap, it's grand...

He told her she needed to put in her PIN number and she turned her back to him as she did so. Maybe she thinks I'm about to take advantage of her, he thought, worm my way into her affections and rob her blind.

Let's take the road before us, and sing a chorus or two, come on it's lovely weather for a sleigh ride together with you...

He left his basket where he had put it down and walked out. He knew where he was going. There was a dive in the west end of town. An Irish bar with a steel door and a spyhole. It consisted of a single room, three television sets and a great Dane given licence to roam. The barmaid - blonde, young and friendly - showed a lot of bra strap and the clientele were mostly men in working clothes – jeans, overalls, steel toe-caps and the like. Builders' vans parked outside. Painters and decorators. One of the regulars was a woman of considerable age whose face was lined with cracks and crevices life had gouged out over the years. She sat alone drinking stout, occasionally going outside to smoke and chat in a voice sounding as though her larynx had been primed with heavy-duty sandpaper. He was heading there now down a long road leading from the stadium to the park, a distance of maybe a mile. An industrial estate with its spiked steel gates and razor-wired fences was, apart from the non-descript terraced houses, its only real feature. That and the pub. He walked with momentum. The sky was flat and grey and the wind biting.

No one looked up when he walked in. The old girl was there with her glass of stout, two young men were playing pool and an older man with a red face and acne sat at the bar with a pint of lager and a burger in a styrofoam container. The barmaid smiled and as she poured Elliot's Guinness he looked at her cleavage. He asked for a large malt whisky and as she stretched to reach the bottle he looked at her tight jeans and red bra-straps. The lighting as though it was nicotine-stained. He stood at the bar, added water to the whisky, downed it and asked for another. A couple of glugs of Guiness. He downed the whisky and asked for another. He looked into the glass. It looked like amber, the bare bulb reflecting in it's swirls. The clack of the pool-balls. It was six pm and there he was. The dog was off its chain and he wasn't scared of it.

ACKNOWLEDGEMENTS

I offer heartfelt thanks to Mary O'Hara for her support and for offering a shrewd and vital piece of advice. I also offer unending gratitude to Ana Sanchez Valiña for her encouragement and her tireless assistance with the proof-read and edit. I couldn't have completed this without either of you.

24450704R00149

Printed in Great Britain
by Amazon